DESTINED

DESTINED

HELLCAT RELEASED™ BOOK THREE

MICHAEL ANDERLE

Copyright © 2022 by Michael Anderle
Cover Art by Jake @ J Caleb Design
http://jcalebdesign.com / jcalebdesign@gmail.com
Cover copyright © LMBPN Publishing
A Michael Anderle Production

LMBPN Publishing
PMB 196, 2540 South Maryland Pkwy
Las Vegas, NV 89109

Version 1.00, June 2022
ebook ISBN: 979-8-88541-676-4
Print ISBN: 979-8-88541-677-1

THE DESTINED TEAM

Thanks to the Beta Readers
Larry Omans, Kelly O'Donnell, Rachel Beckford, John Ashmore

Thanks to the JIT Readers

Dorothy Lloyd
Zacc Pelter
Dave Hicks
Kelly O'Donnell

If I've missed anyone, please let me know!

Editor
The SkyFyre Editing Team

DEDICATION

To Family, Friends and
Those Who Love
to Read.
May We All Enjoy Grace
to Live the Life We Are
Called.

— Michael

CHAPTER ONE

Dante was about to plunge through the door into the wasteland beyond the threshold with his pulsecore carbine firmly in hand when he sensed something amiss. He stopped and glanced over his shoulder at Nasreen.

"What's wrong?" he asked her.

Nasreen was fiddling with equipment. Specifically, the small but unwieldy rig she wore near her collar to keep her high-end camera in place.

She sighed in ragged exasperation as her gloved fingers worked with nimble speed. "The power cell got jostled again when we landed. I need to reconfigure this thing after we finish so this shit doesn't keep happening. Wait, we're already live. The light wasn't on. Whatever, I'm sure they have a real-time censor to bleep out the word 'shit.' There's always a slight time delay."

Dante scowled. "We have more important things to worry about than whether or not a bunch of people sitting around on couches and sipping soy tea can get their daily fix of excitement by watching us try not to die."

From somewhere deeper within the shuttle, the captain

barked, "Hey! Get moving. We can't hover this low for long without damaging the thrusters."

"Okay," Nasreen snapped. "Yeah, fine, we're good now. Let's go." She released the camera rig, allowing it to settle back into its usual place, and hurried toward Dante. By the time she came within arm's length, he'd vaulted out. She followed him at about five feet.

Dante's boots struck the ground, a paradoxical mixture of dust and mud. The lower-lying portions were soft and squishy, but rubble, rocks, and debris were everywhere. They were all coated with fine-grain particles of dirt, sand, and powdered stone, blown through by the frequent windstorms that enveloped so much of the broken wreck of planet Earth.

The facility they were raiding was in a lonely, desolate area, removed from the nearby city of Bucharest, Romania. It lay on a flat plain with the ruins of old walls sprouting from the ground and dead trees reaching toward the sky. Ahead of them was the compound, protected by high concrete walls. The main building itself was smaller than Dante would have expected at only three stories tall. He could barely see the roof beyond the wall.

Most of his attention stayed focused on everything else. The first rule of plunder raids while Dirtside was to be constantly alert to danger. To *assume* that danger was everywhere.

"Clear so far." He kept his pulsecore high at his shoulder, muzzle down but ready to raise and fire at the first sign of serious trouble. There were quite a few Dirtwalkers in Bucharest. The human population there hadn't been as badly devastated as in some other places, and there was sufficient food to raid for them to live a crappy existence. However, there seemed to be no tribes in the compound's immediate vicinity.

The real danger would come from the wildlife if there was any.

Nasreen plunged forward, catching up to Dante and toting

her gun the same way. "Good deal. E-zex and the Hellcat going in once again. Sit tight, boys and girls."

Dante was glad he was looking away from the camera when she'd said that since he grimaced. Having a loyal audience was nice to increase their fame and fortune. He didn't understand why she had to keep talking directly to the viewers like that, especially while being so dramatic about it.

At least it served to remind everyone of who they were. Or, rather, who they pretended to be.

The pair jogged through the frosty muck. It was winter in the Northern Hemisphere, and the temperature hovered right around the freezing point. There wasn't enough atmospheric moisture in the area for any snow to fall, but the water in the muddy ground showed faint signs of ice.

Their ultimate target was a database stored in a secure vault in the facility's heart. Said database contained vast reams of scientific and industrial data. One of the firms the pair had invested in wanted access to it to jumpstart one of their nascent research and development programs.

Remarkably, the prize was on an old-fashioned perishable flash drive that was susceptible to the elements. The vault it was in required a constant power source to function. According to their intel, the advanced underground generator powering the storage area had remained intact and working in the many decades since most of humanity had abandoned their mother planet.

This also meant its security systems would still be alive and well. Crude attempts at theft would only trigger the self-destruct mechanisms in place as a last-ditch measure. Getting the drive out intact would require the attention of a specialist.

Despite her limited career as a Marauder, Nasreen had years of experience in corporate espionage and infiltration. As far as lateral career shifts went, making the switch to Marauder-Breacher was a natural and perfectly viable move for her.

The pair ran forward. Orbital photography had suggested that the facility's walls would be difficult to scale, and cracking through the gates might take too long given the time they'd be spending on everything else. Besides, the viewers always enjoyed seeing things blow up.

So, they had brought the means to go *through* the walls.

Dante took out an explosive charge from his pack. It was a lower to middle power grade model, big enough to bring down a wall and certainly dangerous, but small enough to be manageable. It could be remotely detonated from up to two miles away. He ran straight toward the wall and stuck the charge onto it at head height, then pressed the button to put it in standby mode.

Nasreen watched and covered him from seventy feet away. When no Nightmutts emerged from the landscape to challenge them, she relaxed a little. They still didn't know what lay inside the compound, though.

Dante ran back. "Okay. We're ready to go. Get back behind that foundation." He pointed to the pitiful remains of another wall several feet behind them. It was still sunk into the ground deeply enough that it ought to provide some cover. Plus, their armor would protect them to an extent.

Nasreen explained as much for the benefit of their viewers, but she kept passing it off as learned speculation on her part or asking rhetorical questions.

"...the blast radius will be impressive, won't it? Our suits are rated for this kind of thing, assuming we're talking about run-of-the-mill shrapnel and debris..."

Dante ignored her since he still found the performance aspect of the whole thing silly. He'd been doing stuff like this on a purely professional basis—*without* an audience—for years.

Both dropped to their stomachs behind the broken wall, staying tight to it, and Dante took out the tiny detonation device. An unbreakable cap secured the button, and after popping it open, he had to tap it in the proper sequence. Accidentally blowing up the charge was all but impossible.

"Ready?" he asked.

Nasreen smiled. "Born that way."

He shook his head and depressed the button once, twice, and held it down for one second, then briefly a third time.

A visible shockwave expanded from the wall, translucent but impressive, followed by the noise of the blast itself. The sound blockers in their helmet headsets kicked in. The technology also neutralized the excessive report of gunshots and the like, reducing the deafening explosion to a mere fuzzed-out purr of feedback.

Concrete, metal, and polymer sprayed out from Ground Zero, along with a rising bloom of fire and smoke. The wall collapsed around a good thirty-five-foot stretch. They waited until the echo faded and the wind cleared the smoke before they stood.

"Well, then," Nasreen quipped. "It appears the charge did its work successfully. We got our money's worth on that one."

Dante coughed. "Yeah. Now let's move in." He jogged out, back across the frosty mud, but slowed as he came closer to the ruined wall. "E-zex. Something is moving in there."

"I see it too." She dashed to his side, fingers moving gingerly over her carbine. "Ohhh, shit."

The compound's interior was a nice, simple layout. The square yard held few obstructions other than a handful of lamps along the cracked and derelict sidewalks. The main building was in the center. Two walls had decayed and fallen before Dante's charge had blown up the outer protective wall.

Within the main structure, huddling around what had to be the power source for the vault with waves of heat rising from it in the chill air, was a cluster of bugs. *Big* bugs.

They resembled scorpions but were the size of large dogs, and most of them had fluttering gossamer wings like a dragonfly. They had all taken to hopping and scampering around. Some hovered in midair on rapidly beating wings in a half-panic. They chittered and *squeaked,* turning their black insectoid eyes toward the two human intruders. Their pincers *clicked.*

Dante growled, "Shit is right. I'm surprised the blast didn't scare them off. Let's see how they react to explosions that affect them." He raised his carbine and fired three shots.

Pulsecore rounds were lower velocity than traditional lead bullets. They lacked the same long-range penetrative capabilities of a high-powered rifle but made up for it in sheer potency. Each round was a tiny plasma grenade that created a fiery burst of green light about the size of a human head upon impact. They were dangerous to all in the hands of the untrained. They were lethal to enemies when wielded by those who knew what they were doing.

Dante knew what he was doing.

The plasma rounds detonated in quick sequence near the center of the bug cluster, although he'd made sure to aim away from the bulge in the ground that seemed to be the vault's power source. The crackling green bursts splattered two bugs, reducing them to little more than shards of chitin and sticky organ paste, while two others hopped back with damaged claws or wings.

Nasreen raised her carbine for a follow-up volley. When the bugs charged, shrieking horribly, she let loose.

The pair fired until they had only a couple of shots remaining in their magazines. Green flashes lit up the compound's interior as the mutated creatures died by the dozens. Nearly thirty of them perished in the massive volley. The others, frenzied but not suicidal, changed course and scuttled off to the compound's far reaches. Those with intact wings beat them furiously to rise on the wind and fly over the walls, escaping into the half-frozen wasteland beyond.

Silence set in. Plumes of smoke rose from the many scorched patches where the plasma blasts had worked their magic.

"Okay." Nasreen exhaled. "That was a tense moment. If those

things had gotten closer, we might have had serious issues. This is exactly why we always bring the best weaponry we can afford. No place on Earth is safe from Nightmutts, whatever subspecies they might be."

Dante stepped over some rubble. "Yes, we know."

Following him, Nasreen snapped, "I'm not talking to you. Not everyone knows as much as you do about this stuff. First-time viewers appreciate a little background info."

Dante's only response was a low throaty sound. He wondered if their precious audience found his indifference to their entertainment off-putting or if they thought it was funny. Later, when they were safely back in orbit, he might consider looking into such things.

While Nasreen looked over the odd mound that housed the power supply and the vault proper, which lay toward the back of the main building's central chamber, Dante stood watch near the edge of the rotted wall. They'd routed the surviving bugs, but they might be stupid enough to come back and try again. Or there might be other varieties of Nightmutt lurking nearby, curious about the commotion. He ejected the spent mag from his gun, saved it for later, and snapped in a fresh one.

Then Midas spoke up in his synthesized voice, directly into Dante's brain. *"Sir, I detect movement all around us. It exceeds the number of bugs you dealt with. There was nothing on the earlier tech scan, so it's likely more creatures cowering around the wall."*

"Good. We'll be fine."

Midas was an AI implant that Dante communicated with telepathically. Dante hadn't been enthusiastic about having a second personality drilled into his skull, but Midas had proven extremely helpful if sometimes annoying in the months since his installation. He'd also developed character, and when not pestering Dante to buy more upgrades, he was pleasant enough.

Nasreen explained, somewhat to Dante but mainly to the fans, "Dismantling the layers of security on this thing is a meticulous, intricate process. Admittedly it doesn't make for the most exciting part of the stream, but some of you might find it fascinating. Some individuals have expressed a desire to see *everything* we do here, in all its glory, so they can get an idea of what is truly involved in the art of plunder."

Dante was pretty sure Nasreen scripted her little monologues in advance, but given her background as a spy she might have been making them up on the spot. Quick thinking was one of her stronger points.

He also reflected on how valuable their fans had become, as silly as the whole celebrity idea was. The most rabid and enthusiastic viewers tuned in for every job stream they posted, gradually driving up numbers as they brought friends to watch or spread the word through other means of communication. Each new milestone in viewership brought with it more clout and new opportunities for lucrative sponsorship. E-zex and the Hellcat were becoming household names.

Time passed as Nasreen went through the painstaking process of disabling each safeguard individually, using a variety of specialized devices as well as wetware hacking techniques. Some of the tools of her trade were beyond Dante's understanding. He originally made his name as a "general purpose" Marauder before changing his identity and rebranding himself as a more combat-oriented Reaper. Advanced breaching was a specialty he'd never acquired.

Nasreen stood, exhaling loudly. "Got it!" In front of her, the vault's doors slid open. "Next, I'm going to—wait, getting some interference." She shut off the camera feed.

It was a necessary deception. She didn't want half the world to see or hear her as she made a copy of the database with an outlet attachment in her suit and uploaded it back to their client's servers. Someone might try to intercept the upload if they knew she was doing it. After that, she would proceed with the nominal operation to pluck out the flash drive.

She was nearly done with the upload when the enemy forces attacked.

"Fuck!" Dante exclaimed as two or three heavy rifle bullets zipped through the air near his face while pulsecore rounds exploded around the building's periphery. Dark silhouettes, clearly humans in heavy armor, appeared from nowhere. Over a dozen of them surrounded the compound.

Dante threw himself to the ground and crawled behind a large chunk of the fallen wall. It wasn't much for cover, but at least it offered him some concealment. He stuck his carbine over the top and fired a short spread of five rounds toward the spots where most of the heat had come.

Nasreen screamed, "Goddammit! Who are they? I thought this area was clear! I'm almost done, too. Shit, shit, shit!"

Dante hoped she was smart enough to grab the drive and run for it rather than wait too long for the copy to upload. He would have suggested it, but there was suddenly so much gunfire that she wouldn't have heard him.

Two Reapers burst into the compound proper, one toting a heavy rifle, another a pulsecore. Dante's heart sank at once.

It was a hardcase team—a specialized, elite unit wearing the heaviest armor available. Hardcase raids were rare, given how expensive the equipment was, not to mention armor of that nature was difficult to maneuver in. Whoever had funded these guys had deep pockets and expected them to triumph quickly through overwhelming force.

Speed, stealth, and agility might be the only chances Dante and Nasreen had.

The two men noted Nasreen's position the instant they were inside the outer wall, but it took them an extra fraction of a second to aim. Dante already had his weapon trained on them. He fired four rounds at each. All but one of the shots found their mark, and the two figures were rocked and tossed around by the little green bursts.

The closer of the two had a smoking hole in his armor. Blood leaked from it. He tried to struggle on, but the life was draining out of him, and he slumped over before he could counterattack. The other Reaper was luckier. The pulsecore rounds hadn't struck him directly enough to get through his armor, although they'd still cracked it. The impacts had stunned and disoriented him and maybe snapped a few bones.

Dante rolled away from his meager concealment and dashed into the central structure as more shots burst in the air all around them. Nasreen was hovering above the podium where the flash drive lay with a wire still plugged into her suit. She practically bounced on her feet in her impatience to finish.

"Come on, come on, *come on*," she urged. "There!" She snatched the drive and spun, ready for battle. Her timing was perfect. If she had delayed more than one extra second, Dante would have seized her by the shoulders and bodily removed her from the premises, mission failure or not. There were never any future job offers for the dead.

Nasreen pivoted to see another Reaper breaching the compound from the opposite end. She fired three shots at the same time her adversary fired two. One of his struck the edge of a wall, exploding there before it could reach Nasreen, and the nimble woman rolled out of the way of the other. All three of her shots struck the Reaper around the upper chest and face. His head bent crazily to one side, blood leaking from under his smoking helmet, and he collapsed.

Dante grabbed her by the waist and hauled her toward the thinnest part of the advancing ring, where there was also a narrow gap in the outer wall. "That way," he barked. "Fire and maneuver, but mostly maneuver. We can't outshoot them all."

"Got it," she gasped.

He covered while she went first, moving as fast as she could while Dante sprayed pulsecore rounds in three directions, trying to keep the Reapers pinned down or disoriented. As soon as he finished shooting, he ejected his empty mag and dashed after his partner, trusting her to cover him briefly as he caught up.

It took her half a second longer than he'd like, but she came through. Pulse rounds streaked through the air to either side of him, and enemy fire briefly ceased while he was exposed. They slipped through the crack in the wall and bolted across the muddy field.

Midas pointed out, *"We're heading in the wrong direction. The ship is that way."* The AI then simulated a green arrow toward the left of Dante's field of vision, pointing toward their shuttle.

"I know," Dante growled. "Be quiet for a minute, okay?"

"Sorry. I was only trying to help."

When he thought about anything other than immediate survival, Dante wondered where the hell the Reapers had hidden. Obviously somewhere nearby, but they must have had *outstanding* cloaking tech to avoid being picked up by their earlier scan from the equipment aboard the ship.

Once again, whoever was funding these guys had spared no expense.

Dante also noticed the Reapers were firing seemingly at random, but he put two and two together quickly enough. They were shooting at the podium, hoping that he and Nasreen had left the flash drive behind. They were shooting at the power source. More gunshots and plasma bursts in the distance meant they'd probably attacked Nasreen's ship.

Something within him went cold. The Reapers weren't merely on a regular swipe job where they bullied a rival team to harvest the fruits of their labor, using violence only long enough to get what they wanted. Rather, they were on a scorch and tally run—a mission where the objective was to destroy anything of value and kill all involved targets.

Beyond that dismal truth, there was no time to speculate further.

Nasreen shouted, "I uploaded the copy. We still lose money if the drive gets—oh crap!"

Dante came up beside her and saw the confirmation of his fears. A small contingent of the hardcase Reapers was firing pulsecores at the ship. Their hired pilot had wisely ascended in the hope of escaping, but the way the craft drunkenly swayed from side to side meant they might have wounded him already. Nasreen could fly if the man died, but if they lost the ship, they were fucked.

He put a hand on her back and urged her straight across the plain, where they could use a nearby ravine to get out of sight while taking a direct path closer to the ship. It also meant that if the Reapers caught them there, they'd be sitting ducks.

They reached the edge of the ditch as an armored figure emerged from behind a tree. Rather than firing lead or plasma, it threw a small cylindrical device at them. A distinctive blue light shone from its core.

Something strange happened then. *"No!"* Dante and Midas cried out at the same time.

The EMP grenade went off in the air about five feet from Dante's face, close enough to point-blank for him to take the full brunt. The shockwave blasted him back on his ass. Nasreen staggered and swayed, but she aimed at the man and loosed half a magazine at him, blowing a smoldering hole through his midsection before he could finish the pair off.

Dante crumpled as the electromagnetic surge ripped through him. It paralyzed his muscles, electrified his bloodstream, overwhelmed his synapses, shorted out his suit, and attacked Midas, threatening to annihilate him.

He fell over. His brain simply stopped working for a second, which stretched into other seconds. Within his mind, he heard something like a scream of horror from Midas as the AI shut down and failed.

Nasreen sobbed, "Oh, God! My suit... What if that thing wiped the drive? Fuck, fuck. We still have the upload. Oh, God. Dante! Are you all right?"

When he didn't answer, she fell to her knees to grab him and pull him to his feet. He groaned and twitched, alive but barely conscious, shuddering under the EMP's aftereffects.

Trying not to panic, she dragged the man into the ravine and blindly pulled him along, simply trying to get farther away from the Reapers, who continued to close in and harass them with random fire. She couldn't see where their ship had flown off to. She hoped the pilot had neither died nor decided to abandon them in favor of flying straight back to the Stations.

A quarter of a mile later, the ravine ended, and the pair emerged onto flat ground. There was no sign of their shuttle, and dark, heavy clouds were rolling in as the cold winds picked up in strength. In three directions the horizon thickened with black figures. She didn't know how many Reapers there were in total, but it appeared that the dozen or so who had assaulted the compound were only a fraction of the total force.

They were effectively surrounded, badly outnumbered and outgunned, and had no means of escape. Dante could barely stand, much less fight.

Nasreen exhaled and closed her eyes.

"All right, Dante," she declared in a soft voice. "I'm sorry we ended up like this, but I'm going to sell my life dearly, okay? You seem like the 'go down fighting' type, so that's what I'll do on your behalf. Deal?" She reloaded her carbine and waited for the Reapers to come within range.

Dante groaned, burbling as another neuroelectric spasm went through him.

Then, above them, high-powered engines screamed: the engines of a shuttle. But the craft that emerged from the clouds wasn't theirs. It was something else, cheaper and heavier than the one they'd taken but still agile enough. It rocketed toward the enemy force, and its side hatch fell open while barely slowing. An object of surprisingly large size tumbled out, and whatever it was, it was human enough to handle a pulsecore. It opened fire while still in midair, green shots streaking down toward the Reapers.

Nasreen gawked. "The hell?"

The figure landed with a loud *clank*. It looked like a big, heavily armored man wearing a hooded cloak. He continued to fire while darting to and fro, moving at irregular intervals to confuse his foes and seeking cover wherever he could find it. At least one or two of the Reapers dropped dead under his unexpected assault, and the others converged behind a hillock to confer on tactics for dealing with him.

Nasreen's line of fire had opened, too. The Reapers were barely close enough for accurate pulsecore shots. She aimed and blasted an entire magazine at them, hitting and wounding one or two. They stumbled back, briefly tried to return fire, and joined their comrades in a defensive huddle. Meanwhile, the mystery gunman continued to pin them down with his speed, accurate shooting, and strange way of moving.

The shuttle turned in a broad swoop and came back toward where Nasreen and Dante crouched. As it moved sidelong behind them and slowed its descent to a hover, another miracle happened. At least, it seemed miraculous under the circumstances.

The bay door opened. Whoever was flying the ship was welcoming them aboard.

Dante was on his feet again, staggering and gritting his teeth. He moved in the right direction although he still swayed like he was severely drunk. Nasreen fired a few more shots at the Reapers to cover them. Then she leapt to Dante's side, put her free arm around his midsection, and heaved him toward the yawning door.

The shuttle had descended about as low as it could go, about two feet from the ground. With Nasreen's help, Dante clambered over the threshold and rolled into the craft's bay. Nasreen was beside him, pulling him farther in and trying to watch everything at once with her gun braced against her hip.

The hardcase men outside tried to rally. They weren't blind or stupid and saw their quarry getting away.

The unknown combatant who'd joined the battle against them interposed himself. His armor deflected or stopped a volley of lead bullets. He opened fire once more, his aim preternaturally good. Precise bursts of fire rained down on the enemy. One man fell dead, and three others cringed back, stunned or wounded.

Dante's head swam, and his vision went in and out of focus. Jittery tremors kept coursing through his body, paralyzing him every moment or two when he was preparing to stand and get back in the fight. The shuttle was moving again, its hover becoming a slow, rising swoop away from the Reapers.

Nasreen spoke somewhere above him. "Are you okay?"

"Yeah," he half-lied. "Just, ummm…" His brain flickered back into uselessness.

He looked toward the front of the shuttle. Seated behind the console and controlling the craft was Ambrose Igento, Dante's former pilot.

Dante groaned. His neural activity was too disrupted for him to form sentences or to think too hard about what this new development might mean. He could only process the fact that it was unexpected. And probably bad.

"Nas-Nasreen," he gasped. That was all he could say. He hoped she would notice everything he had seen and get the hint. So far, he couldn't see or hear her. She was somewhere above and behind him. He didn't know what she was doing.

The shuttle sped up, then slowed again as it came closer to the battle's flank. There was a lull in the fighting as the Reapers took cover to reload and rethink their plans. It was all the time the bulky figure needed to dash away from them, putting a couple of thick concrete walls from a collapsed building between himself and their guns.

Dante's gaze refocused on the spectacle outside. The mystery combatant had gotten ahead of the shuttle and was standing there, waiting for it. Ambrose didn't slow the craft. Instead, as it passed, the bulky man leapt straight into the bay door.

For a second, Dante thought he'd hallucinated it. The man had cleared a fourteen-foot-high distance from a *standing* jump. He'd timed it perfectly. The bay door closed behind him as the shuttle changed course again, veering to starboard and picking up speed as it ascended.

Again, it took a moment for Dante to process everything going on around him. When the huge man had landed within the ship's bay, the deck had vibrated with a loud metallic *clank* that far exceeded what a human, even a heavily armored one, should make when landing on a synthetic deck.

He looked at their other rescuer. The figure was shrugging off his cloak, and a nimbus of bright red hair appeared around his head as he removed his helmet.

Nasreen gasped. "Oh my *God.*" After all her bravery through the ordeal, hearing her suddenly sound like a terrified little girl was almost heartbreaking.

Dante only stared at the hatefully familiar, barely human face. It grinned at him with metal teeth.

"Long time no see, *pendejo,*" Mr. Hyde growled. The metallic reverb of his horrible voice echoed through the shuttle.

CHAPTER TWO

Dante had climbed back to his feet and discovered he could stand and walk shakily, right in time for Nasreen to take his hand, guide him to one of the seats, and strap him in for the rest of their flight. She was silent and clammy and looked like she wanted to be sick.

It was because of Hyde. The fact that the cyborg monstrosity had only laughed and wandered into the cargo hold, leaving them be, was somehow *worse* than if he'd immediately tried to crush their skulls with his bare hands.

What did the bastard want them alive for?

Dante sat staring straight ahead, thinking of Nasreen. She didn't often come across as frightened or vulnerable, but when she did, he felt oddly compelled to hold her, soothe her, and tell her everything would be all right. Not that he'd *done* that before. Still, it seemed warranted.

Now, though, he could not. They had to sit tight until the end of their passage through space.

Fortunately, Ambrose was an excellent pilot. Better than Nasreen, Dante had to admit. Ambrose specialized in flying. It was the only thing he'd done for a living since Dante had first heard of him.

Nasreen was a generalist. She was *good* at quite a few things but *phenomenal* at only a couple. Looking at her, he felt a sudden, slightly absurd urge to shake her hand for how far she'd come as a Marauder.

Although still not on *his* level—most people weren't—she'd progressed by leaps and bounds, learning the fundamentals faster than at least two-thirds of the other rookies he'd witnessed. Having a background in industrial espionage and private detective services helped.

Dante's gaze drifted toward the cockpit, where Ambrose's squat form sat in focused but aloof concentration. His hearing focused on the cargo hold, where occasional clanking and whirring sounds, combined with echoing profanity and guttural laughs, wafted toward them.

His jaw clenched, and his teeth ground together. *They might be better off dead,* he mused. It was possible that getting their heads blown off by the hardcase Reapers would be a better, cleaner, more merciful fate. Anything might be superior to being "rescued" by the two living people he hated the most.

As though intuiting his thoughts, Nasreen looked at him, put a hand on his forearm, and whispered, "I don't know what they have planned, but we're okay for now. Even if they're taking us back to you-know-who, we'll have a chance to get away. Something."

She was right. She was also probably reassuring herself as much as him. Dante had never been good at figuring out other people's emotional states or inner thoughts. He regarded such things as secondary to the facts of the external world, especially those necessary to accomplish whatever task lay before him. Still, he'd spent enough time around Nasreen to get a better feel for how her mind worked.

Of course, even if that weren't true, there would be no question to whom "you-know-who" referred.

On the plus side, the shuttle was coasting along nicely. Ambrose had navigated through a couple of dust storms and around some space debris with virtually no effort, and they were already feeling the grip of the Atlantica Stations' artificial gravity. Soon they would be home.

Unless, of course, Hyde succeeded in delivering them right into Cormac Slaine's lap.

Before Dante could pursue that unsettling thought, something happened in his brain, like the return of a sense that had shut down—as though he could hear nothing, and sounds suddenly became audible again. Midas was coming back online.

The faint impression of the AI's existence, a sympathetic thought pattern that underlay his thoughts and which he'd grown accustomed to over the months, rekindled itself. Then, after a moment of hesitancy, Midas's familiar voice spoke up.

"Sir. I'm sorry to inform you, but severe electrical damage has compromised several of my subroutines. I'm afraid we'll need to make a diagnostic and repair run, one that will require significant and intensive effort and proper tools. There's no way to repair them from the outside, and I don't believe you possess the know-how. We will probably need to return to the clinic in Berlin where they first installed me."

Dante frowned. "That doesn't surprise me. It's not your fault, Midas." He spoke softly, then thought better of it and instead directed his mental voice toward the AI, making no sound. *"We're not in a good place right now. We got rescued, and guess who it turned out to be?"*

Since he was already projecting his musings into the AI's processor, Midas figured it out almost immediately.

"Oh, dear." The artificial voice sighed. *"That is discouraging, isn't it? I can't guarantee my continued functionality until I'm repaired. I seem fine for now, but I could still have sudden errors, which may affect you. Might I offer to go offline until we can get my subroutines fixed?*

That way, any malfunctions of mine will leave you unscathed. Most likely. I cannot be certain."

Back in the cargo hold, something *clanked* and shuddered. Dante's hands clenched into fists. *"Yeah. Please do that, Midas."*

He looked at Nasreen. Something about the cold, determined, yet oddly fatalistic look in her eyes suggested that she was thinking much the same thing he was. Namely, they would probably be locked in a desperate, mortal struggle against Hyde in a matter of minutes. The huge ex-Reaper hadn't harmed them. He had seemingly *meant* to save their lives. But he was psychotic. There was no way to truly understand him and no reason to trust him.

Midas registered a last flicker of hope and empathy. He sensed that after he went offline, he might never switch on again because his host was dead. Then he fell silent, leaving Dante to whatever fate awaited him.

The mechanical whining sound grew louder as heavy metal feet clomped toward them. During a couple of the noisiest footfalls, Dante surreptitiously loosened the straps on his seat but left them lying in place to make it less noticeable. Now that the Stations' gravity was kicking in, there was less need to remain secure.

Dante inhaled. Beside him, Nasreen breathed out. Then both watched as the cyborg once known as Eduardo H. Curtidor stomped out and stood before them.

He grinned again like a feral dog about to tear into a helpless rodent. The paradox Hyde embodied struck Dante anew. His body was mostly a machine, the product of highly advanced and sophisticated technology. Yet nearly everything about the man was primitive, brutal, and animalistic. Modern science had served only to make him more effective as a crude, predatory beast.

Yet there were rumors, backed up in part by reliable documentation, that Mr. Hyde was very old. At least in late middle age, or perhaps even elderly by normal human standards. He could not have lasted so long in such a dangerous trade by being stupid.

Hyde gestured at Dante's lap with his gauntlet. "Your straps are loose. What, were you planning to jump up suddenly and surprise someone? I would *never* have expected something like that from you. Ha, ha."

Dante cleared his throat. "We're back in Station orbit. There's no need to stay fastened in. You seem to be doing fine while walking around free."

The huge man shrugged. "I can magnetize myself to the hull if need be. Fuck. You thought we were going to fight again, didn't you?" He turned his cold eyes to Nasreen. "You too, sweetie. Ha. Last time I saw you, you ran as fast as I've ever seen a lady move. You didn't piss yourself, did you, *chica*? Hope not."

A tremor went through Nasreen's body, despite her best effort to keep her cool. Dante couldn't quite tell if it was anger or fear. Probably a bit of both. "No," she stated.

"Well." Hyde chuckled, leaned back, and stretched his massive, armor-sheathed chest as he put his hands on his hips. "I would love to get another shot at both of you. A proper showdown against both at once. That would be fairer since only one of you at a time would be too easy."

Dante's lip curled. Hyde had defeated him the last time they'd met, but it had been *close*. Damn close.

Still, what he was saying so far indicated that he didn't intend to kill them anytime soon. Dante listened, remaining alert to any tricks.

The cyborg rumbled on. "But no, not yet. Killing you two fuckheads would be a pleasure. Heh, heh. It would be hard to decide which should go first and which should have to watch while the other—"

Ambrose called from the cockpit, surprisingly loud, and cut off Hyde amid his little fantasy.

"There's no reason to talk about things like that, is there? Mr. Hyde isn't in the business of killing us right now. He came to save me not long ago. Let's focus on why that is. Shall we, Mr. Curtidor?"

Dante kept his eyes on Hyde, but much of his attention went toward the pilot. Somehow, Ambrose's half-sincere, almost smarmy comment induced a deeper rage than anything Hyde had said. His jaw muscles tensed, and a flash of red crossed his vision. After all, Dante knew up front that Hyde was a monstrosity. But he had legitimately believed that Ambrose was his friend.

Hyde's bestial face contorted in annoyance as though forced to listen to a small dog yapping from behind a fence.

Nevertheless, Ambrose went on. "Yes, when Hyde came to help me, it was, oh, a month or two after someone else saved me from murder. Two assassins came for me while I was drunk and on my way home from a recital."

Dante tried not to snort. Ambrose had turned out to be a surprisingly talented pianist but playing for a glorified cocktail bar wasn't quite a *recital.*

"Those men had to be working for Slaine Solar Solutions. SSS has been trying to tie up all its loose ends, gradually eliminating everyone who knows the truth about their practices. I don't know who saved me that night, but I'm no fool. It was you, Dante, wasn't it? I can't say why I think that. Somehow, the pieces all fall together right. Who else could it have been?"

Nasreen squinted at Dante, half-furious and half-concerned.

He ignored her for the moment. "Yeah. It was me. I was going to let you die. You can probably guess why. I decided against it." He exhaled slowly. "For some reason."

"Well," Ambrose continued, brushing off the allusion to his betrayal of his former captain. "Slaine is a persistent man. He tried again. Someone else came to save me the next time. The big, charming fellow you see back there."

Hyde laughed, a sound like thunder rumbling over the wreckage of a battle.

Ambrose concluded, "He has come to the rescue for all three of us. You might even say we owe him. You can probably guess why someone like him would do such a thing. Slaine has begun to see *him* as a loose end, too. Isn't that right, Mr. Curtidor?"

Hyde's face darkened, growing uglier but somehow less frightening as his mood turned serious. Outside, the vast dome of the nearest Station drew closer.

"Yeah." Hyde's nostrils flared. It was one of the few facial motions that were still entirely organic. "Don't get any ideas that I *like* any of you. You're pieces of meat. I'm not doing anything because I care about your well-being."

Dante smiled a little. "That's okay, Hyde. If you'd said you wanted us to live long and prosper, we wouldn't have believed you anyway."

The hulking cyborg narrowed his eyes, suggesting grim respect more than anything. "It's 'cause I need you. We have, what's the fucking term for it, uh, common cause. You guys have skills. I'm good at what I do. But I only really do one thing."

It was unnecessary to state what they all knew. Hyde *killed*. It was why he existed. For all his ruthless arrogance and general barbaric demeanor, he seemed aware of the fact. He wasn't a man who would have an easy time making a living in most other trades.

Dante pointed out, "Yes. Though you didn't *quite* do it last time we met, did you?"

Nasreen added, "Same."

Hyde stared back at them. It was like looking at a shark from behind the secure wall of an aquarium tank. The hunger to devour was there, but the creature knew it couldn't act on its urges. Yet.

The cyborg's voice fell to what passed for a whisper crackling with static feedback. "Once we're done dealing with SSS, I'll have to smooth out those two wrinkles in my otherwise nearly perfect record."

Dante didn't doubt that he meant it. What surprised him was that Hyde was becoming more eloquent than he thought. The man usually spoke in a way that suggested a level of intelligence barely up to speed with most adult humans. Maybe he was smarter than he let on.

Hyde went on, "I need you because it helps to have a pilot, a spy, and a stealth expert. You two aren't too bad as fighters, either. Not as good as me. But acceptable. The four of us could make a big impact on our mutual adversary."

Dante shook his head at how the monstrous synthesized voice pronounced the terms. "Possibly, but it's a crazy idea. I'm surprised you know a word like *adversary*."

Nasreen nodded in agreement. "Yeah, it has, like, four syllables."

"Shut up," Hyde grunted, more in mild annoyance than anything. "We have things to talk about. You are the ones who know less than you think. Your stunts have threatened SSS in a big way. You're making them look bad, undercutting their business, and making politics more difficult. But you don't seem to be aware of the real situation.

"SSS is connected to something bigger than only the organization Cormac Slaine built. It's part of a whole fucking network. That network is going to start showing off its supremacy. Soon. It'll be more than sending a Reaper crew after you. You don't know all the tricks they have in store."

Dante's stomach roiled, partly in aggravation at how cryptic Hyde was being but also because if he was telling the truth, everything had abruptly become far more complicated.

"How the hell could you have learned all this? Did you see evidence of it? You basically said you're nothing but hired muscle. Do you mean they let you in on all the sensitive inner workings of the organization?" Dante had his suspicions about how the brute would respond. Still, a clear answer was by no means guaranteed.

Hyde turned his head to look out the window as they approached the outer reaches of a major landing bay. Other ships and shuttles floated past.

"Exactly, Shale. They see me as a blunt instrument. A very *effective* one. They don't think I'm smart enough to pose any kind of a threat except the physical kind. Ha, ha. They don't always notice when I notice. They don't care what I see or what I know, particularly. But I pay attention to things. I've seen where the fruits of their special harvests go."

Nasreen spoke in a low voice. "You mean the o-harvests?" The undertone of revulsion in her voice was unmistakable.

Hyde nodded and looked back at the pair. "Yeah. What the fuck else would I mean? Ha, ha. I've killed some people to protect that information. The usual *pendejos* in law enforcement, private investigation, and stuff. They kept looking into all these shady places we used as fronts and shit. You know how it is."

Dante nodded. He'd killed many people too, but only in survival situations, and usually Dirtside where there was no law to speak of. The way Hyde spoke so casually about murdering public servants and private citizens served as a useful reminder of what he was.

"Strands," Hyde added, his artificial voice taking on a buzzing purr. "All these strands connecting them. Like a web. Atlantica— all the Stations together—is a web, but there are a bunch of different spiders spinning in the corners. They're allowed to do it because they offer some prey they catch to the other group, the bigger spiders at the center.

"It's something I've known for a long time. Didn't make any real difference to me. Again, I'm a blunt instrument. Now the spiders think they can bite *me*. Fuck that. So, I'm using what I know against them. That's where you *people* become useful."

Dante marveled at the fact that Eduardo Curtidor had tried to paint an elaborate poetic metaphor and half-succeeded. The information he hinted at was far more interesting.

"It works both ways, Hyde. You know we're gunning for SSS. You'll be useful to us, too."

The cyborg made a snorting, barking sound that resembled someone banging a microphone against a hard surface. "You think you're soooo goddamn smart, Shale. Yeah, we're using each other, whatever. You don't know the half of it. This group, these people behind Slaine...they've been part of his whole rise to success. He didn't do it all on his own. They go back farther than he does. All the way back to Old Atlantica on Earth. I remember when Atlantica Metro went up into orbit. They were around even before *that.*"

Nasreen's mouth fell open. "You *remember?* That was seventy years ago!"

Hyde laughed. "Look at me. Does it look to you like most of me *ages*, little girl? Yes, I remember. I was a young man. Stupid, violent young man. I didn't want to get too old to keep doing what I do best. So, I invested in myself. It was worth it. I'm still going strong at my current age."

He grinned, showing off his perfect artificial teeth, and the horrible fact of his mere existence was never clearer. He was an unnatural life-form, a thing which should not be.

Trying not to shudder, Dante interjected, "Atlantica. What about it?"

"It's always been the dirty heart of everything that happens in orbit," the brute continued. "It always had more than its fair share of shady groups and big scary conspiracies, going back to its founding in the, uh, the 1950s and '60s. Something about that place, the Atlanticore crystal and all the ancient shit they unearthed there, drew those people like flies. Whether they were the same old devils waiting for their next chance or new demons sprung up from the chaos after we abandoned the Earth."

He was referring to the rumors that a secret society had

dominated Old Atlantica. Certain rather paranoid people, right up until the present, liked to theorize that the same organization had persisted into the current year.

Hyde went on. "They're always the same, whoever they are. They try to justify it by saying, 'Oh, we're protecting humanity. We're smarter than you are. We know more. Let us run everything.' They guided things in Atlantica for a long time, and they still do now in the Stations."

Nasreen muttered, "That's an old conspiracy theory. You had better not be making this up based on crap you heard some crazy drunk rambling about to distract us."

Before Hyde could respond, Ambrose called, "We're docking. Get ready. They will not like it if we spend too much time idling, so we best wrap up our conversations, yes?"

Hyde snarled, "Shut the goddamn hell up, you fat little fuck."

Ambrose fell silent, glowering.

Hyde turned back to the pair seated before him as the ship glided smoothly into the bay. The noise and interference were minimal, as though Ambrose was deliberately doing his job as well as he could, specifically to spite Hyde for his dismissal of him.

"I can kill people who think they're in no danger," Hyde boasted with an unpleasant twinkle in his eye. "This group propping Slaine up is too big for me alone. I'm not stupid. I can't take them down completely. But I can cut the strings that connect them to SSS. Then it won't be worth their time and money to protect Slaine and his stupid company. At that point, they won't care if they're watching a news stream and seeing me holding Cormac Slaine's heart in my hand."

He extended his gauntlets and flexed his fingers. Nasreen recalled how close she'd come to being seized by the neck with that hand—how cold, hard, and powerful it was, and how easily it could have crushed the life out of her. It wasn't much of a stretch to imagine him ripping a person's heart out of their chest.

Dante quipped, "We get it. So, for the time being, you share a common interest with us in revenge against SSS. And you, Ambrose, are along for the ride because I'm guessing you like being alive."

"Correct," the pilot remarked in dark resignation.

Dante looked at Nasreen. "What do you think?"

She glanced at the men around her. "I don't like it. I generally don't work with people who thought killing me would be funny. " She forced herself to look Hyde in the eye. "If what you say is true, there is a certain logic to it."

The hideous mechanical face distorted slightly to accommodate the size of Hyde's broad, toothy grin. "Good."

CHAPTER THREE

The problem with space travel these days, Nasreen lamented to herself, was that it was even less anonymous than it had been a few years ago, which wasn't saying much. These days, dockmasters collected as much information as possible. In many Stations, it was a requirement to comply with government policies.

Her misadventure not too long ago, in which she'd gone to erase video footage of Dante's face only to run into Hyde, had directly resulted from the docks' increasingly draconian and intrusive policies. For the time being, there was nothing they could do to avoid it.

Except lie and cheat, of course.

"Hold it." She raised her voice and sharpened her tone in a way that instantly got the attention of Dante, Ambrose, and even Hyde. "Nobody leaves this shuttle until we have our cover identity taken care of. I can probably manage something within five minutes or so, but I need you all to cooperate."

Ambrose had left the cockpit and wandered closer to the seating area, although he still hung back at a safe distance. It was obvious that he didn't want to be any closer to Hyde—or Dante—

than he had to at any time. "Is that necessary? This isn't the same Station we left from. We departed from Paris. When we—"

"Yes," Nasreen interrupted him. "It *is* because I don't want to come back here later in the middle of the night to change data or wipe security footage. It's easier to do it right the first time."

Hyde caught on to what she was referring to and chortled. The sound made her borderline nauseated.

Dante turned toward her while shrugging his coat onto his shoulders. "Okay. What do we need to do?"

"We'll fabricate fake identities for Ambrose and Hyde to sever any immediate or obvious connection between the two of them leaving Paris and re-arriving here." Here was Pentapolis, formerly known as New York City.

Ambrose protested, "The shuttle is registered to me."

Nasreen waved it off. "Don't worry about that. I'll swap out your registration for ours. Meaning, the ship we left behind on Earth, which those Reapers have probably blown to hell by now anyway."

"*Probably,*" Dante emphasized. "They might have stolen it, making our lives difficult."

He was right. "Yes, but we should be able to register the info before they can get it back to the Stations, in which case it would turn up as stolen or unregistered on their end. Then either they'd have to flee and destroy it anyway, or everything will get tangled in red tape long enough for us to think of something else."

Hyde let out another growling, reverberant laugh. "And the fake identities? How do you convince someone that I'm a normal person? For fuck's sake..."

She still could barely believe she was *helping* a creature like him. Her brain wasn't operating at full functionality, she suspected, because part of her was still abjectly terrified of him. It took a not-insignificant force of will to suppress the memory of her flight from him and how close he'd come to snapping her neck.

"For starters, put that cloak on to hide yourself a little. I'll handle the rest. I keep a bank of false identities I can draw upon when I need to. For myself, but also for anyone else I have to work with. Now give me your ID cards and let me use the console."

It took closer to six or seven minutes than five. Long enough, she had to admit, that the dockmaster might be getting suspicious about why they hadn't yet emerged or sent their info to the facility's system. It wasn't *too* uncommon for travelers to pause to gather their things or decompress from the stresses of space flight, but lingering was discouraged. And the docks weren't all that busy.

For Mr. Hyde, she selected "Mario Ramirez." The name reflected his vaguely Iberian or Latino heritage, although the populations of the Atlantica Stations were mixed enough by now that a person's name didn't necessarily have much to do with their ethnicity. The nonexistent Mr. Ramirez was an old combat veteran who'd been through the medical system many times. It might help explain Hyde's various augmentations if anyone was rude enough to ask about them.

As for Ambrose, Nasreen wasn't sure what his heritage was so she randomly picked a profile with the name "Adam X" and paired it with a background of a former commercial pilot, now retired after making some money trading stocks. She briefly explained this to both men.

Hyde smirked. "An old soldier," he mused. "Not too inaccurate."

Ambrose merely shrugged. "That's fine. At least I'm still a pilot. Commercial pilots are rarely much good, though. All they do is fly in circles around the Stations. They rarely go outside the artificial gravity, into space proper. Is that how you think of me?"

Dante said, "Shut up, Ambrose. Play along until we're out of here."

Ambrose flinched and kept his mouth shut after that.

The quartet emerged, and all noticed the dockmaster and one of his lackeys striding toward the craft. They'd been seconds away from the embarrassment of having to be ordered out to register themselves.

Nasreen waved at the man. "Hi. Sorry for the delay. We have a sick man here." She gestured at Dante. "Food poisoning."

The dockmaster's nose wrinkled. His distaste was strong enough that he was in a hurry to get done with them. After Nasreen gave him their identities and the ship's credentials, he simply recorded them and waved them along, leaving his subordinate to park the shuttle in the storage bay. At no point did he say anything other than the minimal words necessary to process them.

As they walked away from the dock, Nasreen sighed. "Ahhh. I see the legendary New York politeness is still a thing."

Pentapolis was so-named due to the five boroughs of the ironically named Old New York. Each had originally been raised on its own, then fused into a single city once in orbit. Collectively they were one of the largest metropolises among the Stations, having absorbed much of the population of the former United States and Canada.

They proceeded into the town proper. Like its Earthbound namesake, it was a crowded, bustling city, oddly old-fashioned compared to the ultra-modern likes of Celestial Seoul. The Americans, paradoxically given their nation's youth back on the planet, were among the more sentimental peoples in the new orbital world.

As they strolled toward the nearest bus station, Dante spoke up. "I said before that the Reapers might have stolen our ship. I doubt it, though. They were on a scorch and tally run. Destruction of the target. They weren't only trying to hijack our shit. Our pilot is probably dead and the ship scrapped and vaporized. We'll have to account for that."

Nasreen's gut clenched. The pilot had been a nice enough

man, hard-nosed but decent. She hadn't *known* him, but it pained her to think he'd been murdered simply for being in the wrong place at the wrong time.

"Yes, I will find ways to smooth that over. Also, at some point I'll have to check in with our client and report the bare basics to him. He did at least get the copied data beamed to his servers, which is the most important thing, but he wanted the flash drive if possible. We'll take a pay hit for that if it's damaged."

"Whatever," Dante mumbled. "We have enough money, and this goes deeper than that particular job. Oh, that reminds me, did you ever turn your camera stream back on after you started copying?"

That, too, was something they would need to address. "No. We'll have to touch base with the network to assure them we're still alive. A feed going dead like that and staying offline for hours isn't common."

"Hey," Hyde interrupted, his echoing guttural voice about as welcome as a Nightmutt in a fancy restaurant, "where are we going, anyway? Ambrose and I were on the run, you know. We don't *live* anywhere right now."

They were almost to the bus station.

Nasreen put her fingertips to her temples and rubbed, closing her eyes to relax and focus her thoughts. She exhaled slowly through her mouth.

"I have a couple of boltholes here in Pentapolis. Nothing spacious or luxuriant, but it will give you a place to stay and lie low while we figure everything out. You should be safe there. I keep the security of my places under strict lock and key, and I have ways of receiving word through the grapevine if anyone starts sniffing around them or tries to take them away from me. Come on, then. The closest one is in New Brooklyn."

She stepped out onto the walk beside the street and headed into the bus station. Dante glided close behind her yet never seemed too intrusive. Hyde clomped behind them in the rear, moving slower than usual to decrease the volume of his heavy metallic footfalls. Given his height and size, he still kept up without much trouble.

Ambrose waffled. He slowed down and sped back up, unsure who he should keep closest to. His slightly smug demeanor while piloting the shuttle had evaporated now that he was out of his element and at the mercy of the two people who most frightened him. If anything, he seemed less scared of Hyde than of Dante. His fear of the towering cyborg was still significant.

"We—ah, um," he stammered, addressing Nasreen, "we, meaning myself and Mr. Curtidor, will both be staying in the same small place, you mean?"

Nasreen wondered what the hell he had expected. "Yes. As I said, I'm not rich enough to offer you high-end accommodations. Having you together will greatly reduce the amount of risk management I have to worry about."

Ambrose let out a groaning sigh of defeat and continued to shuffle along. Hyde chortled in amusement. The mountainous figure seemed to appreciate the humor in the situation since it involved someone else's suffering.

The ride to the apartment in question wasn't long, about fifteen minutes. Human traffic in Pentapolis was constant, as though trying to live up to the old slogan about New York being "the city that never sleeps." It wasn't as suffocatingly thick as rush hour periods in some other large Stations.

Hyde's enormous size and evident meta-human status drew rude stares from curious or anxious fellow travelers. Some of them tried to see what he was hiding under the cloak. He simply glared at them until they stopped.

Once they exited in a lower-income area dense with high-rise housing projects, Nasreen had them huddle around her at a near-empty street corner.

"Okay, as I said, this place isn't fancy. It's not a proper safe-house so much as a stopping-over point, but you two will have to make do." She pointed at Hyde and Ambrose. "The other advantage is that it's easier than a 'real' apartment to burn."

Ambrose's mouth wrinkled. "What do you mean, burn?"

Nasreen waved dismissively. She had lapsed into the old pro lexicon of a freelance spy, forgetting that not everyone would be familiar with the terminology. "Severing all my connections to the place, eliminating the records, covering up the fact that I ever had ownership or even interest in it. That sort of thing. In other words, if something comes up, I can delete its existence from my portfolio without much trouble, provided you guys get the hell out when I tell you to."

"Sure," Hyde rumbled. "Take us up."

Five minutes later, they located the bolthole at the end of a narrow hallway on the seventeenth floor of one of the projects. The whole way up, locals gave them a wide berth. Hyde's presence tended to have that effect on people. Despite having some of his usual energy sapped by the EMP incident, Dante didn't look like someone worth messing with, either.

Nasreen used a burnable ID app on her sphere to open the door, then stood aside and let the men go in first. "Here we are. It's not much, but it's a secure place for you to stay for the time being."

Hyde predictably barged in first, the apartment barely containing his massive frame. It consisted of little more than a bunk with two beds, a table that doubled as a dining surface and desk, a minimal kitchenette facility, and a bathroom with a shower stall. There was no room to move around, only to survive.

Ambrose didn't try to hide his disappointment. "Ohh. It's like a closet." He hunched his shoulders and looked at his roommate. There would be no way for him to avoid Hyde, whom he still feared and loathed. The two would be on top of one another during their stay.

Hyde made a static-laden snorting sound. "Whatever. I'm

used to much worse. Wasn't always a *high-end* Reaper. Ha, ha. Slept in a few dumpsters back in the previous century. I remember those days..."

Nasreen gave Ambrose a chip card. "Here. There's an active account on it with some money. Enough to pay your bills and order food for about the next four weeks. Don't overspend on expensive stuff. Make yourselves comfortable, otherwise. We'll be in touch."

Dante added, "We'd love to stay and have a beer, but I'm pretty sure I need professional help." His voice dripped with a degree of bitter sarcasm unusual for him.

Hyde laughed. "You're just *now* figuring that out, Shale?"

"Better late than never." Dante turned away from the cyborg. "You're probably *beyond* help. Thanks for rescuing us, though. That almost makes up for trying to kill me on the o-harvest run. Now the score is halfway settled between us, and you're merely a big, ugly, unpleasant guy I used to work with."

Hyde's grin was as bestial as ever. "I don't see it that way. Remember—at some point, if we win, I won't *need* you anymore."

Nasreen suddenly recalled her first meeting with Hyde, and again it took immense self-control to maintain her composure. "Sounds like fun. We need to go. Relax, and don't do anything stupid, okay? Bye."

They left with no further words, shutting and locking the door behind them.

As they emerged from the building a bit later and wandered toward a vacant lot that looked quiet enough, Nasreen mentioned, "There are hidden cameras there. I'll check up on them periodically to ensure they don't try to run away. Or to see if Hyde has killed Ambrose yet."

Dante nodded. "Good idea. It sounds like they have been on the run together for a while. I wouldn't have expected they'd make it work, but people can always surprise you."

Nasreen put a hand on his arm. "You mentioned professional help. You probably should see a doctor. Also—"

"Berlin," he finished for her. "Midas came back online for a minute in the shuttle, but he's all messed up. He offered to shut down until we could get him repaired. Physically, I don't think I need anything that rest can't cure, but assuming Dr. Kieffer knows how to do a basic medical checkup and stick machines into people's brains, I could use one of those as well."

Nasreen tugged on his arm, and they walked away from the housing projects. A few locals passed but ignored them, likely on their way to work or running domestic errands.

"We'll do that tonight if we can. If not, we should head back to Seoul. Or we could rent a place here. I'll call the clinic and see what they say."

Dante shrugged. "Yeah. The sooner, the better. I'm okay, I think. But things have changed in a big way. Whoever financed the team that hit us, they weren't fucking around."

Nasreen hugged herself as they crossed the street. The air here, as in most Stations, was climate-controlled, but New Yorkers seemed to prefer somewhat cooler temperatures than she liked. "So it would seem. Slaine could afford it, I think, but I suppose it adds weight to Hyde's claim that other people are propping him up who are even richer and more powerful than he is."

Dante made a low growling sound that emerged from deep in his chest. "He's full of shit if you ask me. Hyde, I mean. No way to be certain. I don't buy it. Either he's setting us up for something, or it's some sick joke of his like he thinks it's more fun if he adds a bunch of conspiracy theories into his little story."

Nasreen cocked an eyebrow. "Did you know him before he, um, abandoned you?"

"Not really. But he's insane. I believe he's on the outs with SSS. Someone as unstable as him wouldn't be an asset to Mr. Slaine forever. I'm having a hard time buying this crap about a shadowy organization that goes back to the Old World. A 'web of spiders,' as he put it. Trying to be a fucking poet."

Dante's mind tended toward the literal. It made it easier to separate true from false and cut back on the bullshit. He didn't like metaphors. Hearing such attempts at flowery language from a beast in human form, like Hyde, was somehow worse than if it had come from someone for whom that crap was more typical.

"It's not unheard of for secret investment groups to have their fingers in multiple front companies. Or organized crime. Maybe Hyde was being melodramatic. The gist of what he was saying isn't as far-fetched as you seem to think."

She pulled out her sphere and found her contact info for the AI clinic. Beside her, Dante stared at the false sky of the Station's dome that separated the city from the void of space and murmured, "Yeah. We'll see."

CHAPTER FOUR

Nasreen saw that Dante was still gripping the bar with a deathly tight grasp, to the point that the whites of his knuckles showed through his olive skin. Yet he'd passed the first half of the ride standing perfectly still, leaning slightly on the pole that supported the overhead bar, and staring at his feet, unspeaking.

He looked unwell. There was nothing obvious about it, but Nasreen could sense it so to speak…a dimming of light, an obstruction in his energy or something. It wasn't only the holographic masks they wore to subtly alter their features.

She nudged him. Their car on the shuttle bus wasn't too crowded, relatively speaking. It was about three-quarters full. She still spoke in a low, soft voice.

"Hey. Are you doing okay?" She wondered if it had come out sounding excessively gentle and concerned. If so, that might embarrass or annoy a man used to being self-sufficient.

Dante blinked and rolled his shoulders. "I'm fine for now. I don't think I'll completely recover until this is over. But I'm functional. Just tired."

She nodded. "Okay, then. Hang in there."

To reduce complications and hopefully speed up the process,

they'd caught a shuttle on a continuous line across what had once been the entire Western world. From Pentapolis it went through Londonburg and Nouveau Paris to their appointment in Deutschheim—or as many people still colloquially called it, Berlin.

As they passed Londonburg, Nasreen's palms and scalp grew itchy and sweaty. The combination of the two was one of the few nervous reactions she'd never managed to fully control or eliminate. Fortunately, most people couldn't notice it.

Nothing happened, though. Her cryptic fears that Londonburg's elite might have installed a new and more intensive passenger scanning system, that something about either of them had tripped a silent alarm or alerted a watchful eye, had proved fruitless. As far as she knew, they were still safe from Cormac Slaine, his agents, and his mysterious and powerful backers.

Unless someone was following or tracking them, making no move until they reached their destination. Nasreen had dealt with situations like that before, and so had Dante. There were ways to avoid scrutiny if it were the case.

When the vehicle passed through the massive tube connecting the Paris dome to the Berlin dome, Nasreen did a hasty mental calculation of how long it would take to walk to the clinic from a stop an extra mile or half-mile away from their usual departure point. They had left early to accommodate such a tactic, so they ought to be fine.

Two stops past their usual exit point, they disembarked in a newer, cleaner, and more boring part of the city.

Dante spoke for the first time since Nasreen had checked on him. "I only hope they've prepared the equipment and shit they'll need. We told them what the problem was when we made the appointment, so they'd better not do that fucking thing doctors like to do where they pretend to know nothing about why you're there and make you repeat everything you already put in the initial report. Doctors, and mechanics."

His voice sounded weak and slurred rather than its more common sharp, brusque cadence, and it was unusual for him to complain about minor inconveniences like this.

Nasreen patted him on the shoulder. "There, there, dear," she began in a half-mocking, motherly tone. "If they make us wait too long, I'll take you out for ice cream later. Yes, I made sure they were aware that we need this taken care of as soon as realistically possible. I'm sure they got the message because I mentioned that with Midas so messed up, he could get hacked a lot more easily—which might allow someone to trace his origin back to them."

"Oh," Dante muttered. "Good."

Despite how feeble he sounded, he maintained a brisk walk as they moved between major streets and narrow alleys. A couple of disreputable characters eyed them with malignant curiosity, only to change their minds and let them pass unmolested after sizing the pair up.

Nasreen knew Deutschheim better than Dante did. She led the way through the city as they worked back toward their destination, approaching the clinic at an oblique angle from their usual route in the past.

Finally, they came to an alley where they could see the building that housed the clinic. Nasreen checked the time. They were nearly fifteen minutes early, as planned. They crept to the mouth of the alley, keeping close to the wall where its shade pooled around them and hid them from easy sight. They also gained a better view of the clinic and anyone who might show up there—anyone who might have followed them, for example.

Nasreen watched. One person emerged from the building and walked away, but the only foot traffic was people passing. She glanced sidelong at her partner.

The long journey, and the added stresses of having to be more careful than usual, were taking a toll on Dante. He leaned against the wall, functional but fatigued. Nasreen didn't dare speak aloud but wished she could reassure him that they were almost home, so to speak, and could at last take care of him.

Another ten minutes passed, and nothing seemed amiss. Their official arrival time was in three minutes.

Nasreen exhaled. She tugged on Dante's sleeve, and the two moved down through the alley. They kept to the shadows until they emerged abruptly into the lighted avenue and strolled to the building's front doors like casual pedestrians on a mundane errand.

Once inside, Nasreen rapidly scanned the lobby for anything that looked out of place or new faces. All was normal, and the receptionist was someone she'd seen working at least five times over the last year.

Nasreen turned her head to click off the holographic mask. It hadn't altered her features too much—the more pronounced the effect, the less convincing it was and looked blatantly artificial. Although her mask had been subtle, it was enough that if she kept it on as she approached the desk, the receptionist might be confused or alarmed. By turning it off well before her face was in clear sight, she could avoid unnecessary hassle.

She smiled at the receptionist as she drew closer. "Hello. We're back for another checkup. It might be a longer stay this time, I'm afraid. He seems to have come down with something serious." She poked Dante in the ribs.

He grunted and nodded. Then she heard him *click* his mask off, and she cursed herself for not verbally reminding him to do that earlier. The clinic understood that sometimes its patients had to be discreet. With the woman recognizing Nasreen, all should be well.

The receptionist squinted at Dante's face to confirm that he, too, was someone she knew. "*Ja*, of course. Fill out the usual forms and the doctor will see you."

Nasreen accepted a small tablet and went through the motions of filling out the necessary electronic paperwork. Since they were right on time, they needed to wait only five minutes or so before a nurse beckoned them into the back area and took them down the elevator to the secret operating floor.

The subterranean lobby was like a colder, more spartan replica of the one on the ground floor. Here was where the real business took place. Here, the clinic made the bulk of its profits off illegal or quasi-legal AI implants and improvements.

To Nasreen's pleasant surprise, Dr. Kieffer, the specialist who'd first implanted Midas to begin with, appeared to greet them almost immediately. "Miss Joelle. Welcome back. I understand that this is a matter of some urgency, so I was able to reschedule another patient to get you in tonight. You are a valued customer here."

She almost laughed. "Thank you, Doctor. We'd also like you to do a basic medical checkup on Mr. Raksha." While she trusted the man, they had never revealed to him that Dante Shale was Dante Shale, instead only giving Kieffer aliases. "Jordan Raksha" was the name Dante currently used in his persona of the Hellcat, although he'd used "Gregor Luciano" before that.

Dante spoke his piece. "I got hit with an EMP. While wearing a full suit. And while Midas was active. I could barely walk or think for close to an hour after that. I've been tired ever since. No obvious major injuries, though."

Kieffer raised his eyebrows in concern. "Yes, that can sometimes cause complications. We will look you over thoroughly before we plug into Midas. Yes?"

"Sounds good." Dante inhaled deeply. "Let's get it over with."

The three of them went to the same room where Kieffer installed Midas. Dante stripped down to his underclothes and sat on the couch while Kieffer sanitized everything and prepared to examine him.

When it was over, the doctor concluded, "You appear to be fine so far. We must also do scans, however. If there is damage, it is probably in your brain since the AI was most affected. After having an AI implant for a long time, the brain begins to integrate with it on a, how do you say, bioelectric level. Damage to the AI can become damage to the human brain."

Dante clenched his jaw and balled up his fists. "And nobody fucking told me this was a risk when you first drilled the goddamn thing into my head?"

Nasreen frowned at him but kept silent since it was a legitimate question.

Kieffer flinched. "I did not know you would be in danger of EMP exposure. It is a rare risk factor. Common electrocution can also cause such problems. I apologize for not emphasizing this when we spoke in the past. If there is damage, we can repair it. I will be back in a minute."

He nodded to them and excused himself.

Nasreen came over and sat beside him. "I should have warned you as well, but frankly, it didn't occur to me as a realistic possibility either. After all, no one told *me* that Reapers sometimes use EMP grenades against humans."

Dante scratched his head. "Yeah, yeah, it's all my fault. Whatever. If Kieffer is right, let's get it fixed. Midas annoys me half the time, but it's good to have him around. Especially if Slaine is turning up the heat against us."

Nasreen frowned as though she was about to say something but hesitated and kept quiet.

Kieffer and a nurse returned with a cartful of strange equipment. They had Dante lie back on the couch and hooked him up to a headset connected to some sort of scanner or computer, which they used to gain a better assessment of Midas' condition. And the state of Dante's gray matter.

The doctor's face was grave but not horrified or despondent, which was at least somewhat encouraging.

He reported, "Yes, there are problems, but also solutions. After the EMP struck, Midas attempted a hard reset, which is how an AI normally deals with a common error. In this case, the reset may have done as much damage as the EMP itself. It has compromised some of his systems. It is made worse because of the complexity of his programming. The enormous number of upgrades and subroutine packages you had installed means there was more that could go wrong."

Once more, Dante gritted his teeth. "Blame Midas himself for that. He never shut up about wanting more upgrades."

Looking at the screen, Kieffer shook his head. "Repairing all the damaged pathways would be difficult. I suggest, instead, that we wipe the programming clean and start over from the beginning. You may lose some of the upgrades, but it will be the most efficient way of ensuring you have a functional AI."

Dante thought about it for a second. "Wait. Does that mean it would erase Midas', um, personality?"

"Yes. You would have to begin with a new operating system, as you did when we first installed him."

Nasreen watched, fascinated, as Dante stiffened and looked straight up at the ceiling. "No. I refuse, then. Midas is... I don't know. We have a good working relationship. I promised him I wouldn't erase him as long as he behaved."

Kieffer's shoulders slumped, probably because the alternatives meant more work for him. He and Dante argued the point for a couple of minutes. Nasreen observed them but stayed out of it. She wasn't too shocked when Dante prevailed.

"Yes, that is fine." Kieffer relented. "We understand. We can attempt to, ah, 'trim' the corrupted files and nonfunctional subroutines. This will take some time, and it may mean that you will still lose most of the upgrades."

Dante's nostrils flared. "Fine. Get rid of whatever you have to as far as the extra stuff goes. But don't touch his core program. Those are your parameters, and I insist that you stay within them. If we lose all the junk he made me buy, fine, but Midas himself is to remain intact."

The doctor pushed his chair back from the console. "Very

well. We will begin the operation immediately. Since it will be more invasive than wiping the system clean, you will have to stay overnight to rest and recover. Is this acceptable?"

Dante flicked his gaze at Nasreen, who nodded. "Yes, that's fine."

Kieffer stood and went to fetch the nurse again to assist him, along with all the stuff he would need. While they waited, Dante inquired, "He said *operation*. Does that mean he's going to be cutting shit out of my brain with a scalpel?"

Nasreen prodded the sole of his foot with the tip of hers. "I doubt it. He'll probably inject a few nanobots and do it remotely. So instead of a knife carving things out, it will be more like little bugs eating up the corrupted dendrites, or whatever they're called. I forget. Kind of like how primitive peoples used to put maggots on wounds since they would eat the necrotic tissue but leave the healthy stuff, which prevented infection."

Dante sat halfway up to glare at her. "Are you trying to get back at me for teaching you this line of work to begin with? Because that's the sort of thing you'd say if—" He stopped abruptly, noticing how angry he sounded, and drew a deep breath. "No. Sorry. I didn't mean that. But goddamn, woman. I don't like anything inside my head, least of all hungry bugs."

"My apologies," Nasreen quipped. "You do like it when people give you the straight facts instead of beating around the proverbial bush, don't you?"

He lay back down and tried to relax. "True."

Sure enough, when the doctor and the nurse returned, it was with a new piece of wheelable equipment that Dante recognized as a nanobot control console. He had never been the recipient of one himself, but he'd seen them in videos, not to mention at hospitals in the past when recovering from injuries or watching over partners who required similar care.

It included a long, thick needle for delivery of the bots. Fortunately, there was also an anesthesia rig.

Dr. Kieffer tried to smile. "Please. Relax. You will not feel anything, and I have done this many times before."

Dante inhaled slowly and deeply. "Do what you have to do. Wake me up when it's over."

———

Nasreen stood outside the room, conferring with the doctor. Dante lay asleep on the couch within. The operation had concluded about twenty minutes ago, and they had left him unconscious. The anesthesia was still in partial effect, and they'd thrown in a common sedative for good measure.

"Okay," Nasreen began. "How much time will he need to recover? We may be extremely busy soon, so I hope it won't be too lengthy of a convalescence."

Kieffer grimaced. They had come in toward the end of his usual workday, and he was now a good hour and a half past the point when he would normally have been home relaxing. Bags were forming under his eyes.

"I am afraid I cannot tell you what you wish to hear. He will need extensive rest. Where we trimmed the subroutines, there are wound channels—too small to cause problems that will not resolve themselves, but they will need to heal. The AI, Midas, must reintegrate with his brain. When he wakes up, have him turn Midas on and speak to him for a short period, then shut down again. Keep doing this for longer and longer periods each day for at least a week."

Nasreen looked at the floor. A week of limited functionality might be too long. "Yes, I understand. How active can Dante be? Physically and mentally."

"He should not do much. No strenuous exercise, excessive stress, or thinking too hard about the universe's fate. He must get more than an average amount of sleep, medically induced, if need be. I will give you a supply of sedatives on your way out. This will help his brain adjust to all the changes that have taken place. If he pushes too hard, too quickly, the brain may not be able to heal."

Under the circumstances, this was one of the worst prognoses Nasreen could have received. Short of the operation's failure and Dante's permanent mental disfigurement, anyway.

"So be it, Doctor." She slipped too easily into her spy-diplomat way of thinking, where lying felt as natural as breathing. "We will do our best."

CHAPTER FIVE

Dante's jaw hung slack, his eyes were only half-open, and he stared at the juncture of the opposite wall and the floor. He also kept clutching the bed's headboard as though he wanted to slump back over and found it physically difficult to remain sitting upright.

"I'm fine," he said.

Nasreen stood over him with her arms crossed. Her right thumb and forefinger stroked her chin and lips as she eyed him like a piece of equipment whose functional integrity was in question.

"I'm not so sure about that, Dante. You look like you got drunk last night, then got beaten up and left in a dumpster. Well, minus the blood and dirt. You know what I mean."

With his free hand, he rubbed his eyes and ran his fingers through his disheveled hair. "Whatever. I had robot bugs eat a bunch of stuff out of my brain, didn't I? Am I supposed to look *good* after something like that?"

She allowed herself a tiny smile. "I suppose not. Dr. Kieffer did say you would need a lot of rest for at least a few days."

She deliberately kept the length vague rather than mentioning his actual recommendation of a week. They both wanted Dante back in action as soon as possible. Now that she saw how badly messed up he was, second thoughts were becoming impossible to ignore. If they tried to advance the recovery schedule, the earliest they might get any use out of him might only be five or six days instead of seven. She'd hoped he would be functional after two or three, but that appeared out of the question so far.

He coughed, reached for the glass of water she'd brought him, and downed it all in a long, slow draught. When he finished, he gasped. "Okay. What am I supposed to do now? Physical therapy or something?"

"After a cup of coffee and a light breakfast, you're supposed to switch Midas on for a short period to begin the reintegration process. Then turn him back off so you can recover before resting once more. Keep repeating that until you're back up to speed."

Dante groaned. "How do I switch Midas on? It's not like they installed a button on the side of my skull. He did that shit on his own, mostly. Can he hear me?"

Nasreen blinked. He had a point. AI implants were dependent on commands, and a defunct one might not be able to receive any input from the host's voice or thoughts. "I'm not sure. Try thinking about him hard and telling him to wake up, something like that."

Muttering under his breath and massaging his temples, Dante closed his eyes and concentrated. About five seconds later, his eyes flew open as his body jolted and nearly knocked him out of bed. Nasreen started forward to catch him, but he managed to steady himself in time.

"Whoa! Okay, Midas is back. You okay, buddy?"

He fell silent, although his eyes remained alert as he and the AI had a quiet conversation within the privacy of Dante's brain. Or so Nasreen assumed. When he continued to say nothing aloud after four or five minutes, she finally decided to pester him.

"Well, what does he say?" She brushed a strand of hair back from her face, hoping she'd pitched her voice right. She wanted the correct implication of slight impatience and nudging command, but not to the point of making him defensive.

Dante leaned back and looked up at her. "He's, uh, not all that coherent. It's like he remembers some of what happened but not all. I've been trying to explain it to him, and every time he tries to 'feel out' for things it's like someone is eating up my thoughts and blanking me out. Shit. I'm tired."

His head drooped.

Nasreen frowned in concern. "All right, I see. Tell him to go back into hibernation, then maybe you should lie down." They had both forgotten about the coffee and breakfast, but she suspected he might need more sleep before worrying about such things. He'd already been out for a little over twelve hours.

Dante mumbled, "Midas, shut down. We'll do this again, uh, tomorrow, I guess."

A shudder went through his body, then he relaxed. He rolled back and slumped into the bed, his eyelids growing heavy and his face going slack with exhaustion. "I'm tired. Need a little extra nap. Then..."

He passed out.

Nasreen stood and watched him for a short while, making sure he was okay. His sleep appeared natural and healthy. That was the *only* good news. Everything else she had witnessed since waking him up suggested the operation had taken a *lot* out of him.

He wouldn't be back in action soon enough. Trying to force it could be as dangerous as Kieffer had warned, and if they waited six, seven, or eight days to make their next move against SSS while regaining the attention of their fanbase, their window of opportunity might well be past.

"Dammit," she sputtered, turned, and strode out of the room. "I'm going to have to do everything myself. Or hire someone to help me, which costs money, and you never know who you can trust with jobs like this."

She gravitated toward the kitchen. Already she could see that it would be necessary to spend a fair amount of time away, pulling strings and preparing for what was to come. Dante might wake up without her around to attend to him. She prepped a pot of coffee, made him a sandwich and left it in the preserver compartment, and thought over what she should do next.

Ambrose. Ambrose might be of some use, although she didn't know him well and had no reason to consider him particularly trustworthy. Still, he needed her, and as a former member of Dante's crew, he possessed some useful skills.

Nasreen found one of her spare spheres and left a voice message on it, explaining the situation to Dante. She set it to broadcast via motion sensor as soon as he wandered away from his bed. Like many modern, decent-quality domiciles, her apartment in Celestial Seoul had a built-in intercom messaging system. Those were easier to hack than small individual devices. She had disabled them in all her safehouses.

She drew a deep breath. "Okay, Dante. Rest well, I guess." She left the sphere on a chair near the bedroom door's threshold and exited the apartment, headed for the shuttle bus and Pentapolis. Messaging Ambrose via a secure channel would *probably* work, but she'd rather speak to him in person. She wanted to check up on him anyway, to make sure Hyde hadn't torn him into small pieces out of boredom.

Unfortunately, Nasreen caught the bus during the last of morning rush hour, so the compartment was packed, and progress was slower than it would have otherwise been. Shuttle buses ran along tracks laid out with the specific intent of speeding up traffic and reducing delays. However, the tubes that connected the different Stations could still become congested since multiple tracks merged to fit through them properly. There were several tube junctures between Seoul and Pentapolis, and the shuttles had to take turns.

When she finally arrived, Nasreen reflected that she probably should have made breakfast for herself along with Dante. She would have to see if Ambrose and Hyde had any leftovers.

The housing project was peaceful aside from a few kids playing out front and a handful of slightly disreputable-looking characters lounging at the end of one hall, but they ignored her. When she came to the right apartment, she let herself in without knocking but announced herself as soon as she was over the threshold.

"Hi, it's me." She closed the door. "Ambrose? Uh, Ed?" She wandered into the kitchenette.

Ambrose was hovering over a pot of coffee with a cup in hand. "Yes, hello," he greeted her, none too enthusiastic. "We are fine, before you ask."

"Good." She glanced around. "Is Hyde here?"

"Yes." Ambrose sighed the way a man might after admitting he had a probation hearing in the morning. "How is Dante?"

She explained the situation to him. His facial expression didn't change. He only nodded as he poured coffee and sipped it.

"I see. Well, it's for the best since—"

"I need someone to help me with the next phase of the operation against SSS. I hoped you would volunteer since there's no way Dante will be back on his feet in time, and I don't want to wait too long. We need to get our livestream channel back online, recapture people's interest, and continue to chip away at Slaine's profits, not to mention his reputation. Breaking into a facility of his would be a good start if we think we could find anything scandalous."

Ambrose visibly cringed. "I, ah, suppose I could fly you somewhere? But that's about all I would be good for, and I do not feel up to it if I'm honest. I don't have your or Dante's skillsets. I'm only a pilot. And, um, a pianist. Sorry."

Shrugging awkwardly, he turned and slipped away, making it obvious that he didn't want the conversation to continue. It would have been easy to corner him in the tiny apartment and browbeat him into compliance, but she didn't feel like it. Instead, she helped herself to what remained of the coffee and some oatmeal with fruit paste.

While she had her light breakfast, she stared out the small window, which didn't provide much of a view, only more of the projects. "Nothing is ever easy," she murmured.

Behind her, machinery whirred, and the space around her dimmed as a giant figure blocked the light.

"I can help," Mr. Hyde said. "It's boring as shit here, anyway. Nothing to do except fucking with Ambrose's head by talking about what I would have done to him if he hadn't accepted Mr. Slaine's offer of working with us. Heh. Stuff like that. Or heading into the cellar and killing rats."

Nasreen was about to comment that the second activity wouldn't have occurred to her, but Hyde had more to say.

"Strangely unsurprising, isn't it? That rats, of all things, would manage to survive and follow us to the stars and would end up thriving in the same kinds of places we worked so hard to drive them out of back on Earth."

It made sense, then. Hyde was old enough to remember life on Earth before humanity's departure. Hence the continuity of vermin from planet to orbit had personal relevance to him. Nasreen had been born in the Stations. She'd visited Earth in its current ravaged state, but she had no individual frame of reference for what it had been like before the Stations went up and people fled into the refuge of space.

Nasreen blinked and cleared her mind. "While I'm sure you would like to get out more, and I've seen how well you can fight, the job I have in mind is more focused on stealth and subtlety."

"Okay." He snorted. "You can do that shit, and I'll protect you." He attempted to smile.

It wasn't so very long ago that he'd tried to do the complete opposite. She gazed vacantly at the wall to avoid fixing him with a death glare.

"That *might* work, but I'm not sure. What I have in mind isn't merely a smash-and-grab operation but an ongoing campaign where we make SSS untouchable through the Hellcat and E-zex channel. We'll turn it into a propaganda outlet or informant hub, where we not only shine a light on what *we* know SSS has done but also gather info. That will allow us to pursue leads dropped by others who may be aware of further misdeeds. It will be more effective if we get feedback from other raider-types who have appeared on our channel in the past."

Hyde nodded, the machinery of his body making only the faintest of whirrings. "That sounds fun," he purred. "I can be more subtle than you seem to think. I worked for them, remember. I know most of their secrets."

Nasreen had almost forgotten about that. He had a point. "Yes, that would be helpful. Do you know of any sites we could conceivably gain entrance to where they're involved in illegal activity?"

He let out a short, barking laugh. "Of course! You said before that the o-harvesting was your favorite of their little side activities. I know where a lot of those stolen *huevos* are going. Hitting that place would be a good start."

Nasreen couldn't disagree. Proving Slaine's involvement in the black market for ovaries would get everyone's attention and make it easier to get people to notice their various other, lesser crimes.

Then she put her hands on her hips and glared. She wasn't glaring at anyone, simply at a point beyond the wall that represented her frustrations with some of the poor luck they'd had lately.

"There is one serious problem to consider. Dante and I were live-streaming that breach job. I turned the cam off for reasons of our client's professional privacy, saying that we were having technical difficulties. Then we were attacked and got distracted before you showed up to save the day. Not to mention, that EMP grenade killed the device altogether so there was no turning it back on afterward even if we'd wanted to."

Hyde chuckled. The sound sent a low, unpleasant vibration through the air, not to mention the floor and walls. "Yeah. Makes things complicated when tech fails, doesn't it? My body holds up pretty well. Most of the time. Hydraulic instead of electronic, mostly. I avoid a lot of issues that way."

Nasreen tried not to shudder. Dante had mentioned that Hyde's usual nickname was a contraction of "Mr. Hydraulic," the moniker he'd used as a Reaper years ago before his terrifying reputation led to most people shortening it.

Banishing all unsettling thoughts of the man's past from her mind and returning to focus on the main issues at hand, Nasreen continued, "It would be nice if we could develop more tech that is resistant to EMPs, but what's done is done. Anyway, we returned to the Stations mostly incognito and haven't been in contact with much of anyone, aside from the client. Most of our viewers, and the community in general, probably think that Dante and I are dead. Which is bad for business."

"True," Hyde growled.

CHAPTER SIX

Hyde was grinning and smirking an awful lot lately. Nasreen hoped it simply meant he had a good, positive feeling about their course of action and was in an upbeat mood. It still made her skin crawl and her soul quake with dread, however.

"So," he rumbled, looking down at her, "you don't look enthusiastic. What's the matter, did you have to *convince* yourself to go out on this little job with me? Ha, ha."

They were standing on the platform beside a major circuit route, waiting for the shuttle bus to show up. No one else was present, but other commuters would probably wander up in the next few minutes as its scheduled arrival time drew near. Above them, the artificial lighting that emanated from the dome was dimming to nighttime levels.

Nasreen cleared her throat as she employed calming techniques. It would behoove her to keep her cool, no matter how much she might want to lash out at the man and tell him exactly how she felt.

"Mr. Curtidor," she began, using his real name to ensure she had his attention. "I am well aware that your mind doesn't work the same way as most other people's. While you may be somewhat more intelligent than I had at first suspected, you suffer from slight deficits in things like empathy and social referencing."

He stared at her, his face oddly skewed as though he wasn't sure whether to be amused or befuddled.

She continued. "Therefore, I will allow that you may have trouble understanding how an average person could be uncomfortable about working with you after the first time we met. You murdered someone in front of me and tried to kill me. For the typical human, this unpleasant experience creates a negative impression. Overcoming it may take time."

She inhaled deeply. "Although I will grant that you also saved my life more recently and have made an effort to behave yourself since then. Which is appreciated."

For another two or three seconds, Hyde continued to gaze at her dumbly. Then he erupted into a buzzing fit of snorting and scoffing sounds.

"Pfft, okay, whatever. What, you trying to tell me I was the only person who ever tried to kill you? The shit we do for a living, I figured it happens all the time."

Much to her annoyance, he had a point. "I have been in life-or-death situations before, but the one in which we met was very unexpected. I also, ah, had never seen anyone quite like you before."

Another of his low, rumbling, buzzing chuckles. "I keep forgetting how scary I am." He stretched his arms behind his head, causing the metal parts to rustle while the hydraulic-powered cybernetics made a faint whirring sound. "A lot of the time, I feel like I'm still a kid."

Nasreen ignored the statement since it only made her gut roil that much more in discomfort and worry. Hyde was practically ancient in addition to being a professional murderer. For such a person to think of himself as an overgrown child was almost like an abomination against nature.

Other commuters, mostly native Koreans but also various

foreign residents or visitors, approached the platform to join them in waiting for the shuttle. Most gave Hyde a wide berth. He'd disguised his features with a large, hooded overcoat, but his sheer size and bulk still drew a certain amount of attention. Not the good kind.

The bus pulled up, and in silence the pair trudged in, finding a quiet spot near the back corner of the middle car. The ride wouldn't be a long one. Their destination was an innocuous-seeming facility within Celestial Seoul, albeit on the city's far side.

It was a place Hyde had heard about during one of his various bodyguard jobs for Slaine. A front business, of course, where SSS' customers and affiliates carried out the worst of their business behind the scenes.

Nasreen ran her fingertips over the fabric of her collar, which mostly concealed her new camera rig. It was smaller than the one she'd worn Dirtside on her last expedition as E-zex. The pictures and sound quality wouldn't be as good, but it would still be sufficient for a decent livestream. A violent exposé, one might say.

Although actual violence brought with it a lot of complications, it made for a good show. Not to mention Nasreen was pretty sure the potential targets had it coming.

Hyde had explained earlier how things went down at the facility. On the surface, it was a combination of a plastic surgery clinic and day spa, an all-purpose beauty care establishment. Behind the scenes, SSS' inner circle of trusted employees counseled wealthy persons on their reproductive health, including the outlawed transplants of stolen Dirtwalker ovaries. They also transplanted testicles, but those were less common since the effects of living in orbit were harder on women than men.

Prices got negotiated in the back rooms, and sometimes things took the form of an auction. The "fruits" of Slaine's illicit exploits, as Hyde called them, were doled out to high bidders ovum by ovum. They could also place orders for future products if none were currently available.

Nasreen's hands hung loosely at her side, but they balled into fists. That SSS was able to get away with o-harvests was bad enough by itself. Dante was ultimately in his current miserable state precisely because of Slaine's perfidy.

The shuttle slowed as they reached their stop and the automated voice system announced the location. The doors opened and out flowed half of the car's passengers, including Nasreen and Hyde. The giant cloaked man led the way, deliberately taking them down side streets to separate from the crowd. Occasionally he doubled back or took long scenic routes to throw off anyone who might be trying to scrutinize their movements.

When they were almost there, Hyde paused and said, in a low, grinding voice, "We go in the side door, so we bypass the first layer of security. I can kick it down if you want, or you can try to hack it or something. I'll show you where."

Nasreen nodded. They moved on.

The clinic was a two-story silvery-blue building shaped vaguely like a filled-in horseshoe. There were probably more levels under street level. The back of the building was curved, and the front was square. Hyde pointed toward an alcove along the side that contained an entrance.

Nasreen didn't move. She waited and watched. They were behind a fence in the shadow of a tall banking center and had decent concealment to observe the place. A pair of sentries tricked out in heavy armor and toting shock batons marched past.

They passed again about a minute and a half later. Hacking through the door would have to be quick. Unless Hyde could neutralize them without anyone noticing.

Seemingly intuiting her concerns, the cyborg mentioned, "Oh, pretty sure they have cameras watching all the entrances and exits. You should do something about those."

She muttered, "Yes, thanks for telling me." She pulled her sphere out of her pocket and brought up a variety of scanning and hacking programs.

While Hyde fidgeted in boredom and irritation, Nasreen found the frequency the external cameras operated on and jammed them without being too obvious. Someone watching the feeds within might notice and come out to check, but she was confident that she hadn't tripped any alarms.

Hacking the door the remote way would take too long, she decided. But she did have another nanobot solution on hand, one that could disable the mechanisms of virtually all doors, albeit at the cost of doing permanent, noticeable damage.

They were going to be filming and broadcasting the whole endeavor anyway. Getting away with it unseen and unnoticed wasn't exactly part of the plan.

Nasreen held up a hand, signaling to Hyde to wait until she was ready. Once the guards moved past the next time and passed out of sight around the corner, she swiped down. Then she burst out from behind the fence and raced across the pavement to the door, pulling the vial of nanobot solution from a pouch within her jacket as she moved.

Behind her, Hyde moved across the pavement at a steady clip —whirring and clanking all the while. Nasreen cursed mentally. It was almost impossible for the brute to move without making any sound. They would have to rely upon speed.

She popped open the vial, found the tiny aperture nearest the door's lock, and upended the vial right on top of it. The drops of dark liquid—so colored because it was swarming with tiny mechanisms—disappeared into the structure and began eating away at everything they encountered that was metal or most types of industrial-grade polymer.

Nasreen glanced back over her shoulder. Hyde had tramped two-thirds of the distance across the lane. By taking long, powerful strides, he could move quickly while making less noise than if he'd broken into a full jog and risked cracking the pavement.

She looked back at the door and watched faint steam rise from the areas the nanobots were eating away. They were programmed to seek out the wires and accouterments of most high-end alarm systems, plus destroy locks. They could do it in about forty seconds.

She'd lost count of exactly how long it had been, but the guards would sweep by again any minute now. Unless they'd heard Hyde's heavy footsteps and gone to gather reinforcements.

The door fell ajar as Hyde entered the alcove.

"There," Nasreen gasped, pulled it open, and slid through. Hyde came in behind her and pulled it shut.

Within, a short hall led to another, larger, perpendicular corridor. It went to the front lobby to the right and deeper parts of the facility to the left. As they went to the intersection and ensured no one was present, they faintly heard the two sentries stomping up outside.

One of them said, "Hey, the door's ajar." The other responded in Korean. It seemed they were trying to decide whether to investigate or fetch the rest of the security detail.

Hyde growled, "Hold on."

Before Nasreen could protest or attempt to stop him, he lunged back the way he'd come, flung open the door, and bowled straight into the two men.

Nasreen winced as their short, choking cries cut off amid the general whirring of angry machinery and bodies *thudding* to the pavement. A moment later, Hyde trudged back inside, dragging the guards with him. "They'll probably live."

"Okay," Nasreen whispered. "We agreed to try to avoid killing anyone if possible. Somebody will notice that they're no longer on their rounds or checking in, so let's move fast. Now that I'm inside the building I should be able to disable the internal security systems from here. Just, um, cover me."

Hyde chortled, deposited the two injured and unconscious men in the corner, and stood guard while Nasreen pulled out her sphere again.

This time the signal was close enough to home in on the facility's network and activate a couple of dormant malicious viruses. She'd sent them earlier in preparation for this moment. Once awakened, the programs rapidly located the weaknesses in the clinic's internal camera and microphone setup and dug in their claws, paralyzing them until a knowledgeable professional could remove them.

Nasreen smirked, allowing herself a brief second of self-satisfaction. She'd earned enough money to be able to afford the very best in black market hacking software. Not to mention her skills were considerable even when she only had mediocre stuff.

"Okay," she told Hyde. "Onward. I figure it makes sense to have you in front. After all, I'm the brains of this operation, and you're the brawn." That last comment was mostly narration for the audience's benefit.

Hyde scoffed, "Well, yeah."

As they went down the left hallway, Nasreen glimpsed more guards moving outside through a window opposite the side door they'd come through. A pit of dread suddenly opened in her stomach, but she forced herself to ignore it.

The door beyond was the hermetically sealable variety, like those found in an airlock on a deep space craft. It was probably a measure to keep diseased people away from the relatively delicate environment within the clinic proper. She only hoped that Hyde wasn't carrying any weird infections or STDs. Checking him beforehand would have been wise, but it was impossible to think of *everything* in advance.

The door opened without difficulty. Hyde clomped in with Nasreen close behind. She wasn't sure how much time they had before the next wave of guards noticed something was amiss, but it couldn't have been much. There was virtually no way they would attain their objective without making a mess.

Once the door sealed itself behind them, they were in a short, narrow, tube-like hallway, brightly lit, but the obvious camera nodes were inactive. Since Nasreen had already disabled their microphone system as well, and the doors appeared to be sound-proof, there was virtually no chance of anyone hearing her. She spoke down toward her mic, keeping her voice low anyway to be safe and feed into the atmosphere of clandestine activity she was going for on the stream.

"It's strange how many guards there are here. True, everyone needs to protect themselves from crime, and a place like this that caters to wealthy clients will naturally attract its share of body-guards and the like. We're seeing hardware and staffing normally found in a government facility or major corporate headquarters. It's highly conspicuous...and only makes me much more curious about what we'll find here. Stay tuned."

Hyde ignored her little speech and stared straight ahead as the next door opened. It disclosed a small room that functioned as a security checkpoint to control access to another corridor beyond it.

It was well-staffed. A guard stood looking right at them. Behind him were two others at a desk and another in the corner, all armed with shock batons and razorfists.

The front man had glazed-over eyes. The instant the door started to part, he robotically droned, "All right, before you proceed, I'll need to check—*oh my God!*"

His eyes bulged in shock and horror as they focused on the familiar face of Eduardo H. Curtidor, who was grinning again.

"No, you won't," Hyde said as the man scrambled to draw his baton.

The other three leapt to their feet as Hyde's massive, armored hand shot out. It struck the man and grabbed him around the chest and shoulder in the same motion before picking him up and hurling him back. He sailed through the air and crashed into the closest of his comrades. Both men tumbled to the floor as sparks rose where one's baton electrocuted the other.

Nasreen stepped to the side to get a better view of the checkpoint room as Hyde waded into it, growling in his low, buzzing voice. Another guard, a stocky woman, came at the cyborg from the side. She thrust with her razorfist, but the blade glanced off Hyde's steel-sheathed ribs leaving only a scratch.

Hyde clamped a hand on her head, jerked her roughly aside, and punched her midsection with his other fist. She made a strangled yelping sound and flew back, doubling over and spitting up blood, before crumpling to the floor.

One of the two men who'd fallen in a tangle sprang up, charging at Hyde with a crackling baton. The other stayed on the floor. Meanwhile, the fourth guard who'd been in the corner sidestepped around the table to flank the hulking attacker.

He hadn't seen Nasreen. As he came in front of the doorway, she lunged, kneed him in the kidneys, and wrapped her arms around his neck. His reflexes were good, and he resisted her instantly, ruining her takedown, but her form was good enough that he couldn't do much else.

The door behind them was closing, bringing its edge near the man's head. Nasreen pivoted and let him fall into the opening. The pressure dented his helmet and sent a spasm through his body. The door retracted again as the man went limp. Nasreen pitched him forward so his head collided with a hard surface a second time, in this case, the wall. He slumped, down for the count.

Hyde appeared to have broken the arm of the man attacking him and cracked his skull for good measure. He was currently throttling the last of them, who was the guy who'd greeted them at the door. The man's face turned red as Hyde lifted him, and his feet kicked uselessly in the air.

Nasreen's stomach clenched. "Stop. Don't kill anyone unless you have to."

Hyde's massive head spun toward her, his red hair and beard rippling like flames, and his mouth twisted into a brutal snarl. Then he exhaled and simply tossed the guard aside. The man slammed into the table and fell over again onto the floor, unconscious but alive.

Nasreen rushed over to the guard with the cracked head. He still lived, although he might die without treatment. She pulled out a pair of sealant patches and put them over his head and arm wounds, then dragged him aside and laid him down in a relatively comfortable position. Next, she injected a stimpack into the woman, who appeared to be bleeding internally from the powerful abdominal blow. She might have had a hernia.

If the security detail knew about the o-harvests, she couldn't summon *that* much sympathy for them. For public relations and damage control, it was always better to avoid needless fatalities.

Hyde stood, glowering at her. "I'm not built for fighting that puts people in bed with a headache over the weekend. I pinch a man's cheeks, and his head comes off. If we were going to be all pacifistic about this, you shouldn't have brought me."

She snapped, "I didn't have much choice since Hellcat's still out of commission. Do your best, okay?"

He made a low grating sound, like two vibrating pieces of metal shoved against one another in an industrial grinding device.

Walking toward him and trying not to cringe at the prospect that the brute might suddenly turn against her, Nasreen peered into the hallway ahead. It bent around a corner about ten feet past the checkpoint and was otherwise featureless. The checkpoint itself was in the form of an electronic scanner that would certainly have set off a silent alarm if either of them passed by it without being cleared.

Nasreen examined the desk. The impact of the guard's body

had badly damaged the console. "Dammit. I might not be able to disable this thing the clean way."

"Okay. The dirty way, then." Hyde kicked the scanner device, snapping it off in a screeching eruption of sparks and metal fragments. It flew across the room to crash into the opposite wall. Where it had been originally, exposed wires steamed.

Nasreen sighed. "Crude and noisy, but effective. Now let's go. Remember, I need to find their computers or any other tech that might store their data and transaction records. Your main function is to allow me to do that."

"No shit," he grunted.

Fortunately, there was another sealed, soundproof door after they rounded the corner. It contained a small transparent window that disclosed an expansive, luxurious floor space beyond, like a lounge or lobby. Valued customers likely spent time there. The soundproofing was to prevent them from being disturbed by any ugly business the guards might need to engage in.

Nasreen spoke into her camera's microphone. "Here, we come to the belly of the beast. This appears to be the clinic's main customer area, where they peddle legitimate and illicit services. We don't yet know exactly what sort of degeneracy we'll witness here, but we have a damn good idea."

She grabbed the door, flung it open, and burst into the room beyond, with Hyde crashing in behind her to spread his metal hands.

The lounge wasn't much different from any other spa, although it was extremely fancy. Everything seemed to be silver or blue and white marble. Fountains sprinkled, velvet covered the chairs and couches, statues glimmered, and overhead in the rear, interestingly, a golden sun sculpture hovered above it all.

Today, several esteemed clients had gathered for a closed presentation. Most of the seats had been moved to the back, forming a semicircle in front of the platform under the sun. Eight or nine people, mostly couples dressed in exceedingly tasteful outfits that stopped short of ostentatious, sat and listened.

On the platform stood a nondescript, well-groomed man in a business suit, pointing with a silver wand at various items spelled out on a screen. A security guard hovered behind him, and two others stood at the wings of the seating area.

The man on the platform had been in the middle of droning on when the pair had burst in.

"...and included with the premium implantation care package is our money-back, one hundred percent satisfaction *guarantee* that the products are viable and conception will occur." He paused and looked at the intruders. "Um, excuse me, this is a private session. Hey, who the hell are you?"

The guard nearest the door blurted, "Fuck, it's *him!*"

The men and women of the audience gasped, clucked, or screamed as Hyde thundered with laughter, throwing the cloak off to expose all the details of his unmistakable, monstrous frame. He waded toward them.

The first guard aimed a wrist-mounted dart launcher and fired. Hyde simply turned and took it against his shoulder. The dart sparked and fell uselessly to the floor, repelled by his heavy armor.

Then Hyde picked up a chair as easily as if it were a spoon and hurled it. It exploded against the guard's face and chest, knocking him almost four feet back and leaving a trail of blood droplets in the air behind him.

Nasreen dashed around the seated crowd to the rear, flanking the central platform, which was her main target. While the guard on the near side deployed his razorfist's blade and prepared to engage Hyde, the one on the far end hefted a shock baton and came at Nasreen, his face contorted with fear and anger.

He feinted, then swiped. He was fast enough that the baton rustled the air beside Nasreen's head, singeing the ends of her hair. She'd expected a move like this. It was part of the standard combat training for most executive security forces. She blocked his next downward diagonal strike with her right hand while deploying the wrist knife hidden beneath her left.

The blade stabbed into the man's leg above his knee, and he crumpled with a squawk of pain. Nasreen yanked the baton from his grasp as he fell. Then she turned toward the crowd, who were about to flee, and barked, "Nobody move!"

Across from them, Hyde had picked up the remaining guard with both hands and held him horizontally over his head. The man shouted and cursed in Korean, but to no avail. Hyde threw him into the wall where he first *crunched*, then tumbled and lay still.

Nasreen gave a nod of grim satisfaction. "Opposition neutralized," she said into her camera. "Now, let's see what 'implantation care' means, exactly." She allowed the cam to get a good view of the screen, where whoever had put the presentation together listed the procedures the company performed to ensure that the ova were functional.

Then she focused on the face of the man in the business suit and those of all the people in the audience. She asked the presenter, "Okay, where are your files of recent shipments, recent customers, transactions, and all that fun stuff? Don't make Hyde squeeze the answer out of you."

Hyde took a clanking step forward. The chaos of battle had rustled his hair and beard, and he grinned horribly at the clucking mass of customers before turning his gleaming eyes toward the presenter and flexing his huge, armored hands.

The man trembled. "You, ah, you can access most of that info from a console in the locked office. End of the hall, down that way." He pointed. "I'm not supposed to give any of that out. Oh, God. Don't you realize what they'll—"

"No," Nasreen snapped. "I don't, because it doesn't matter. You need to focus on what *he'll* do if you don't shut up and cooperate. That goes for all of you. Hyde, watch them. This shouldn't take long."

She hid her growing nervousness that SSS' auxiliary forces would show up at any moment. There had been more guards outside, possibly checking from the front lobby, after all.

As Hyde stepped up to the platform and flexed his massive, hydraulic body for everyone to admire, Nasreen hurried across the lounge toward a hallway branching off from the side. As the man had said, there was a door at the end of it. The lock was a conventional, mechanical knob device. She simply kicked the door and broke free the casing so it swung away from the busted polymers.

The office was medium-sized but nicely furnished, with lots of fine imitation wood and various ferns and paintings. Nasreen clicked on the light, found the console, and powered it up. It had been idling rather than entirely shut down, so she didn't have to wait long for all systems to be running.

"Good," she commented. Remembering the viewers, she added, "At last, the big reveal of who exactly is paying for the product. We can no longer deny it's a bevy of stolen ovaries, harvested from the living bodies of hapless Dirtwalker women in direct violation of inter-Station law."

She imagined some of the people back in their homes gasping in horror.

Predictably, two layers of security protected the business files she sought, but neither was as robust as she'd feared it might be. They would keep run-of-the-mill employees from stealing company secrets or delay more skilled espionage agents, but there was nothing Nasreen couldn't handle given a bit of time.

That was the problem. Her inner countdown clock, her amorphous intuition as to how long she had to complete the job, was growing close to its end.

Using her sphere's battery of potent hacking applications as well as various tricks she'd learned about how to hack corporate consoles directly, she attacked both layers at once. An automated hack activated by her sphere ate away at the inner one. She brute-forced the outer with a probability algorithm that reduced the time it took to cycle through every possible combination of characters. Computing speed had advanced well beyond the bad old days, but such methods could still be excessively time-consuming if one didn't know the shortcuts.

The screen abruptly flickered, and the first layer vanished. The second was weak enough thanks to the automated program that Nasreen hacked it in half the time of the first.

Thus, the absolute dirtiest of the place's laundry opened before her.

"Ohh, this is something," she quipped, ensuring her camera was recording it all. With it being live-streamed and automatically archived, there was no need to make a separate digital copy, let alone a physical one.

"Look at all these 'sales' of equipment from SSS, which they generously offered at the lowest prices I have *ever* seen for this kind of medical technology. And the 'bonuses' for employees who seemingly have bounced back and forth between the clinic itself and various SSS research and development sub-firms. Fascinating."

Then, her eyes almost glazed over as they wandered over the bombshell of bombshells. Everything thus far, while still momentous, was *expected*. The final bit was not.

Nasreen inhaled. "The list of customers—those who have received the stolen organs for personal use—includes none other than Cormac Slaine himself."

She had seen enough. Now felt like the time to get the hell out of here.

Rather than destroy the console, she left it. That way, if there was a formal trial, the clinic would have to produce the device as evidence, and it would be highly suspicious if they were somehow unable. Or if it got damaged despite her leaving it alone. Or if it had undergone the kind of professional wipe-job that an expert of Nasreen's caliber could detect upon examination.

She ran out into the lounge. All eyes turned to her. "Hyde! Let's go. We have enough to implicate your old boss. He's on the goddamn *customer list.*"

The presenter standing awkwardly beside the giant cyborg clapped both hands over his face and hung his head, moaning.

Hyde gawked. "Shit, that's fucking funny. *Papi* running around with stolen *huevos.* Explains so much! Ha, ha."

Nasreen added, partially in response to Hyde and partly for the benefit of the fans, "Apparently, all the solar power in the universe wasn't enough to fix things for Mr. Slaine."

CHAPTER SEVEN

Hyde dropped the heavy couch in front of the door. "Have fun!" He cackled, and the walls vibrated disturbingly with the metallic reverberations of his awful voice.

He and Nasreen had hastily herded the presenter, the customers, and the wounded guards into the same suite of offices where Nasreen had accessed the spa's records. Trapping them within, albeit temporarily, would ensure that no one could actively interfere with their escape.

There was an uncomfortable moment when Nasreen caught the gaze of one of the women among the clients. In addition to being terrified, she looked hurt and put-upon, as though she didn't understand why Nasreen and Hyde were doing this to them. Perhaps in her mind, she was a victim of her infertility, and they were taking away her dream of having children.

It was an unsettling thought. Still, the solution offered by the spa, not to mention by SSS and their unscrupulous minions, involved stealing that same dream from someone else.

Jogging back through the lounge and presentation area, they looked around for alternate exits that might get them out of the building but found none. Unless they wanted to ascend to the second floor and try to leap down. It occurred to Nasreen that Hyde could probably manage that without getting injured, but she could not, even if he carried her.

Their only option was back to the checkpoint and through the sealed security hallway, then through either the same side door they'd entered or through the front lobby.

Hyde growled, "I doubt we're getting out of this place without getting into more trouble. We drew a lot of attention to ourselves. Heh, heh."

Nasreen was inclined to agree. She still had the shock baton she'd taken from the guard she'd downed. It would act as a decent force multiplier, but if by some chance the remainder of the garrison was bigger than anticipated, or if they'd called in reinforcements, it might not be enough.

She tapped the camera at her collar. "So far, our egress is going smoothly. But there's a chance that SSS may have more surprises waiting for us." It felt odd, behaving as though she was telling a story when the events she was referring to could lead to her death within the next few minutes.

They passed the checkpoint and entered the short tubular hall without incident, then emerged into the small intersection where their original entrance point lay to the right. Hyde went first. After rounding the corner, he halted, and Nasreen almost crashed into him.

The door Nasreen had disabled with the nanobots was missing. No longer merely hanging loose, someone had removed it altogether. She could see nothing else amiss. But...

Thunderous *bangs* rang out overhead, and three points on the front of Hyde's suit spewed out sparks in tandem with metallic ricochet sounds. The giant cyborg was jostled back about half a step by the impact of the shots.

"What the shit?" he bellowed, in a mixture of sudden rage and sheer disbelief. "They're using *guns!*"

Nasreen jumped back toward the middle of the intersection

and reflexively ducked into a crawling position to get her head out of the way. Dante had emphasized during her Marauder training that anytime someone opened up with firearms, the first thing to do was remove oneself from the line of fire—unless one had a clear and immediate shot back at the perpetrator.

Then Hyde did something that was every bit as shocking and unexpected as the gunfire itself was. He walked forward and stuck his head out through the door, looking around. Another shot rang out, and he retreated, taking the bullet on the shoulder, where it left a dent. It looked like the slug had flattened against the metal and stuck there.

Hyde turned and marched back toward Nasreen, his hideous face twisted with disgust. "They put snipers on the roof across from us, and five or six guys are charging the door." He sounded almost calm, as though he weren't so much panicked as exasperated.

Nasreen sputtered, "Lobby!" She dashed for the door to the front of the building, which they'd bypassed on the way in. "They're probably covering that, too, but at least we'll have room to maneuver. We *cannot* get trapped in this hall or driven back into the building's interior."

"Yeah, fucking obviously."

Nasreen flung the door open, then ducked as soon as she crossed the threshold. The reception desk hid her from sight in less than a second, but before she passed beneath its edge, she saw five men in armor, all toting rifles or submachine guns, turn or startle in place. They'd seen and heard her. Now the shooting gallery would begin.

Hyde roared, his voice shaking the foundations of the building, and barreled out behind her, cracking part of the doorframe and plunging straight for the chair that idled behind the desk, as crackling gunfire filled the lobby. Bullets struck him, doing little damage. He seized the chair and hurled it at the closest member of Slaine's paramilitary hit squad.

The chair's leg clotheslined the man, probably shattering his jaw and perhaps breaking his neck, and he toppled over like a felled tree. Hyde snatched a short-barreled rifle from his grasp, then dashed back toward the desk.

Nasreen huddled on the floor, trying to keep the desk parts reinforced with marble and polymer in front of her since bullets tore straight through the artificial wood. As Hyde stomped up beside her, he dropped the gun into her hands.

"Here. I'll take the rear." Then his hydraulic implements whirred, and he ducked back into the corridor from which they'd come, right in time to meet the first guards who had been charging the side door a moment ago. A man screamed, metal whined, bones crunched, and more painfully loud blasts filled the enclosed space.

Nasreen fumbled with the gun in her hands. She had never used this exact model before. Most of her experience was with pulsecores. It was similar enough to one or two other weapons she'd used months ago so she got the gist of it.

However, she had less than a second to ensure it was in battery. While the rest kept her pinned down with short bursts of covering fire, one of the surviving goons circled to the side of the desk to find and execute her.

Nasreen rolled over to meet him, her brain struggling to put together everything she knew about close-quarters projectile combat. The rifle had a round in the chamber and Hyde had managed not to damage it when grabbing it. It seemed to have at least half a magazine of ammo left.

At the first sign of motion, the dark silhouette of the point man moving to the corner of the desk, Nasreen opened fire, squeezing off five rounds while the gun tried to jump in her hand and spat empty casings to the side. The bullets tore holes through the upper portion of the desk, sending wood fragments scattering through the air, and the man behind it let out a strangled cry and fell from sight.

The others kept shooting. Nasreen poked the gun around the edge of the desk and fired everything remaining in the mag toward the last three men. She didn't think she hit anything, but two stopped shooting while they took cover.

Then she cast the rifle aside and snatched the other gun, the one belonging to the man she'd killed. It took half a second too long to yank its strap away from the dead guy's arm, but she managed to get it before the barrage began anew. As bullets slammed into the floor and desk's edge around her, she had to duck back for cover. There was no time to grab a spare magazine.

"Shit, shit, *shit*," she gasped through gritted teeth. The current rifle was about half empty. It was unlikely to be enough ammo to take on the last three guys at once, particularly not while pinned down in an awkward spot.

The goon positioned between the other two switched to semiauto and took single shots at Nasreen's rough location. The other two fell silent. They were moving in from both ends, trying to catch her in a pincer maneuver.

To the right, a lamp hung from the ceiling. Nasreen sucked in her breath, aimed, and fired two shots. At least one struck true, severing the cord and sending the lamp plummeting to the floor. She couldn't tell if it hit the man approaching from that direction, but he shouted something like a curse. It had surprised him and thrown him off his game, if only for an instant.

Nasreen rolled in his direction, lay on her belly, and aimed around the other edge of the desk. The hitman was regaining his balance. The lamp had fallen right in front of him, and he'd nearly tripped over it. His submachine gun's barrel pointed close to three feet to Nasreen's left.

Behind his helmet's visor, his eyes bulged. Nasreen shot him three times. The first two rounds struck the heavy plate protecting his chest and merely jolted him, but the third took him in the throat. Blood spurted, and he crumpled with an awful gurgling noise.

Then the other man pounced around the opposite side of the desk. He caught Nasreen in his crosshairs a heartbeat before she could adjust her position, and her heart felt like it tried to jump out through her throat.

Hyde roared back into the lobby, wielding a bent and warped rifle in one hand like a club. The stock struck the goon's hands and knocked the weapon from his grasp. He tried to backpedal, but Hyde's other fist was driving toward him with the speed and power of a small vehicle.

It struck him square in the chest, caving in the armor plate and crunching his ribcage. He flew back, spitting blood.

The last of the five men guarding the lobby opened fire on Hyde with a fresh magazine on full auto. Hyde cringed back under the barrage. Some of the metal that sheathed him was cracking, and it looked like he was bleeding in places. Although far better protected than a normal human, he wasn't invincible.

Nasreen stood straight. It was probably what the last man would have least expected. The muzzle of her rifle passed over the goon's helmet, and she squeezed the trigger as he noticed her and tried to turn his weapon on her.

The rifle in Nasreen's hands crackled, and her foe's helmet grew a nasty indentation. He shuddered, lost his balance, and toppled over as if drunk. He wasn't dead but badly disoriented and probably had a concussion.

Hyde did a standing leap that took him ten feet across the lobby, crashing next to the fallen hitman and rattling the floor. As the man desperately tried to rise to his knees and bring his weapon back up, Hyde seized his head with both hands and twisted it sharply. It spun nearly three hundred and sixty degrees and made a soft *crunching* sound. Hyde released it, and the man fell back.

It was silent. Nasreen remained keyed up and jumpy. She spun back toward the door to the hallway they'd come from. "Did you get all of them back there?"

"No," Hyde snarled. "They're probably coming around this side right now. Two, I think."

He was wrong, though. At that moment, heavy boots pounded the floor from beyond the door behind the desk. Nasreen threw herself aside to get out of the line of fire and backed away from the desk toward Hyde. The men about to charge into the lobby paused. They had lost the element of surprise and become bottlenecked.

Nasreen stepped carefully over the body of the man she'd shot in the throat. He had a pulse grenade attached to his vest. Cocking an eyebrow in appreciation, she plucked it off.

"My friends," she said into the camera, "they've crossed the line in deploying firearms against us. That is how serious they are about stopping our activities." She hoped the two or three guys approaching from the hall would think she was distracted. She pulled the pin on the grenade.

"For all their reckless willingness to potentially damage the dome itself, which is one of the cardinal sins of all the Stations, they seem oddly reluctant to inflict any major property damage on this place. I am in no way similarly constrained, thank you very much." She tossed the grenade into the doorway beyond the desk, then turned, sprinted, and waved frantically at Hyde.

He grinned stupidly, then snatched her by the waist and took a few bounding, half-airborne strides away from the lobby. She tensed in dread at the feel of his metallic hands on her but didn't protest, although the harsh yet fluent motion of his unnatural gait made her sick.

The grenade went off. A sphere of green light briefly engulfed the rear of the lobby and the halls behind it, blasting large, burning pieces of the building's superstructure far into the air and raising a pale cloud of superheated steam into the sky above. Parts of the walls and ceilings collapsed inward, quickly smothering most of the yellowish-green flames.

Hyde looked back and laughed. "Ha, ha! That was great. I

hope those fucking snipers were in there too. Probably not, though. I think they're still up there." He gestured toward the building opposite the spa, where the first of the hit squad had taken potshots at him a few minutes ago.

He let Nasreen go, and she fell to her feet, immediately putting the huge, armored body between herself and the snipers' likely position. Her timing was impeccable. A single bullet struck Hyde's thigh right where her torso had been less than a second earlier.

Hyde bellowed, "Hey! You fucks. Come down here and *fight!*"

Nasreen raised her rifle, trying to get a bead on the sharpshooters. The only thing she could see was a couple of dark flickers moving across the roof away from them. She could attempt a long-distance shot, but she'd probably miss. If she did, the bullets might travel deeper into the city before falling on someone's unsuspecting head. Or they might damage the Station's dome.

She exhaled. "They're running away. We won, for now. The authorities will be along soon enough. Let's move out." She started toward the street beyond the front of the building, wanting to cover maximum distance in minimum time while also avoiding the route the fleeing snipers seemed to be taking.

Hyde's grating metallic voice echoed from behind her. "Hold on. Nobody else is coming. Have a look at this."

Nasreen paused. She could think of many things she would rather do than linger here right now—drink room-temperature coffee, clean a toilet, file her tax return, get a root canal—but she forced herself to turn around. For all his crudity, Hyde sometimes had a knack for noticing important things.

"What is it?" She walked toward him.

He stood over two of the paramilitary goons. One's helmet had cracked in the battle, and Hyde had pulled the other's off. Both appeared dead, although there was perhaps a slim chance they'd survive once the medical cleanup crew arrived.

Hyde gestured at their faces. "I know both men. I mean, not in the sense that I bought Christmas presents for their *hijos* or anything, ha, ha. I saw them around at SSS. They're on Slaine's payroll. Or one of his front companies, on loan, something like that."

Nasreen drew closer and bent slightly so her camera aimed at the men's frozen, contorted visages. She'd made peace with the necessity of violence, but the sight of dead human beings was still deeply disturbing no matter what. It made her hair stand on end that Hyde could joke about things like these men's families after he'd ended their lives.

Clamping down on such unsettling thoughts, she focused on the implications of what Hyde had said. "So, SSS themselves caught wind of what we were doing and resorted to excessive and illegal force to stop us. They endangered the civilian population of this neighborhood, and indeed the entire Station, by deploying ballistic weaponry here." Many of the people watching the stream probably could have got the message without her pounding it into their heads, but it never hurt to be clear.

She paused for effect, then added, "Not only did they engage in reckless and hazardous actions in their desperation to stop us, but they failed."

CHAPTER EIGHT

When Nasreen returned to the Celestial Seoul safehouse, Dante was up. Not merely awake but on his feet and walking around. It had been five days since the operation and two since the raid on the so-called spa.

She stopped to examine him. "Hello. You're looking somewhat better. Maybe not entirely back to normal, but I'd say you've made a lot of progress. You're getting shaggy looking, though."

"Yeah, I know," he conceded as he poured himself another glass of water. "That tends to happen when you sleep twelve to sixteen hours a day for close to a week and can barely move around. But yes, I *am* better."

She closed the door, got a glass of water, and sat at the kitchen table. He moved over to join her. She saw the gears turning within his head as he decided that sitting would be more comfortable than leaning against the counter.

Nasreen was about to inquire how the Midas integration process was going, but a second before she could ask, Dante spoke up.

"Tell me what happened. You were out with Hyde doing

something, weren't you? I think you told me, but my memory's fuzzy. Anyway, glad you survived."

She pointed out, "Hyde survived too before you ask. We found what we were looking for. Made a bigger mess than I wanted, but there was no way to execute a job like that without some heads getting cracked. The information we uncovered was exactly what I expected. One thing stood out, though..."

She told him.

Dante had been finishing his water. He nearly choked on it as his cheeks bulged and he snorted, trying not to spit it out. He swallowed the remainder and slammed down the glass. "Slaine himself? Is he married? I never looked into that. Whatever, it doesn't matter. This is big. It means there's no way the son of a bitch can try to pin the o-harvesting operation on some middle manager who was 'acting alone' or that type of shit. When SSS goes down, he'll go down with it."

Nasreen's fingers drummed against the table in growing excitement. "Exactly. Before we get into the tedious details, tell me how your recovery has been. And how things are going with Midas. I'm curious how close you two are to being fully integrated again."

Dante frowned. He must have wanted to press on with the Slaine stuff. Still, he knew well that having himself and his AI back to maximum functionality would be vital to the ultimate fulfillment of their plans.

"I followed the directions you and Kieffer gave me. I've turned him on every day, for a little longer each time, pushing him harder but not to the point of hurting myself, that sort of thing. Yesterday he started to feel close to normal again. Almost everything he said made sense, a one-eighty from how he was right after the operation.

"I kept him on for a good hour and a half before my brain got too tired. His personality is still recognizable. He keeps expecting some of his upgrades and subroutines to be there and gets confused and angry when they're not, but he's adjusting."

Nasreen sipped her water. "Ah, good. That means everything is working the way it's supposed to. Have you turned him on yet today?"

"No. That's the next thing on my agenda. Might as well do it right now." He put two fingers to his temple and directed his thoughts inward, activating the AI simply by focusing enough neural activity directly on it to stimulate it back out of its slumber.

Within his mind, he felt Midas awakening, reaching out and expanding into the channels he occupied, melding his artificial consciousness with Dante's organic one.

"Hello, sir. I'm back online. Do you need me for anything specifically? Wait, yes, I recall now. We are slowly reintegrating ourselves over a week. I could be wrong, but I believe I'm at the end of that process. I cannot perceive anything more I can do to connect to the pertinent parts of your mind more efficiently. Unless, of course, we were to purchase several upgrades, which I would highly recommend. Are you feeling all right? You still seem a tad lethargic."

Dante smiled. "I'm mostly better. Maybe one more day. I'm glad you're feeling like your old self again. Sorry about the lost upgrades, but it was the only way to save the core of your programming. Otherwise, we would have had to replace you altogether."

There was a faint tremor of emotional discomfort that affected them both at the same time. *"Yes, I quite understand, and you have my thanks. Now, where—wait. Wait!"*

Dante stiffened, abruptly seized with anxiety as both he and the implant perceived that something was wrong.

Nasreen reached out and touched his hand. "What is it?"

"I don't know," Dante muttered. "Midas, talk to me."

The AI did not. He was silent for long enough that Dante feared he'd fritzed out or encountered an unexpected bug or damaged circuit and couldn't adapt around it. Then, at length, he declared, *"I fear we have a rather serious problem. I've been scanned and copied. It happened, ah, several days ago, if I'm not mistaken. Someone made a copy of a substantial portion of my stored data. Possibly all of it."*

Dante's face fell. His hands clenched and his eyes narrowed. "How many days ago, Midas?"

"One moment." While Nasreen watched, the implant reviewed his recent history. *"Five days, or possibly six. The period before then is difficult to see. That's when I was in dormancy after the EMP incident."*

Dante's fist pounded the table. "God *fucking* dammit!" His water glass fell over on its side.

Nasreen's eyes widened in alarm. "What is it?"

Pushing back in his chair and pulling himself to his feet, Dante rasped, "Someone at your trusted clinic in Berlin copied a bunch of Midas's info while I was under. Midas says someone scanned him five or six days ago, and he's certain they made a copy of a bunch of his files. Is that standard procedure with these things?"

Nasreen's mouth had formed into a small circle, and her eyes darkened. "No, it is not. It's completely against their normal policies. Either someone got the idea to sell your data to the highest bidder, or Slaine outright purchased them sometime before our last visit."

"Yeah," Dante agreed. "They fucked us, either way. Who? Kieffer?"

Nasreen's eyes rolled sidelong toward the wall; she concentrated. "I doubt it. If Slaine is blackmailing him, it's possible. I'd suspect a lower-level employee, one of the nurses or technicians. Someone with access to the equipment but didn't play a direct role in the surgery. That would be my guess."

Midas piped up. *"The details are becoming clearer. I now have the exact time at which the copy scan took place. If we could access the clinic's records, including network signatures and power expenditures on the day of the surgery, we could compare that against my records, who was on duty, and what machinery they were operating at such-and-such time."*

Dante relayed the information.

Nasreen frowned. "Finding out who's responsible is important, but if this happened five days ago, they must have sold it or passed it on already. Tracking down the culprit will point us in the right direction as far as damage control, but the damage has happened."

Grumbling under his breath, Dante focused on keeping in touch with Midas on the technical details. The AI sent them to Nasreen's messages. She powered up her sphere and immediately looked up the information she would need to begin remotely hacking the clinic's computers, as well as their power bill and network activity.

In a low voice, she commented, "Good thing I made sure to get their IP address and check what kind of security software they use right before you first had Midas installed. Not that I suspected them of anything, but better safe than sorry."

Forty minutes later, Nasreen had gathered and reviewed everything they needed to know.

She clenched her jaw. "A technician named Ergun. I barely know him, but I believe I saw him around the place a couple of times before. Chances of him being our culprit are around ninety-nine percent.

"As near as I can tell, he also copied some of the information in their computer system about me. It wasn't a random act of identity theft because he felt like making extra money that day. Someone put him up to this, specifically because of who *we* are."

Dante still looked tired, but he was visibly regaining much of his usual vitality. "No surprises there."

Nasreen added, "We can't rule out that it might be some deranged fan of the E-zex and Hellcat show or a rival consortium of Plunderers who want to sell it to our stream competitors, or some crap like that. Realistically, yes, it's likely to be Slaine."

Dante stared into the distance. "Slaine didn't know who we were beforehand, though. He was aware that our alter egos have been messing with his operations. But he didn't know that I'm Dante Shale. Did he? He thought I was Jordan Raksha. This is embarrassing, but I wonder if Hyde might be right. About the 'big spiders.' The people *behind* Slaine."

Nasreen froze in place as something within her went cold. "If that's the case, we have a major problem. Kieffer's clinic is very privacy-focused while also being off the radar of most people, even the rich and powerful. If Hyde's shadowy conspiracy is real, then they're every bit as powerful and omnipresent as he seems to believe."

They spent another hour conferring with each other and Midas over what to do and how to do it. Ultimately, they concluded that they had to seal the leak even if the info had already passed to its buyer. It would send the message that they weren't helpless, and it would allow them to learn how much their foes knew.

They would need help.

"Ambrose," said Nasreen. "He's not the most enthusiastic person, but I think he might be our best bet."

Dante scratched his chin. "Maybe. He's been more helpful lately. He can fly. I *want* to trust him again, honestly. But talking to him and Hyde at the same time is too complicated. They're completely different personalities, and they don't trust each other."

"Separate them," Nasreen proposed. "We can get more out of Ambrose if Hyde isn't breathing down his neck."

After a moment's pause, Dante quipped, "Yeah, and I can't help thinking that if we blurt all this out to Hyde, he'll get impatient, decide we aren't worth the trouble after all, and try to kill us both. No offense to your skills or our quality as a team, but it would probably take more than the two of us to beat that fucker. I hate to admit it, but he kicked my ass back on Earth. The day everyone thought I died."

Nasreen's gorge rose. She and Dante were both good enough that Hyde had failed to murder them, granted, but she feared her partner might be right. Trying to fight the monstrous cyborg head-on would be a supremely stupid risk.

She sighed. "All right. I'll message Ambrose. Then we'll have to hope he's smart enough to accept our offer without screwing anything up in the meantime."

Ambrose hurried up from the housing project's darkest corner with a coat over his head, melding into the shadows across the alley where the next building over blocked most of the street-lamps and overhead faux stars. Watching him, Dante felt an odd twinge of pride. When he wanted to, Ambrose wasn't half bad at moving without being seen or heard. For an amateur, anyway.

"Okay," the squat pilot greeted them in a low, breathy whisper. "He's asleep. Still, I'll feel much more comfortable if we're far away before we discuss anything. I think his, er, augmentations give him enhanced senses as well. He wakes up quite easily and never has trouble falling back asleep after he finds out what disturbed him."

Dante scouted ahead, determined they were in the clear, and waved for them to proceed. He, Nasreen, and Ambrose went down the alley before re-emerging onto the main lane and the sidewalk adjacent to the street that would take them deeper into Pentapolis.

Nasreen mused, "That's interesting. I wondered if Hyde slept like a normal human being or if he slept. It almost sounds like a computer going into standby and flicking back to life instantly if a fly farts nearby."

Despite his nervousness, Ambrose laughed in a half-embarrassed way. "Yes, that's a good comparison. He sleeps when he wants to. I believe he can 'power himself down,' much like a machine."

Dante nodded. "Shit. That's one regard in which I envy the bastard. All these advances—cities in space, plasma weapons, collapsible holograms, and all the other stuff we've invented since Earth got fucked—and science *still* can't do much to help the average person get a good night's sleep."

They were strolling along freely with the housing projects falling far behind them.

Nasreen turned to Dante. "That's not true. Those sedatives were doing a fine job keeping you down while you recuperated, weren't they?"

"Yeah, down and out. I'm not sure how much of it was the drugs versus the aftereffects of the operation itself, but either way, sedatives like that aren't something you want to take all the time. You can't *move* after you wake up. If you ever spend a night Dirtside or in certain neighborhoods, that's not worth the extra shuteye."

Ambrose cleared his throat. "*Anyway*, I understand you had something important to tell me about? You insisted that I help you? I don't want to, but I suppose I owe you."

Dante smiled. "Correct on all counts. Midas, do we have any listening devices nearby or anyone suspicious around?"

The AI replied in Dante's head, *"Nothing out of the ordinary, sir, although there are some standard city microphones nearby—the usual ones supposed to reduce crime and the like. I'm not sure if you're concerned about those. They pick up so much chatter that it's unlikely much of what we say would stand out. However, their security systems are generally middling at best, so if we're worried about hacking, it might be best to wait until we're out of range."*

His mood darkening, Dante muttered, "After what you told

me earlier, I'm not taking any chances. Ambrose, hold on a minute and we'll tell you all about it."

As they proceeded, away from the unseen public listening devices in question, Nasreen clarified some of the less sensitive aspects of the situation.

"We thought it would be better to talk to you alone because your roommate, well, he has skills at a few specific things, but this is a job for *your* skills. Plus, it helps to have someone who's, you know, sane."

Ambrose shrugged the coat a notch or two farther up. "Thank you. I'm glad you think I'm sane."

"Most people are, compared to him," Nasreen clarified.

Midas notified Dante when they hit one of the dead zones between the effective ranges of the various street microphones. Usually said zones were near busy intersections because those places would produce too much noise for anything to stand out, not to mention crime was more likely to occur along the fringes of well-traveled areas rather than in the thick of them.

Dante scanned their surroundings one last time before he spoke. "Okay, good. Ambrose, we mainly need your services as a pilot. Those are more useful than your skill as a pianist. Someone stole something from us, so we're going to abduct this person and interrogate them until they give it back."

Ambrose coughed, probably to cover a mewl of horror. "Abduct someone? Should we be breaking the law right now?"

A cluster of teenagers ambled past, eyeing the three nastily but leaving them be. When they were out of earshot, Nasreen observed, "We're all fugitives already, in one way or another. What does it matter if we add kidnapping to the equation? Besides, he worked for an illegal medical practice to begin with, *and* he stole from us first."

Ambrose sighed. "I suppose that's one way of looking at it. I only hope you have a plan to keep us from getting caught. More specifically, what do you want me to do?"

Dante and Nasreen stopped, blocking Ambrose off so he came to an awkward halt two feet away from them. They'd both agreed it would be better if he were standing still. Sitting down would be even better, but they couldn't expect perfection.

Dante caught his gaze. "We want you to pilot a stolen multi-taxi-class shuttle while we intercept the guy we're after as he's about to catch a ride. If we do it right, he might mistake us for the real thing and get in on his own. If that fails, we need you to do the maneuvering and hold steady while we jump out, grab him, and haul him in. It will probably be in a crowded area, so things could get dicey."

Nasreen added, "Don't worry, I'll be able to procure the shuttle a day or so in advance, so you'll be able to do a little practice flying. I'll handle all the red tape of making sure it's cleared to fly in the sector of Deutschheim we'll be in."

Ambrose stared at them both. Then his gaze fell, and he stared at the ground. He rubbed the sides of his head and drew a couple of deep breaths. "Who in the world is this person we need to do something like *that* to get? Kidnapping in the middle of a crowded platform? Cheating the taxi administration of Berlin?"

Dante wasn't good with rhetorical questions, so he simply answered everything the pilot had asked in the most direct fashion possible. "He's an employee of the clinic where I had Midas implanted. Doing it this way makes it easier for us to escape because with taxi clearance it will take them longer to unravel that we're not who we say we are. If we tried to load him into a private vehicle, they'd be able to pinpoint us much more quickly."

Ambrose chewed on his lower lip. "I don't like the idea. It can be done, but 'can' and 'should' are two different things. Also, what if Hyde finds out you're leaving him behind? How do you think he'll react?"

Nasreen brushed a strand of hair back from her face. "We thought of that. We'll play to his ego and have him bust up a gang of small-time hoods on the grounds that we think Slaine sent them to spy on your bolthole. They're not.

"Don't worry. They're hyperamphetamine dealers, and the authorities tried a couple of their members for rape and murder not long ago. They're not exactly innocent victims despite having nothing to do with our situation. Think of it as we're having Hyde clean up the neighborhood a little while we pull off the abduction."

"Yes, that may work," Ambrose murmured.

Dante put a hand on his former friend's shoulder. "Ambrose. You've been good and cooperative since you came back. By rights, I should still kill you, but for a traitor, you've been pretty reliable. Don't betray my trust again. *We need you.* If you understand what that means, we can tell you the whole story."

Nasreen raised an eyebrow. Although still rather curt as emotional speeches went, it was unusual for Dante to discuss human feelings the way he had. He must have still had a soft spot for Ambrose despite everything that had happened.

The pilot made a sour expression that was like an odd mashup of a grimace and an attempt at a pleasant smile. "Yes, I understand. I feel bad about what I did if that wasn't already clear. Let me make it up to you. By doing what I do best."

Dante's face relaxed, growing borderline friendly and warm, as opposed to his usual intense yet cool alertness. "All right. Great. Do *not* tell anyone about this, but Midas got hacked. Someone copied a bunch of information from his records and has probably passed it on to you-know-who, or possibly even the people Hyde refers to as 'big spiders' or whatever. That would be *bad.* This is the kind of thing where we cannot assume that anyone is on our side."

Ambrose's eyes widened. "Yes, that's concerning. The last part is an extremely good point. What if Hyde himself was involved? He's been closer to you than anyone else lately, aside from myself and Nasreen. He may have arranged to acquire that information to hold it for ransom. Use it to buy himself a place back in the 'web,' as he calls it after SSS gets taken down."

Dante and Nasreen exchanged a glance.

Nasreen's nostrils flared. "That could be. Although he's not exactly a master of subtlety, Hyde is smarter and more devious than he lets on. At his unnatural age, it makes sense that he would have learned a few lessons by now. Anyway, that's all the more reason to keep him out of the loop on this. Nobody says *anything* about where we will be or what we'll be doing. Not so much as a hint."

Dante grunted, "No shit. The bastard openly admitted that he plans to turn on us and try to kill us, to prove a point or something, as soon as we no longer have a common goal."

Ambrose shuddered. "Don't worry. I have no desire whatsoever to make him angry at me."

CHAPTER NINE

Many taxis were small, automated pods designed to accommodate only one or two passengers at a time. The more traditional type still piloted by human beings that could fit a larger number of people had nonetheless persisted. They were a common sight in Deutschheim and most other Stations. The one Nasreen had procured would hold four to five individuals, exactly the capacity they had in mind.

Dante was starting to wonder if it wouldn't have been a better idea to get a bigger one, intended for six or eight. It would have been more conspicuous and less nimble while flying, but at least they would all have more room to maneuver.

Ambrose snapped, "Watch it!" then added in a crestfallen whisper, "Sorry, Dante. I'm used to more elbow space than this when flying a craft."

"Yeah, I get it. I'll stay out of your way. Nasreen, are you sure you don't want to switch places?"

He and Ambrose were in the front seat, which was large enough for both of them to sit, but considerably less convenient if they had to *move*.

Nasreen was in a stylish and provocative dress that was low-cut up front and short at the bottom. She rested in the back seat with one leg crossed over the other. "Yes, I'm sure. Admit it, Dante, the optics of having me handle this part outweigh the fact that you have slightly more upper-body strength than I do."

Dante made a low, wordless grumbling sound and turned back to the viewscreen. "Fine. But tech stuff like this is your specialty."

She raised a finger. "You were the one who told me how important it was to have a good set of *general* skills. It's not like you're a completely useless amateur when handling comms and surveillance stuff."

Since she was right, Dante said nothing.

They had been spying on Ergun, the technician at the AI clinic, all day, using a small, camouflaged drone. Between direct observation and their review of the clinic's records, payroll, and scheduling information, they knew when he'd be getting out of work and what route he would likely take to go home. Like most people, he walked straight to the nearest public transportation platform. The trio did experience a brief hiccup when he detoured slightly to purchase a falafel from a roadside stand. Still, once he had his food, he returned to his usual·footpath, eating as he walked.

Once he'd come close to the platform, Ambrose powered up the taxi and flew it out of their hiding place. They'd waited in an abandoned garage not far from another, functional one where other taxis sometimes lodged for repairs. Ambrose merged seamlessly with the flow of other, legitimate hover traffic.

They got pinged by the oversight agency almost immediately, but Nasreen's fake credentials served them well. No one bothered them as they made their slow revolution around the platform, waiting for their fare.

Unsurprisingly, a few other travelers were trying to flag them down.

Dante exhaled in a ragged, impatient way. "Come on, Ergun.

Hurry the hell up. If we keep circling without picking up any obvious customers, it'll look much more suspicious."

Nasreen remarked, "Not necessarily. Remember, we accounted for that part."

Grunting again, he returned to the screen. "Okay, he's almost here. I'm going to cut the drone loose since there's a nice gutter here for it to burn itself up in." He flicked a couple of switches. The camera feed vanished as the drone dive-bombed into the gutter, where it self-destructed out of sight of the public.

Then Ergun appeared in person, stepping onto the rear of the platform. He was a relatively small man with a round face and a bristly black mustache, quite unremarkable looking. He wore a light jacket over his medical coveralls.

When they'd observed him last night, he had chosen to wait for the shuttle bus rather than bother with a taxi, presumably to save money. Tonight, the bus seemed to be running a little late.

Ambrose took the cab down, deftly avoiding another such craft that tried to butt in to scoop up fares and slowed down nearly to a halt right in front of Ergun. The dour little man turned to look at the cab with a questioning expression. Someone else noticed the taxi and began pushing through the crowd toward it.

Dante said, "Now."

Ambrose hit a switch to open the rear seating compartment automatically. At the last minute, Ergun leaned toward it, hesitant but interested. Perhaps now that he was receiving a massive payout from whoever had purchased the info he'd copied, he felt like riding in a bit more luxury than the bus could provide.

He saw Nasreen already sitting there, and his eyes widened. He tensed and froze.

Nasreen was ready for the possibility. She sprang forward, smiling and allowing her face to light up as if in delighted surprise. "Hi!" In German, she added, "Oh my God, it's so good to see you again! Come here. I need to hug you, then let's get going."

She wrapped her arms around his neck and shoulders and hauled him bodily into the cab with a sharp jerk. The instant he cleared the threshold of the taxi's door, Ambrose closed the door and moved forward, picking up speed. Behind them, the other guy who'd wanted to catch the cab waved his fist and cursed heartily.

Nasreen shoved Ergun so he lay awkwardly on his back across the seat, a poor position from which to fight. She deployed her wrist knife, letting him see the sharp, gleaming blade. "Do not move," she said.

Dante looked back from the front passenger seat. "You heard the lady. Give us any trouble, and you're dead. She'll slit your femoral artery and let you bleed to death on the cab floor. It's not our vehicle, anyway, so we don't give a shit. Wait, does he speak English?"

The small man was stunned and frightened but retained enough presence of mind not to panic. "Yes, I do," he stated in a mixed German and Turkish accent.

"Good." Dante quickly checked the viewscreen. The cab's floor cam had replaced the destroyed drone's point of view.

Ambrose had ascended into the highest of the major skylanes. Air traffic was considered more dangerous than rail traffic, and some cities were trying to discourage it. Nevertheless, it remained an important part of the Stations' transportation infrastructure.

Nasreen gave their guest a wry smile. "All right, Mr. Ergun. Do you know why you're here right now? Do you know what we want?"

Ergun scowled. "Yes. There is nothing I can do for you. I have already sold the files. I do not have them anymore." Although terrified, he maintained his composure a little more effectively than Dante had hoped.

This was another problem with having Nasreen on knifepoint duties. Ergun undoubtedly got the message that they intended to harm or kill him if he gave them any shit, but Nasreen looked ravishing in her current outfit. If Dante had hovered over him with a blade, he might have been a little more intimidated.

Nasreen sneered, not missing a beat. "Oh, we'd guessed as much. You can still help us, Ergun. If you help us, you'll get out of this alive with all your body parts intact. If you try to lie to us or refuse to tell us what we want to know, today will be the worst day of your life. And perhaps the *last* day of your life. Understand?"

The technician's eyes darkened, and a palpable sinking sensation radiated from him. His vibe of dread and resignation conveyed that he knew they'd caught him, the odds were not in his favor, and he would be damn lucky if they were as merciful as they promised.

He sighed. "Yes."

Dante nodded. He found torture repulsive, and Nasreen wasn't fond of it either. Roughing people up or scaring the crap out of them was sometimes useful or necessary, but the thought of rendering someone helpless and carving pieces from them made him sick. He'd seen a lot of brutality in his time. If Ergun refused to cooperate, the plan was simply to kill him.

If he played ball, they intended to keep their word. Of course, what happened to him once he was out of their custody and back where Slaine or his benefactors could get at him was none of Dante's, Nasreen's, or Ambrose's business.

Ergun looked at Dante and the back of Ambrose's head. He squinted. The pilot focused on flying them.

Nasreen waved the knife. "Ah-ah. Focus on me, Ergun. Focus on this. My knife is the thing you should care most about right now. We're going to a quiet spot where we can talk in peace. Then you will tell us everything we want to know. There will be no deals, no bargaining. We ask, and you give. You are in no position to ask anything from *us*."

If by some chance he tried to overpower Nasreen, the cab, like many, was equipped with a tranquilizer gas charge, though that would also knock Nasreen out. She could typically handle herself. And Ergun was behaving thus far.

Ambrose took them to an older, run-down part of the former Berlin. He steered out of the skylane at the appropriate time before descending to street level to hover above the pavement on a comparatively dark and lonely road.

From there, they wove through various small lanes until they came to a humble and diminutive private dock facility at the edge of the Station. It linked to the band of artificial gravity and residual atmosphere that encircled the dome. It was designed only for small-craft, short-distance travel around Deutschheim's periphery and perhaps to the tubes connecting it to other Stations. The dock wasn't big enough nor did it have the necessary facilities to handle full-sized spacecraft that could go Dirtside or cut across space to the Stations on the opposite side of the ring.

Ambrose had rented the place out yesterday, saying that as a newly hired, semi-freelance cab driver, he would need a place to park at night to check his vehicle's condition and act as a base of operations until one of the major firms hired him. The people who owned it hadn't asked further questions. They only cared about the money and that he didn't break any laws.

It was too bad about the "breaking laws" part, Dante thought. They would likely be doing plenty of that.

Ambrose landed, took the cab out of sight of the street, and stopped before powering it down. Dante climbed out. "Keep an eye out until we get him secured." He went around to the side of the vehicle to help Nasreen.

Dante muscled Ergun out. He didn't try to fight them while Nasreen kept her wrist knife aimed at his groin. They took the man into a back room, mostly bare but already set up with a chair, cords, and straps. Dante felt the technician's muscles grow tense as he saw the setup. With the Station heading into evening lighting and themselves right on the edge of space anyway, it looked like a torture chamber.

The more scared he was, hopefully, the more cooperative he would be.

Dante pushed Ergun into the chair, tied his hands to the chair's arms, and his ankles to the chair's legs. He ensured everything was tight and that Ergun had no means of breaking free, including tipping the chair over and trying to use its momentum to his advantage.

"Okay," he said to Nasreen. "We're in business. I'm going to check outside. Then we'll get started. Yell if you need anything."

Nasreen smiled. "All should be well."

Dante strolled out front and did a fast scan of the street, barely visible beyond the dock's edge. To his left, the dome's crystalline surface was thinner to accommodate the gate that led into the gravitational-atmospheric band. The barrier was translucent enough to see the blackness of space and the silver of the stars beyond. Below them was the dull brown surface of the dying planet Earth.

Ambrose was still sitting behind the driver's seat of the shuttle cab, staring out at the void. He looked calm but uncomfortable. His mouth puckered the way it sometimes got when he knew something ugly was about to happen.

"Am, you want to head in? I think we'll be okay as far as nobody bothering us. Or if you're bored, you can help Nasreen, and I'll stand guard. It doesn't matter at this point. She's going to handle the main interrogation stuff."

Ambrose cringed. "I would rather stay out here. I'm not interested in participating in whatever you plan to do to that man."

Dante realized they hadn't specifically told Ambrose that actual torture was unlikely to be necessary and probably off the table no matter what. He wanted to reassure his old friend, but there was a chance that his voice could carry to the back room. If Ergun knew they were bluffing, he'd become more defiant. Pulling this off depended on his belief that they *would* do anything to get the information out of him.

Dante shrugged. "Fine, it's up to you. Let us know if you see anything suspicious and be ready to take off in ten seconds if you have to."

"Of course." Ambrose continued to stare straight ahead. The day had been stressful even though everything had gone to plan, and he was probably looking forward to it being over. Talented though he was as a pilot, including under massive duress, he had never been the overly adventurous or gung-ho type.

As Dante walked off, Ambrose stayed in the same position, feigning distaste and fatigue as he'd been doing. Once Dante was out of sight and earshot, and after an extra minute or so, he slipped his sphere out of his pocket, checked something, and tapped a few keys and panels to send a message. He tried to look down as little as possible. It was important not to draw attention to himself.

When he finished, he closed his eyes and slid the device back into his pants. "Soon," he murmured. "Soon this will be over. Finally. Then everything will be back to normal." He paused and permitted himself a small smile. It was more of a smirk. "For me, anyway."

Dante strode back into their makeshift holding cell. Nasreen was kneeling in front of Ergun and speaking softly to him, as though she was trying to be mildly seductive and coldly threatening at the same time. It was the type of subtle, manipulative approach that wouldn't have occurred to Dante but which Nasreen excelled at. She was, after all, a woman as well as a professional spy.

He didn't interrupt but simply crossed his arms and stood nearby, grimacing and trying to look imposing. It wasn't too difficult. People had told him that despite his average height and build, he was imposing even when he *wasn't* trying to be.

"...as well as anyone else they might have mentioned, including couriers," Nasreen explained. "Every single person you spoke to or interacted with. Every name—person, company, organization, even brand of equipment they might have used. Anything or anyone connected to these people in any way. We want it all."

Ergun stared back at her with a kind of stoic deadness of the spirit. He must have known that if anyone discovered his cooperation with them, Slaine or the "big spiders" of Hyde's ramblings would come for him soon after. That at least pushed the risk of death slightly farther into the future. Nasreen and Dante had made it abundantly clear that if he resisted, death would arrive before morning. Guaranteed.

When the small man replied, he said something neither Dante nor Nasreen had expected. Dante fell back half a step despite himself, the way he did to brace himself in a fighting stance if he thought someone was going to jump him.

"I will tell you if you let me see this man who drives the cab. I did not see his face. But something about him seems very familiar."

Nasreen didn't react visibly, but Dante sensed her shock through a subtle shift in her vibe.

She maintained her composure, staring into the man's face. "That's a nice trick. I already warned you, Ergun. You're in no position to make *any* demands of us." Her hand shot out, pinched his arm, and found a pressure point, squeezing it with a sharp motion.

Ergun cried out in pain and alarm, his head rolling back and mouth falling open as his eyes squeezed shut.

Nasreen retracted her hand, ending the pain almost as quickly as she'd begun it. "I don't want to have to hurt you. But you will not receive another warning. Cooperate, or else."

The captive's lips trembled with misery. "Very well. I will begin with how it happened and all the people I spoke to along the way..."

Dante wandered back outside. Nasreen could handle simply recording information that a broken man rattled off for a moment or so. While Ergun's little request probably *was* a trick, as she'd said, it had piqued Dante's curiosity.

When he emerged back into the bay area, Ambrose was still sitting in the cab and staring straight ahead into space.

"Am," he called. "We need your help with something. It'll only take a second. Don't give me any bullshit or try to keep asking about the details, okay? Come here and do it."

Dante had never been much good as a liar. He'd found it was better to rely upon his forthright and intimidating nature to simply persuade people not to question him if the occasion arose that he needed to operate on a falsehood.

Ambrose turned his head with such sharpness that it might have been spring-loaded. His eyes looked enormous. He sat still and dumbfounded as though he couldn't mentally process how little he wanted to do what Dante had said but couldn't bullshit his way out of it.

His hand moved to the door and lay atop its edge. "Oh. Well, yes. I can do that. Give me, ah, a moment, if you please." He swallowed and slowly opened the door before heaving himself out of the vehicle at a pace that was also absurdly unhurried.

Dante watched him. It was obvious that he was stalling. His best guess was that he hoped Nasreen would deal with whatever the problem was in the time it took him to get there, or he simply needed a minute to adjust after the stress of the day's endeavors.

Or...

"Hurry up," Dante prodded. "Something seems fucked up with the pressure in that room, and I want you to spot me while I check it out. Nasreen's busy."

Ambrose sighed as he shuffled toward his old partner at a marginally faster rate. "Okay, yes, fine. I'm coming."

Once he was close enough, Dante put a hand on his shoulder and deftly transposed their positions so Am had to march in front of him. Dante could also poke him in the back to speed him up.

Am didn't react to the trick. He kept tramping forward.

When they emerged into the back room, Nasreen was still crouching in front of Ergun. He looked mostly at the floor, having sunk inside himself as he muttered, giving his lengthy account of how he'd been recruited.

Suddenly, Ambrose sped up. "Oh, that!" He jogged toward the far corner, where he would be behind Ergun's line of sight. "I'll have a look at it right now."

Dante barked, "Ergun!"

The captive's head jerked up, and his eyes widened. He saw the cab driver at the exact moment he passed.

"That is him!" Ergun sputtered, his voice jumping in volume and urgency. "That is the man who came to me with the job—the first one I met in person."

Ambrose stopped. He stood unmoving, facing away from them and staring at the back wall.

Dante drew a deep breath through his nose before slowly releasing it from his mouth. "Oh." He patted his jacket, feeling the outline of his knife.

Outside, rushing noises suddenly grew louder as vehicles landed in their rented bay. Enough of the specifics echoed through the halls toward them that Dante could detect the unmistakable sounds of razorfist blades ejecting from their gauntlets and people tightening dart launchers against their wrists.

Ambrose burst into a run at speeds Dante wouldn't have thought him capable of, shocking all three of them. As he moved, he snatched something out of his clothes and threw it.

Dante pounced, but the thrown object struck him in the arm and detonated. He fell backward as though a heavy pole had swatted him. His head swam, and his ears rang. It had been a miniaturized sonic grenade, a self-defense device of questionable legality that was difficult to use but could be surprisingly effective if one got it right.

Against all odds, Ambrose got it right.

As he toppled to the floor, his hearing temporarily impaired but not entirely ruined, Dante heard Ergun warbling something incomprehensible. Nasreen sprang to her feet and turned as Am shouted, "It's me! All three of them are in there!"

Ambrose Igento had put Ergun in contact with Slaine's people or whoever else wanted the hacked info so badly. Ambrose had acted as the facilitator for the whole thing, probably in exchange for vast sums of money and assurances that he would be left alone.

Dante managed to roll as he hit the floor, then used the momentum to jump back up into a half-crouch. He was disoriented, and it would take him a minute to recover, but he had more experience than the average person with keeping his head after being hit or blasted with something nonfatal.

As he struggled to his feet, Nasreen grabbed his arm and helped him up. "We need to take Ergun and get out of here. We *cannot* let them trap us in this room. Might be able to get out if we can reach the cab in time to stab Ambrose in the face and take over the car."

"Yeah." Dante groaned. "*Might* be able."

He somehow managed to drag Ergun, chair and all, into the hallway, with Nasreen on point. The alluring dress she'd worn for the occasion made it impossible to conceal wrist-mounted weapons. She'd still hidden a tiny pistol-style dart launcher somewhere, and now she held it in her hand, ready to fire. It was better than nothing, but it wasn't a powerful weapon and only carried two darts.

They were about to emerge into the loading bay when the first of the hit squad stormed in.

In the flash of a second before everything turned to violence, Dante saw a lithe but muscular figure wearing light armor and brandishing a razorfist. He held his hand in a position that would allow him to stab or slash at someone's face, chest, or throat as fast as possible without overextending his arm.

He must not have counted on projectile weapons. Nasreen fired the dart launcher directly into his face. After he attempted a quick but inaccurate strike, the reality of what had happened sank in. She'd embedded a toxic dart in his eye. He gasped and crumpled backward. Nasreen snatched a backup knife from his belt and shoved his body out into the bay, jumping over it.

Dante was annoyed that she hadn't waited an extra second for him to let go of the terrified Ergun to reinforce her. He gritted his teeth and left the chair with the small man still bound to it, pulled the razorfist off the dying assassin, put it on, and bounded out into the fray.

There were only three more men. Enough to be a problem, but not as bad as he'd feared. The enemy probably wanted a small, highly mobile, highly skilled group who could strike anywhere in minimal time rather than a large, lumbering army. They had come on a pair of thrustbikes. Each was large enough to hold one passenger behind the driver.

Beyond them, Ambrose had reached the cab door and was fumbling madly to get it open.

Everything was happening at once. Dante had to help Nasreen overcome the attackers, stop Ambrose from getting away, *and* protect the hostage. All at the same time. Somehow. He was good, but no one was *that* good.

"God*dammit*," he raged and hurled himself into the closest of the three onrushing assailants, hoping he could bowl the man aside in time to work his way forward. Maybe he could wound one of the others on his way to catching Am.

The attacker's knife flashed. Dante ducked under it and hooked the man's arm to throw him into the guy rushing at Nasreen. The two collided, stunning one another and nearly falling over, but still blocking Nasreen from the last man.

He hopped to Dante's side, aiming and firing his wrist-mounted dart launcher. But not at Dante.

Dante glanced at the trajectory as one of the small yet deadly projectiles streaked through the air and embedded itself in Ergun's forehead. He stared slack-jawed for a second before his head sank to his chest and his eyes turned glassy.

Dante growled, "No!" and lunged at the assassin. His blade sank into the man's throat as the wrist launcher sent another dart wildly over his shoulder. The man tried to draw his knife, but Dante trapped his hand, twisted the blade to open more of the man's jugular and windpipe, and kicked the bloody corpse aside.

Nasreen had taken down one of the two remaining combatants but landing the killing stroke on the first exposed her to a rib strike by the second. Off to the side, the cab was powering up and starting to move.

Dante could have caught the vehicle if he'd flung himself straight at it and gone directly for Ambrose. He had only a half-second to decide, and Nasreen's life hung in the balance.

He slid at the last of the assassins, scissored the man's leg between his ankles, and twisted, throwing the man to the floor. Then he and Nasreen both pounced on him at once, stabbing him four times in a second. They sprang up from the body together.

Nasreen's eyes widened as she realized what was happening on the other side of the bay. "Ambrose is getting away! And Ergun's dead. Fuck!"

Dante was already climbing astride one of the idling thrust-bikes. They were fast, maneuverable machines, albeit dangerous, and he hadn't driven one in a couple of years. But there wasn't anything else available. "I know. I'll get him."

His hands twisted around the clutch and throttle as he felt the bike's balance, bringing it half a meter higher off the ground into the appropriate hover-level for a quick blastoff.

"What?" Nasreen protested. "You're not going to leave me behind, are you? Bullshit!"

Dante wasn't sure whether to be annoyed or relieved when she jumped onto the makeshift passenger's seat behind him.

CHAPTER TEN

"Hold on," Dante admonished, and Nasreen clamped her hands around his waist. They rose another three feet into the air, drifting forward, then Dante accelerated out of the bay and onto the lonely street.

Ambrose had gone out and turned left. He only had two or three seconds' head start on them, but it might be enough to lose them if things went pear-shaped. Dante had no intention of allowing that to happen. His jaw clenched as the breeze picked up.

As they swept out onto the street, the automated windshield turned on. It was a small, contained gravitational mass field, totally invisible but surprisingly effective at blocking or diverting the rushing air as the thrustbike's speed increased.

Most modern bikes also had similar shields that would deploy along the top and sides if the bike veered too sharply to the side, spun in a circle, or collided with anything, keeping the riders mostly in their seats. Reports had surfaced of bikers ending up with broken bones as they crashed against the shields, but someone analyzed the stats and figured out that *without* them, the bikers would probably have been dead.

Midas had been keeping silent but was aware of everything going on. He spoke into Dante's mind. *"I'll navigate as best I can and track him with a nice green icon showing where—*to your right!"

Dante saw them at the same instant Midas did. Two more assassins rode a third thrustbike, which had remained hidden on the street beyond the bay, waiting in reserve. They must have had strict orders not to intervene unless necessary. Or they weren't entirely aware that their four comrades had botched the ambush and lay dead within the bay.

They undoubtedly realized that Ambrose's cab, plus one other bike mounted by two strangers, weren't supposed to emerge. As Dante picked up velocity, aiming for the green cursor that Midas used to target Am, the other bike rose and rocketed toward them from behind. They were now chasers *and* chased.

Nasreen raised her voice to be audible over the rushing wind. "This isn't good. Too bad we're not Dirtside, or we could blow them out of the air with a pulsecore."

Dante agreed, but in that scenario, the assassins would probably be packing similar heat and could easily return the favor.

Ambrose was pushing the cab to its maximum speed, continuing straight down the street. Because of the time and location, there was little traffic so he could put the most distance between himself and his pursuers.

Dante muttered, "No." He drove the bike hard, doing much the same thing, and accelerating faster due to the smaller vehicle's lighter weight. He was gaining.

Behind them, the assassins lost ground. Then they hit their max velocity and slowly began to catch up.

Ambrose abruptly hung a right into a relatively narrow perpendicular street, almost more of an alley. Dante sucked in his breath and slowed enough to keep them from spinning out of control during the sharp turn ahead.

He leaned into it. The bike slanted at a crazy angle and the shields kicked on to press against them. Right in front of them was an oncoming auto-car. Dante's reflexes remained sharp even if he was out of practice with thrustbikes. He twisted the throttle, accelerating into the turn despite the gut-wrenching sensation of capsizing that seized them both and veered wide around the madly honking vehicle.

Then they were past it, and Midas's green cursor found Ambrose's cab. Dante righted his course and kicked their speed back up. He avoided going full throttle since that was a recipe for disaster if he needed to dodge or turn without warning. It would take longer to catch Ambrose even with the bike's weight advantage, but there was marginally less risk of going *splat* before they did.

Behind them, the two hitmen had to brake and skid off to the side to narrowly avoid being smashed by the car. Had the oncoming vehicle not slowed for Dante a second earlier, it probably would have run them over.

Nasreen was watching from the rear seat. She quipped, "Well, the bastards are still in one piece, but dodging that auto threw them off a bit. Now's our chance to pull ahead."

"Yeah," Dante growled. "I know." He also knew that Ambrose wouldn't maintain one direction or course long enough to allow them to catch up to him. He'd been Dante's pilot for years, and he knew how the man drove. How wily, defensive, and agile he could be behind the console of anything that hovered.

Two important factors were working in Dante's and Nasreen's favor. One, Ambrose was in a hurry. Two, he was trying to get somewhere in particular. Dante wasn't sure where. It was simply a general hunch, a sense of familiarity with the way the pilot handled the cab that bespoke a specific destination as his goal.

Probably, he wanted to get back to Pentapolis so he could beg Hyde to protect him from Dante's wrath. If that were the case, their four-way partnership would be over. It also meant Dante would finally get to settle accounts with both. He tried to look on the bright side.

Sure enough, Ambrose merged onto a no-stop track as they caught up. It was reserved mainly for public transportation, but personal motorists were permitted to use it as a short-term means of getting from one point to another if they stayed out of the way of the shuttles. It was a relic of Germany's famous Autobahn, known for its lax approach to speeding enforcement.

A shuttle was coming up directly on their left.

Nasreen exclaimed, "Shit!" as Dante accelerated, pushing the speed past what even he considered safe or sane. They barely zipped ahead of the hurtling silver front of the shuttle, then slowed once past it to fishtail along the track in the next lane.

The track's magnetic quality helped stabilize the bike to an extent but also made acceleration harder. Once a vehicle had properly merged, it could achieve an even higher maximum speed. But entry and exit onto the tracks were to some extent AI-controlled, with the magnetic forces slowing down other vehicles if necessary to prevent collisions.

Ambrose was bearing toward an exit up ahead. He didn't plan to stay on the track. It had simply been a scheme to lose them.

A glance in the mirror cam showed Dante the other bike, still mounted by the last two hitmen, jet onto the tracks behind them and weave between buses.

To his shock, the assassins' bike jumped the edge of the tracks right into the regular street that ran parallel to it, which was illegal and usually inadvisable. They didn't care, confident that Slaine or whoever else was signing their paychecks would bail them out of jail if necessary.

Dante shouted at Nasreen, "This might be a good thing. Maybe we can get those guys and Am to crash into each other, and all we do is pick up the pieces."

"Well, don't crash *us!*" Nasreen yelled back.

That was the idea.

Ambrose took the exit. He'd waited as long as possible to do so, hoping he would catch Dante by surprise and the bike would shoot past and miss its chance to follow him. Dante had anticipated the move. He leaned in behind the cab, still pushing the acceleration.

Then Am did something that *did* catch them by surprise. He hit the brakes and slowed down.

Dante's eyes widened as the cab's rear thruster, which put out a lot of heat and energy, loomed closer. He was about to flank the vehicle to ram or hijack it when Am poured on the speed again, so the thruster glowed brighter.

Snarling and sputtering, Dante jerked the bike aside, barely missing the blast of flame that came close to engulfing them. The bike's windshield might have absorbed or deflected some of it, but not enough to save them from injury or death. It was a problem unique to bikes and one he wasn't used to dealing with.

Then Dante sped toward the cab's flank again. He squeezed onto the street's median, much to the consternation of other motorists in the opposite lane. The bike fit into the no-man's-land well enough to pull it off but it would only take one idiot who wasn't paying attention to turn them into a projectile launched at the nearest building. Horns honked madly. Dante gave thanks that most regular streets didn't yet have AI systems that could shut down vehicles breaking traffic laws, at least not how he was currently doing.

Sirens sounded in the distance. The authorities had caught on to the fact that a destructive event was tearing through Deutschheim.

Dante followed Ambrose around two more turns where the pilot tried to double back, only for the assassins' thrustbike to explode out of an alley beside them and pin the cab in on its other flank.

Nasreen exclaimed, "What the hell? Are they trying to cooperate with us?"

"Temporarily," Dante suggested. "Maybe."

The hitman seated in the rear looked at them. He raised his wrist launcher, leading the target, and fired. Nasreen ducked as Dante tilted them at a nearly forty-five-degree angle and the dart sailed over their heads. As the shields kicked in and the bike struggled to right itself, Nasreen screamed, "Hey! You assholes!"

Their rivals had pulled ahead of them and now tailed Ambrose closely. Am tried to fire the thrusters again and technically succeeded. A gout of bright yellow flame struck the bike's front, only to be dispersed by a faint cyan glow in the air. The riders remained unharmed.

Dante glanced down at the console. "Oh, for fuck's sake. They have enhanced shields on these things. I didn't notice." There had been an awful lot of commotion. He pressed the button, and the air's electrical quality shifted, the way the atmosphere on Earth sometimes did before a storm. Everything around them took on an ever-so-faint blue-green tint.

Nasreen called, "That gives me an idea. Can Midas hack their bike and disable their shields?"

Excitement swelled. Dante deliberately allowed himself to fall back, pulling away from the median to avoid another pair of onrushing cars. "I hope so. Midas, did you hear that?"

"Yes, sir," the AI responded. *"Right on it. Get a little closer to them, please?"*

Dante grumbled but pulled ahead. If this worked, he didn't want to be too near the results, but it was worth the risk.

Five or six seconds later, Ambrose let off the accelerator again, and the assassins pulled forward, approaching the vehicle's rear in anticipation of disabling it or trying to board. Midas exclaimed, *"Aha! Done."*

Ambrose fired the thruster.

This time, there was no cyan light ripple to protect the assassins. Both cried out in horror as the tongue of fire blasted them out of their seats. Their burning bodies spiraled through the air and crashed into a metal wall a quarter mile back.

The bike itself, scorched and driverless but not totally disabled, wobbled and was about to fall.

"Wait," Midas said sharply. *"I have it. Do we want to keep it? It has a rudimentary automatic steering mechanism that—"*

Dante cut him off. "Nasreen! Can you drive one of these things?"

"Yes. There's no time, though! Ambrose is pulling ahead." She pointed. It was true. Getting rid of the assassins had given him more of an opening to outpace the pair.

Dante sucked in his breath and pulled closer to the other bike, which continued to speed along the road under Midas's inexpert guidance. "Yes, there is. Two heads are better than one, right? Drive this one. I'll take the other. Midas, help me with this. Turn off the right-side shield for a second or two."

Nasreen made a series of incomprehensible ranting and spitting sounds, apparently believing he needed a serious mental health appraisal. Dante stood on the bike, waited until the other was a foot away, then tried to ignore the dizziness and sinking feeling of terror in his stomach as he flung himself into the air.

His hand caught the left handlebar, and one of his feet jammed hard against the lower frame. After the initial sense that he'd pulled off such a ridiculous maneuver, his heart jumped into his throat. He was falling. He was going to plummet horizontally off the rear of the thrustbike the same way the two assassins had.

Midas panicked along with him. Then a solid surface stopped him and pushed him forward. He fell awkwardly into the seat, bumping his groin harder than he would like but abruptly in control of the bike. And alive.

The AI explained, *"I reenabled the shield at the last instant, sir. Here, let me turn the device back over to manual."*

"Thanks," Dante gasped. The console responded to his touch, and he immediately kicked up the speed. Off to his side, Nasreen was wild-eyed with fury, but she, too, had control of her bike. Together, they moved in on Ambrose's flanks, tight enough to remain in the correct lane but off enough to the sides to avoid the thruster flame.

Seemingly without warning, they neared the Station's far end, about a mile from the junction with the tubes that connected Berlin to various other cities in the West. The pilot was bearing toward the one in the center, which went directly to Amsterdam. And beyond it, Londonburg.

The tubes closed around them, darkening the quality of the artificial light, and boxing them in with a steady flow of other traffic and no real egress points to either side. Dante wondered if the Deutschheim cops had figured out where they were or where they were going. If so, they might message the police in Amsterdam to set up a roadblock near the tube's mouth.

Other cars, cabs, and shuttles honked, stalled, slowed, or swerved aside to avoid them as Ambrose drove his vehicle relentlessly forward. Each time the pair of bikes got too close, he tried again to burn them with the thrusters or ram them with the outer hull, potentially smashing them into the tube's walls. Advanced shields could do only so much to protect against massive high-speed kinetic impact.

Dante tried to put himself in the more dangerous positions as they emerged since Nasreen's skill at piloting a bike seemed rusty or mediocre. She was a much better pilot of full-sized shuttles than he was but didn't have much practice on smaller, hand-driven craft. It had been a while, but Dante had ridden bikes all the time when he was younger. It was all coming back to him fast —it had to, to keep him alive.

Between Ambrose's wiliness and the curving, irregular, haphazard layout of the tubes, there was no way to predict *exactly* what they'd encounter around each new bend. Intuition, reflexes, and quick thinking were all they had.

Finally, the tube's exit loomed ahead. As they rocketed out of it, tailing Am closer than the squat man probably preferred, two trios of police cruisers emerged from the city on either side of the opening. They stopped or swerved in circles, their sirens blaring as the three madly rushing vehicles shot overhead and left them behind.

Dante grinned. He'd never liked the Amsterdam police. They always seemed to be stoned.

Ambrose stuck to the express sky lanes, leaving most of the city below them and traversing the narrower and more direct space where the gravity dome narrowed toward its rotunda. As Dante had suspected, his former crewmate had no intention of lingering in the Dutch metropolis. He was headed straight for Londonburg, the home city of Slaine Solar Solutions.

Halfway across Amsterdam, the cab largely stopped its defensive-offensive maneuvers as though Ambrose had resigned himself to not killing Dante and Nasreen. Instead, he focused on covering space and making haste. His goal was to get "home" as quickly as possible.

A light flickered on Dante's console, forming an icon to indicate an incoming message. Nasreen announced, "You've probably reached the same conclusion I have. He's making for SSS headquarters. Over."

Dante spared a half-glance to tap the icon to allow himself to respond, then grunted, "Yeah. He probably trusts Slaine more than Hyde." It made sense that the bikes would all have a private network. The downside was that the assassins' employers might still be listening in.

"Poor bastard," Nasreen remarked. "He thinks they'll protect him instead of turning him into human scrap for botching this whole thing so badly."

Dante's hands tightened around the handlebars. "Not if I can help it."

She sounded shocked. The evening had been full of surprises

for all of them. "Wait, what? We're going to *save* that asshole after he betrayed you again? And me, obviously."

Annoyed that she was trying to argue in the middle of a high-speed chase, Dante shot back, "I'm not saving him. I'm simply not letting SSS kill him. That's my job!"

Nasreen responded with a stream of low yet sharp muttered commentary he couldn't entirely make out, but he was pretty sure the words "stupid," "macho," and "pissing contest" were in there somewhere.

The tube leading from Amsterdam to Londonburg was short enough that they barely qualified as tubes compared to those connecting many other Stations, more of an aperture than a tunnel complex. They blasted through it and evaded law enforcement, this time by a slightly greater margin. Dante had more respect for Londonburg's cops, but they had an extremely large city to patrol, and parts of the Station's infrastructure needed updating.

Which was good news, at least today.

The three vehicles soared past the tube's mouth and descended into the city proper, with Ambrose jumping up and down between mass tracks, regular streets, and sky lanes depending on what would get him to his destination fastest. There was no question where he was heading. The towering structure where SSS ran its central operations, and Slaine often directed his empire lay dead ahead.

The same place Dante had gone before his whole life had changed, setting him on his current path.

He said into the console microphone, "Help me run him onto the shoulder of this street up here. I'm going to try a hostile takeover. It will be easier to stop him from inside than out."

"Are you kidding me?" Nasreen demanded. "You owe me for talking you into getting Midas installed. There is no way any of this would work without him."

Sighing, he conceded, "Yes, you win. Good job. Now let's do this."

Ahead of them, the gleaming spires of Slaine's palatial corporate capital drew closer. There wasn't much time.

Ambrose was rising again, the better to approach SSS HQ from the most direct possible route. The Stations didn't have the same massive wind increase at higher elevations that Earth did, but it still meant death was much more certain if Dante screwed this up. He liked to think he was used to it. His stomach still felt like it was shriveling into a prune at what he was about to do.

Sky lane traffic had advantages for speed if one was doing everything the kosher way, but it could be far more dangerous and restrictive if not. Nasreen came up on Ambrose's flank, trying to force him toward a line of sky-bound traffic on the opposing side. The move diverted his attention from Dante, who shot up above the cab and tried to overtake it. The dome's arc wasn't too far overhead. The smaller buildings below looked like toy models.

Ambrose slowed as the trap began to take shape. He would have to either risk a head-on collision with oncoming traffic or try ramming one bike or the other. As Dante had expected and hoped, he chose Dante's and rose, intending to either send Dante spiraling off to the side or perhaps crush him against the Station's dome.

Dante drew a breath. "Midas, I need you to help me with this. Keep hold of this bike after I jump. Open the cab's doors if you can, and feel free to advise me on any, uhh, trajectory calculations or stuff like that. Also, disable its side shields, but not the top one."

The AI sounded downright nervous. *"Oh, dear. That is a lot to do at once, and I'm concerned for you, sir, to be honest. I'll do what I can. Hold on..."*

Dante increased his speed to hover over Ambrose's front windshield and maintained his position. Hopefully, Am thought he was trying to pull *ahead* and was failing. Nasreen continued to press against his lower flank.

Midas reported, *"I believe I've disabled the cab's gravitational shielding. It had only a minimal amount to begin with. The mechanical doors are beyond my ability."*

"Fine, I'll deal with it. Now disable my shields and tell me when."

The wind suddenly became louder and colder as the invisible barriers around him vanished. He tilted the bike to the side.

After a second, the artificial voice announced, *"Now."*

Closing his eyes and trusting whatever higher powers might exist, Dante hopped off the bike, aware that he was possibly committing suicide in an especially dramatic fashion.

The gravitational shield, like many such barriers on mid-sized shuttle vehicles, had a "squishy" exterior designed to soften, slow, or redirect other cars or random objects in a collision. As Dante fell into it, trying not to scream, it "caught" him the way a mass of soft fabric or sticky liquid would, slowing his descent enough for him to grab the upper edge of the windshield and brace his foot against the top-mounted cab sign. He still felt as though his entire skeleton was trying to rattle itself apart within his flesh, and his brain was trying to spiral out of his ears.

Gritting his teeth against the massive force exerted against him, he pulled himself sidelong toward the passenger's side door. Above him, Midas kept the bike hovering, barely, and Nasreen on the other side of the cab moved closer to distract the pilot.

Cab doors these days relied too much on their gravitational shields to double as anti-carjack devices. Midas had disabled the barrier, leaving only the mediocre mechanical defenses built into the vehicle. Dante deployed the blade from his razorfist and jammed it into the slight gap along the door, trying to damage it enough to open it through brute force. It might ruin the blade, but he could always get another one.

The SSS building was closer now. They would be within its immediate airspace in a minute or two.

Ambrose finally noticed his boarder. His eyes widened, and his mouth formed a perfect circle as he hunched over the console. While he was briefly distracted, Nasreen came up beside him and scraped the edge of the cab—not enough to jolt Dante off, but enough to alarm the pilot.

Dante gave the knife another jerk, and the door made a rushing sound as it opened. Some models did that. The theory was that peaceful compliance was better than violent resistance when it came to thieves. They over-relied on AI to stop the thieves from taking the car too far afield.

His muscles shuddering with the effort, Dante swung down into the opened doorway, kicking the door to propel his body into the passenger's seat. He still nearly fell but somehow managed to wriggle in before the vehicle's momentum could hurl him into the void.

Ambrose cried, "No! No, no, no..."

"Shut up." Dante reached over and punched him in the jaw. It wasn't a very powerful blow since he didn't have space to wind up for one, but it was enough to stun the man and cause the cab to waver in its course. Other shuttles nearby honked in alarm.

Am recovered fast. His elbow shot out, painfully striking Dante's bicep, then the pilot's hand extended to claw at his face. Dante leaned back, twisting for better leverage. He seized Ambrose's wrist with both hands, forcing it down and away. The pilot's other hand maintained the vehicle's course.

A siren went off ahead, and something moved atop the SSS building. It was one of the ballistic defense cannons. High-value private properties often employed them, and so did government structures.

They intercepted out-of-control air vehicles and shot them down with short-range, high-frequency sonic pulses. The blasts had a bludgeoning effect and dissipated quickly beyond a certain distance, making them safe to use against shuttles without the risk of damaging vital parts of the Station's infrastructure.

If SSS hit them with one, Dante and Ambrose were dead. Probably Nasreen and Midas, too.

Dante was still moving his former partner's hand into a wrist-lock. He growled, "Ambrose! Goddammit. You keep picking the wrong side. You're about to be killed by your so-called employers —*again*. Slaine is going to shoot us out of the sky. You fucking deserve it. If that's what you want, I'll stay here holding your hand until it happens even if it means I go down with you. It's up to you. Midas, you still got that bike?"

The AI confirmed that he did.

Ambrose's mouth trembled as he blubbered. "No. None of this was supposed to happen! There is no good option. None of this is fair!"

"Too fucking bad." Dante applied more pressure to the man's wrist, bending it further, and the pilot squirmed. "Either come back with us *on our terms* or get scraped off the Londonburg streets tomorrow after they clear the wreckage."

Ambrose pleaded, "Don't do that. Fine! Yes. I agree. Just get us out of here!"

There was no time to question how sincere he was. The cannons were aiming, and they'd be in range in less than a minute. Dante shouted, "Midas, bring the bike down here. Ambrose, we're climbing out. Don't fuck with me. Do as I say."

It took longer than it should have. Ambrose wasn't in great physical condition. His extreme terror meant that Dante had to physically shove him out of the cab, allowing Midas to manipulate the bike's shield to catch him. Then Dante jumped out, crashed into the pilot, and allowed the barriers to roughly and painfully force them both into their seats. The entire maneuver was embarrassing for someone of Dante's skill.

The siren was deafening. The sonic cannon hummed and glowed, its point aimed at the runaway cab.

Dante barked, "Time to leave," hoping that either Midas or the bike's comm system would convey the message to Nasreen, although he was sure she could guess as much.

Traffic had cleared out due to the obvious emergency developing around them, as well as the tight control SSS kept over its airspace. The two bikes swerved around in dual aerial U-turns and headed back the way they'd come, pushing their speed as the air rippled and sound itself ceased to exist for a moment.

Vibrations went through the sky, rattling their bones and teeth as the sonic pulse cannon fired. The shuttle cab behind them crunched into a pitiful wad of twisted scrap metal. It spewed sparks and flames as it plummeted toward the streets.

It was standard procedure for all potential impact zones on the ground to be cleared of people whenever a cannon deployed. The cab's wreckage ended up leaving an impressive crack in the beautifully sculpted sidewalk that led to SSS's main lobby.

The two bikes speeding away from the scene drew close enough that their riders could almost have conversed with their unaided voices, but they kept the comm system on anyway.

Nasreen observed, "This seems an awful lot like a rescue. I thought you wanted him dead."

Ambrose made a brief humming sound as he clung to Dante's waist.

Dante exhaled. "Be quiet and fly. Oh, and when we get a second, I think we'll switch him over to your rear seat. Might be less stressful for him."

"Yes," Ambrose agreed instantly, massaging his wrist. "Please and thank you."

CHAPTER ELEVEN

Ambrose pouted, his eyes drooping and mouth sticking out the way it did when he was about to sullenly protest something he considered unfair.

"Why do we have to do this? I'm your prisoner again. I'm in no position to leak any information to—"

"*Because*," Dante snapped, cutting him off. "You've proven that you *will* leak information as soon as your position changes. Sparing your life is one thing. Trusting you is another. Now shut up and do as we say."

The squat pilot sighed but said no more. Dante spread the strip of cloth over his eyes, then moved around behind him to tie it nice and tight.

Meanwhile, Nasreen put noise-canceling muffs over his ears. They attached themselves by pneumatic suction, and the flip of a switch freed them. Since they also functioned as hearing aids for the deaf or severely hearing-impaired, seeing a person wearing them wasn't unusual. Of course, Ambrose's hands were already tied behind his back, preventing him from taking the muffs off or altering their settings away from total silence.

Dante threw a large, hooded coat over Ambrose's head and

shoulders. The hood fell far enough in front to hide the blindfold. Pulling the torso portion forward mostly disguised his bound hands.

Nasreen nodded. "All right. Let's move out." She seated herself behind the thrustbike's console. Ambrose slumped against her from behind while Dante mounted the bike beside her.

They had already conferred on where they were going. Dante had held a silent conversation with Midas on it, and Midas had sent a remote message to Nasreen's sphere, making it unnecessary to say anything aloud.

They agreed that the safehouse in Celestial Seoul probably was no longer safe. They'd spent too much time there since they returned from their disastrous last Dirtside mission. By now it was likely that their enemies had discovered the place and begun to surveil it.

Nasreen had written back to Midas.

I have ways of checking on that, but we'll have to get somewhere that *is* safe before we can be sure. Until then, there's another location I haven't used in a long time. I tend to keep it in reserve for emergencies, so it should be clear. I won't say what it is over this line to be safe. Follow me.

As Nasreen powered up the bike, Dante hoped they wouldn't run into anything that would cause them to get separated. If they did, she could attempt to send a message to him via Midas as to where the hell she'd gone, but that posed risks of its own.

She rocketed off down the street, first to the south, then west. She might have been taking them in a loop, but Dante's immediate suspicion was that they were heading for one of the Stations corresponding to Earth's Western Hemisphere. Unless she meant to bypass those and head for Sydney or Tokyo. Most Stations had risen into space relatively close to the city's original locations.

With Londonburg far behind them, they diverted to Neo-Miami. Here was where they'd make the crucial decision. North, or south, or farther west? Nasreen cut across most of the city as quickly as possible, not bothering to try and throw off any pursuers but simply getting to the main hub of inter-Station tubes without delay.

When at last they reached it, she drifted into the southbound lane. Dante's mouth stretched into a smile of satisfaction as it all clicked. They were going to El Dorado.

The El Dorado Station was one of a few that had been built not to emulate any single Earth city but as a collaborative effort between the peoples of many countries who shared a similar culture and had lived together in a particular region. In this case, Mexico had teamed up with the various countries of Central America and Columbia, where the original mythical city of gold was said to be. They'd constructed a Station that would collectively serve their portion of the Latin world. Elements of Mexico City, Guadalajara, Panama City, and Bogotá predominated. Certain neighborhoods had strong influences from other major cities within the area as well.

Dante hadn't been there in years. It was one of the largest Stations in the Atlantica network and would be a good place to disappear for a while. Large stretches of it were little trodden by the average person, let alone the upper class, and even many Plunderer-types had barely explored some of its labyrinthine streets.

They sped into the tube, pulling ahead of a couple of shuttles at high speed. It was borderline illegal, but if a cop was watching they might get away with it unless he was having a bad day. People did it all the time. It was part of how everyone drove when crossing from city to city.

Moments later, they emerged in El Dorado. The tube's mouth was unusually high since the Station sat somewhat closer to Earth than most others. It was like coming out of a cave high on a cliff overlooking a plain or cresting the top of a waterfall that spilled into a massive valley.

Below them, the tube gave way to a set of tracks that sloped down toward the metropolis at an approximately forty-five-degree angle. The dome changed in color and lighting conditions as they descended, going from the night-sky-like effect of space nearer the top to a more normal, overcast, early morning sky closer to "ground" level.

The city itself was vast. Clusters of skyscrapers extended far into the air, surrounded by sprawl, barrios, and housing projects interspersed with parks, areas of greenery, and lively open-air markets where noise and color flourished.

Dante was used to viewing impressive scenes without staring at them long enough to get distracted. He returned his attention to Nasreen, still buzzing ahead of him with Ambrose pressed close behind her. She passed a couple of slow-moving buses, and he followed suit. The road began to level out as the town proper's buildings rose around them.

They dropped their speed to something more appropriate to a dense urban area, and Dante followed her along a winding, zigzagging course. She deliberately took the most circuitous and nonsensical route possible to throw off potential pursuers and perhaps to confuse Ambrose further, not that he would have been able to see or hear anything, regardless.

At last, they came to a small, quiet neighborhood, vaguely representative of El Dorado's lower-middle-class population. Groups of quadruplex condos bordered a central garden area, and a low wall provided basic but adequate privacy.

Nasreen slowed way down, and Dante did likewise. They pulled into a broad parking lane next to one of the buildings toward the rear of the little complex, where their bikes were largely hidden from view by palm branches, the overhanging edges of roofs, and the deep shadows of the other structures. They halted and shut off their vehicles.

Dismounting and removing her helmet, Nasreen quipped, "Well, it's not much, but it's home." She tossed her hair, and Dante couldn't help but notice how good she looked despite being tired, sweaty, and strung out from adrenaline. He had more important things to worry about for the moment, like getting Ambrose into the safehouse without creating a public incident, for one.

"Yeah," he muttered. "It'll do. Nicer than the place where he was before." He pointed a thumb at Ambrose, who seemed jittery with anticipation now that they'd finally arrived at their destination.

Dante helped Ambrose off while Nasreen secured the bikes and opened the side door with one of her various cards. It revealed a stairwell, and she led them to a moderately spacious if sparsely furnished apartment on the second floor.

They didn't encounter anyone else. Everyone who worked in the morning had already left, and those who didn't were still sleeping or busy indoors. Still, Dante had to wonder how many cameras might have caught glimpses of them.

As Dante marched Ambrose into the main sitting room, Nasreen said, "We need to talk. Let's get our friend settled in nice and safe. Then we'll have a little conversation. Shall we?"

Her tone implied that it wasn't going to be a *fun* conversation. Dante could deal with worse. He'd rather they had a beer together and focused on their plans for the coming few days.

They found a comfy chair and turned it to face the corner rather than the window. Then they plopped Ambrose down in it and removed his noise-canceling earmuffs, but not his blindfold.

Nasreen addressed him. "Ambrose, we're going to put these back on in a moment, but first, would you like a drink of water, and are you okay in general? Yes, you're our prisoner, but keeping you in halfway decent condition makes our lives easier since we would prefer you remain alive. For now."

He swallowed, and his voice was noticeably dry and scratchy.

"Yes, please. I would also like something to eat soon if that's possible."

Dante untied Ambrose's hands and stood watch beside him as Nasreen fetched a glass of water and a portable meal of pasta salad with preserved vegetables and lab-grown meat. They allowed him to eat and drink.

Then Nasreen delivered her ultimatum. "We won't go out of our way to harm you as long as you're in our custody. But don't give us a *reason* to, or we *will* harm you. Now the muffs are going back on while Dante and I have a chat. You'll get some of your freedom back soon. But not much."

They refastened the sound-blocking devices on his ears, retied his hands so he couldn't remove the muffs, and left him there. He didn't move or seem interested in trying to escape, but they remained across from him in the same room so anything he might do wouldn't escape their notice.

They faced one another. Nasreen crossed her arms and leaned on her right leg. "All right. Why the hell did you bother to save him? I mean yes, he might be useful to us, but hauling a prisoner around makes everything more difficult. It's not as though he was going to 'get away with it' if we abandoned him. Slaine or his benefactors would have taken him out of the picture within a week."

For the sake of saving time and having other things to do besides stand there and be glared at, Dante took off his coat and detached the various packs and pouches strapped to its interior. They would need to assess their gear inventory before the next phase in the plan could proceed, anyway.

"I don't know," he stated.

Nasreen exhaled sharply and allowed her shoulders to slump. She looked sidelong at the wall and tapped her foot in blatant irritation. "Well, then, you should find out. I'm not necessarily saying it was the *wrong* decision, but it was highly unexpected since you almost killed him not too long ago. With the noose tightening around us lately the way it has been, we can't afford to be irrational or fickle."

Dante almost blurted out that was usually what a man said to a woman, but he bit his tongue. Starting a fight would be useless. By the same token, he intended to stand his ground.

He needed a moment to think. He laid out his sheathed knife and his small but well-rounded complement of medical supplies, plus some of the soft body armor he'd worn. It was rare for anyone to use guns or pulsecores within the Stations, so the extra protection against bullets and explosions offered by heavy armor was unnecessary. The lighter, lower-grade stuff was still pretty good proof against the edges of knives, the points of darts, and the blunt shock of truncheons.

By taking off the armor, making himself more vulnerable and having only his reflexes, lean muscle mass, tactics, cunning, and experience to protect himself, some of the issues and problems churning around in his mind began to grow clearer.

Midas interjected in a low voice, *"Sir, I gather you're confused, and frankly so am I, so I'll try to stay out of this. Your thoughts and feelings are too 'human' for me to comprehend fully at this stage in my development."*

Dante nodded and replied with a vague sense of appreciation, aimed straight toward the AI but not attached to any spoken words. When he did speak, it was to Nasreen.

"I've been thinking it over, and I suppose it's finally starting to make some sense to me. Yeah, part of it is because I don't want *them* to be the ones to finish him off. Part of it is because he might still be able to help us. Not like there's any way I can trust him after betraying me *twice*, but he might know things. After all, your interview with Ergun got cut short."

He finished laying things out on the table, then turned back to look at her.

Nasreen's eyes moved a tad up, then back down. "He—Ergun, I mean—told me a little before we were interrupted. It might be enough to get ourselves started—a lead or two. But yes, I was certainly hoping for more. Ambrose may be able to fill in the gaps in our knowledge. If we persuade him right."

Dante nodded. As near as he could tell, Ambrose and Ergun had set the whole thing up between them, but obviously with the help of intermediaries from SSS. Or worse yet, the shadow entities lurking *behind* SSS.

Flourishing her hand, Nasreen added, "You implied that's only part of it. What's the rest of your reason?"

He supposed there was no use in holding back. His cheeks flushed at the prospect of how ridiculous he might sound if he wasn't careful.

"If I killed Ambrose or let Slaine's minions kill him for the pleasure of watching him die, that would...it would confirm things about me that I don't want to be true. And I feel like they *won't* be true as long as I listen to the little voice in my head. Not you, Midas. I'm talking about, you know, conscience."

Nasreen raised her eyebrows. The skeptical twist of her mouth softened a little. "Hmm. You were the one who taught me the importance of killing when you have the chance during dire circumstances. But, well, maybe you see that as different. Go on."

He did. "If all I did was stomp Ambrose's head to satisfy my anger or take some kind of sadistic joy in watching him suffer and die, I wouldn't be any different than fucking Hyde. Yes, he's helping us now, but we all know what he is. He's not our friend or anyone else's. I don't want to be like him."

To his surprise, Nasreen smiled, and there was real warmth in it. "You're not. Anytime you've been violent, there has always been a good reason behind it. I never got the sense that you *enjoyed* killing, Dante. Maybe a professional satisfaction from a job well done or the rush of combat, but you have never been gleeful about destroying lives as long as I've known you."

He exhaled. "Thank you. That's good to hear."

Silence between them for a few seconds. It was as though something had sprouted and was blooming.

Then Dante blinked, and a sense of alarm shot through him, and he was entirely back to business. Nasreen frowned.

"Hyde," Dante blurted. "We haven't checked up on him. What the hell is he up to right now? Midas, check into it. Any violence or weirdness in Pentapolis. Especially in the neighborhood we stashed him in or involving gangs. But anything that sounds like it could be the work of, well, Hyde."

Midas wasted no time. He sounded almost chipper at being needed again. *"Certainly! I'm right on it. Please hold tight for a moment while I tap into the network."*

Nasreen took a step forward. "I should have started looking into that myself as soon as we got indoors. We're both tired and stressed."

In the back of his mind, Dante grasped that there was a dual meaning to what she had stated. She was half-apologizing for not thinking of the same thing but also implying that she probably still had the energy to rush over to Pentapolis if a fiasco required their attention.

Still, perhaps to reserve her strength, she only stood and rested rather than pulling out her sphere and backing up Midas's investigation with her own.

It didn't take long. After a minute or so, the AI reported his findings. He spoke aloud so Dante wouldn't have to repeat everything to Nasreen. The faint ringing vibration through his skull once again made him cringe, but he tried to ignore it.

"Oh, dear. I am sorry to relay this, but it seems there was a disturbance less than a block from the housing project. General reports of noise and scuffles after nightfall. Then, not long after that and shortly before the police arrived, there was an explosion centered within an old pool house. It leveled the building, causing minor to moderate damage to other structures around it, and everyone trapped within was killed. Six bodies, they've now confirmed. No other details are available from any source I can access."

Again, silence fell over the apartment as Dante and Nasreen looked into each other's eyes. This time it was pregnant with vague dread and trepidation, along with a dose of...relief? Dante wondered if it might be gratitude.

Nasreen said, "He's dead. Probably? I don't think Hyde could survive an explosion that took out a whole building, armor or not. He started to break down under a hail of bullets. Lasted a lot longer than a normal human would have, including one wearing heavy armor, but he's not impervious to major force."

Her tone confirmed what Dante had suspected. On some level, she hoped the monstrous cyborg *was* dead. So did he. He wasn't proud of that. Still, the bad blood between them had never fully gone away, and Eduardo H. Curtidor was enough of a loose cannon that having him on board made him as much of potential liability as an asset. Not to mention, they still didn't know if Hyde had any hand in the hacking plot. He and Ambrose might have cooked it up together.

Dante swiped his hand in front of him. "No. You cannot count someone as dead based on hearsay and 'no one could have survived that' speculation. We don't know that he was in the pool house to begin with. The gangsters might have blown themselves up before he got there. Either way, I'm not assuming anything until I get verification from my two eyes. And Midas, if necessary."

"Thank you, sir," the AI chimed in.

Nasreen narrowed her eyes in concern. "You may be right."

He put his soft armor vest back on. "After all, look what happened with *me*. A lot of people still think Dante Shale is dead, and now more people think I'm dead as Jordan Raksha. But here I stand." He strapped his knife to his hip. "So, I'm going to look for the big clanking bastard."

Nasreen pinched the bridge of her nose. "Don't do that,

Dante. Come the fuck on. Do *not* run off on a wild goose chase and potentially get yourself killed, over *him*, of all people. What's gotten into you lately? You can be ethical without being suicidal. Or wasting precious time."

Anger flared, unexpected and unheralded, at her ingratitude. He bit his tongue to keep from spewing out anything stupid, but only for a second or two. Once his thoughts reordered themselves, he could speak with a little more prudence.

"It's not a waste of time. Hyde may be a monster, but he is a monster whom we are responsible for right now. He's been useful. If he's turned against us, we don't want him running free to cause more problems. If he's still on our side, we owe him something. He's saved both of our lives. Multiple times, in your case. I cannot, and will not, abandon him like someone dumping a dog in the street because they don't want to take care of it anymore."

His tone was harsh but not bitter or furious. He didn't want to antagonize her more than necessary. He also considered the discussion concluded. There was no point in her trying to change his mind.

"What?" Her jaw dropped. "You're acting like a teenager who thinks his new gangster buddies are his soulmates because they were nice to him two or three times and they need someone to be the fall guy when they rob a store. Don't be a moron. I told you mere minutes ago that you weren't a terrible person. You don't have to do this to prove you're some paragon of morality."

He finished suiting back up and took a couple of steps toward the exit. "Sorry. I appreciate your feedback. But you can't stop or dissuade me. I'm heading out, and I won't be back until I find something to clear this up."

Nasreen watched him, sullen but starting to relax again. "You're impossible to negotiate with when you get like this. I won't waste my time. If you insist on this nonsense, at least be careful. Okay?"

"Yeah," he replied, "I always am. Keep an eye on Ambrose and take care of him."

She glanced at the squat pilot, who remained in his chair, unmoving and oblivious. "If you take too long, I might interrogate him without you. We need to know what he knows. Plus, I mean, it would be decent stress relief after everything we did today."

Dante waved that off. "Don't cut him up or anything, but yeah, do what you can otherwise. Also, I recommend that you check with our corporate allies. They deserve to know we're alive. Slaine might be moving against them. If they need help, it would be a good idea to give it to them."

Nasreen smiled with resignation as much as anything. "Okay, fine. Don't be mad at me if I'm enjoying brunch and coffee and you're not."

CHAPTER TWELVE

Midas's report had indicated that the explosion was close to the bolthole where Nasreen had stashed both Hyde and Ambrose, but somehow it seemed even closer when they arrived on the scene. Bits of debris from the obliterated pool house were strewn across the lots and yard right next to the wall containing the bolthole's windows.

On the ride over, Midas had convinced Dante to pay for and perform a quick remote installation of a "manhunter application" used by bounty hunters and the like. It wasn't available to the general public and typically had to be sold through closed industry channels. Midas had enough fraudulent material from Nasreen that it didn't pose much of a problem.

"Fine," Dante had muttered, "but I don't want to get arrested for goddamn ID fraud while we're in the middle of something way bigger and more important. If you want to keep collecting upgrades, they need to be worth the cost *and* the hassle."

The AI had insisted, *"Oh, they will be—this one in particular. It will allow me to search for and highlight clues and stimuli associated with the physical description of the target person. It also automatically monitors all public and semi-private network communications within a given range for any message concerning the same. In our present case, it should not be too hard to distinguish stimuli about Mr. Hyde from those of, well, anyone else."*

With an appreciative nod, Dante had to agree with the last part.

After getting back into the low-income neighborhood in Pentapolis, Dante stashed his new thrustbike in a secure lot nearby, then proceeded on foot toward the site of the former pool house.

Aggravatingly but not much of a surprise, the whole block was swarming with Pentapolis utility employees, a medical crew or two, some construction workers brought in to help deal with the debris, and a bevy of law enforcement officers. The cops would undoubtedly take a great interest in anyone sniffing around for a person who may or may not have gotten caught in the blast.

A ring of citizens had also formed around the periphery of the detonation site. They were concerned about such violence in their neighborhood, but they were mostly curious. No one, so far, had any obvious reason to believe that the explosion was intentional.

Strolling between two of the housing developments, Dante surveyed the main scene. It was hard to see all the details from here, but the gist was easy enough to comprehend.

A fireball had leveled the pool house and scattered pieces in all directions. The ground was black from a fire that had burned briefly. The Stations had automated fire responses in most areas that could deal with unexpected blazes with simulated heavy rain. Fortunately, there was not enough fuel for an inferno to engulf any neighboring buildings. The greater portion of the damage had been from the kinetic, concussive, and sonic effects.

Midas suddenly piped up. *"Oh, the manhunter app has another feature I forgot to mention. It also provides scenarios for likely events that occurred around an investigation scene, based on available evidence. It requires me to disclaim that such speculation is not consid-ered equivalent to that of trained detectives or legal professionals and is not admissible in court."*

"Sure. God, I hate courts. What does it say about what we've seen so far?"

He had his predictions, of course. Roughly, Hyde had got in over his head, and someone had damaged a boiler, generator, or something during the all-out brawl that had erupted.

The artificial voice, still speaking without sound directly into its host's brain, explained from the beginning. *"Well, I processed the initial setup, which is to say, the false story you gave to Hyde to get him out of the apartment, combined with the actual details of what we know about the drug gang. The likely conclusion is that he was reckless or overconfident, got ambushed, and fought too many gang members at once. The battle would have worked its way into the pool house, where Hyde tried to uproot a boiler device, perhaps to hurl it at someone, and ended up igniting a gas line or something of that nature."*

Dante bit his tongue. "That's one smart program. What would humans do without technology to guide them?"

Midas hesitated. *"Are you being sarcastic, sir? Need I remind you of how my manipulations of the thrustbikes' shields during your recent chase saved you from being spla–"*

"No," Dante stated. "I remember well. I was so grateful that I agreed to buy you that new program. Now, we need to find out if Hyde died or if he's off at an underground auto mechanic's chop-house getting his face repaired with a blowtorch or something. Keep scanning all the police bands and news stories, and I'll pretend to be a gawky civilian."

Which meant that once again, he would have to lie and pretend to be something he was not. He recalled something Nasreen had mentioned about how the best lies always contained elements of the truth.

He would be a former Plunderer, then. A burned-out man who would never pass for a normal citizen who had never been

Dirtside. He was retired after an injury last year. He'd heard of the notorious Mr. Hyde before from Reaper crews. Shame the poor bastard got caught in the blast. Wasn't it?

Dante blinked. Embedding himself within a false identity still came unnaturally, although it wasn't too far off from his true self.

He wandered into the crowd, observing who stood where and what areas seemed to be allocated to bystanders to hang around and watch. He stuck to those for now.

An old couple lingered beside a police barrier. "Hi." Dante kept his voice low but not to the point of sounding conspiratorial. "Is this where that blast happened? Heard about it on the news."

The elderly pair both looked at him in unison. The woman, a full head shorter than the man, spoke first. "Yes! The gangs are fighting again, the damn fools. That's what everyone says so far. They have four dead bodies strewn through the neighborhood, including that yard with the basketball court. Our neighbors' kids play there! They found a dead body overnight. Terrible!"

"And," the man added in a gravelly voice, "those four are in addition to the six they've got here. The damn fools."

His wife echoed, "Damn fools."

The man glared at her, then looked back at Dante. "Damn fools indeed. They got to fighting and blew up a gas line while they were at it. I guess nobody wins a fight like that, do they?"

While Dante listened, he kept one eye on the awful devastation itself. The corpses had been placed in body bags and piled into the rear of a refrigerated truck. The authorities weren't doing much to keep the meat wagon out of sight of the public, but at least the bags meant no one could see the condition that the dead were in. The ones caught in the explosion could not have been a pretty sight.

There were ten corpses, which corroborated what the elderly couple had said. All the body bags appeared normal-sized. Dante doubted that Hyde would fit in any of them. Then again, the blast could have mixed-and-matched different parts. Or the heat might have melted some excess metal off the big cyborg's body. There was no way so far to be sure.

Dante directed his thoughts inward, focusing on Midas. Out in the external world, the older couple were rattling off an anecdote about how the same basketball court had been the site of a very nice birthday party that their neighbor's kids had hosted last year.

He asked the AI to recall the image of Hyde, to guess what sorts of metal his armor was, and to perform a scan of the blast site to determine if any traces of it, especially *large* traces, could be found amid the devastation.

"Certainly," Midas replied. *"The difficulty is distinguishing any potential melted or broken body parts of his from similarly damaged pieces of the building itself, or for that matter, the boiler. He was, or is, a* hydraulic *cyborg, after all."*

Dante groaned. Fortuitously, the couple had reached the point in their anecdote when another neighbor had protested the kids playing in the sprinkler system, which interrupted the flow of water to the grass, so the groan was well-timed.

The woman clucked. "I know. It's unnecessary to deny children the right to play in the water occasionally. It's not as though birthdays come more than once a year, isn't it?"

"Right," Dante said.

A pair of cops, a man and a woman, wandered by. They immediately took note of Dante. Law enforcement often did, even when he was dressed as much like a civilian as he could manage.

The man said, "Heeeeyyyyyy. Haven't seen you around these parts, chief. You looking for work with the Plunderer's Local? Hope not. We don't have a Plunderers' Local here."

Dante snorted. "It's *that* obvious I'm a Dirtboy, is it? Hah. No, I was coming here to inquire about housing vacancies. I retired.

Didn't hear about this until I was most of the way down the track…"

He answered a few more of their questions, which they disguised as innocent banter, and Midas filled in a couple of the details whenever he was on the verge of getting tripped up. Once they were satisfied that he had no connection to the night's events, the cops moved on to the refreshments table.

Dante wandered a bit more around the edge of the cordoned-off zone, scanning the wreckage as Midas processed every iota of potentially useful information. When he turned and walked away, shaking his head at the misfortune of the whole thing, the AI finished his analysis.

"Sir, I can say with a reasonable degree of confidence that most of Hyde's body was made of an alloy of steel and some or another modern synthetic material, giving it an exceptionally high degree of resilience."

Dante squinted. *"Isn't steel* already *an alloy?"* Metallurgy wasn't his specialty, but he'd picked up a fact or two over the years.

"You know what I mean. The important part is that the strength of the explosion, as well as the level of heat probably generated by the ensuing fire, were unlikely to be of sufficient potency to either completely tear Hyde apart or melt most of his body. It's statistically likely that if he perished in the blast, he would be mostly intact."

Responding with silent thoughts rather than spoken words, in case any of the nearby residents overheard him, Dante surmised, *"So, he isn't dead. Or at least he didn't die here. He dragged himself off to some-where else, wounded but still functional. Or maybe he did die, but someone else took his body before the authorities got to it. How do we track him?"*

Midas all but chirped, *"That should not be too difficult. The new app can detect the telltale signs of blood splatter and most other types of spoor we enter. I'm punching in the approximate constitution of Hyde's armor, in liquid or semi-liquid form, right now. His exterior may have softened a little from the heat, which would leave residue on the ground or other things he touched. He did have human blood, didn't he?"*

Dante scrunched up his face. *"Um. Some. Not much. Nasreen said she saw him bleeding after he took a few magazines' worth of lead during their raid on that spa place. He's mostly a machine now. If anything, I bet he mainly bleeds water. So that doesn't help much."*

Midas made a "hmm" sound and returned to his calculations as Dante slipped into the shadows, the gaps between places that naturally drew people's eyes. Now was the time for him to disappear. If they picked up Hyde's trail, he didn't want anyone else picking up *his*.

"There," the AI exclaimed. He conjured a green crosshair in the corner of Dante's field of vision, which centered itself as he turned his head.

Dante saw nothing except a patch of unhealthy grass next to one of the more peripheral housing blocks. He didn't protest, though, and walked toward it, taking care to stay out of sight or move as casually as possible if he thought he might be visible to anyone watching from the windows.

Midas explained, *"A small droplet of molten metal. Well, it's hardened, but it would have been molten a few hours ago. And—yes, another one about thirty feet beyond it."*

Dante nodded. *"The grass is tramped down in places, too. Someone with big, heavy feet and a long stride."*

They followed the trail beyond the projects, with Midas highlighting not only metal droplets but also blood, a tiny, scorched spring and socket, and what seemed to be the residue of a pressurized saline solution that may have been what powered Hyde's inner hydraulic operations.

Dante shook his head. *"He must have been hurt bad. I almost feel sorry for him. Seems like he was staggering around. I think it was him alone, rather than someone else dragging him."*

Past the housing complex, the city became a low, narrow cluster of small businesses, depots, tight alleys, and unfinished lots. Traffic buzzed, whooshed, and honked nearby, but they had come to an area that seemed quiet and desolate.

Ahead, in an alcove not far from the street but nestled into a short alley between buildings, was one of the access hatches that led into the bowels of Pentapolis. Most Stations had them. They provided service workers with ways to inspect the complicated labyrinth of plumbing, electrical, and ventilation apparatuses that kept the celestial cities in operation.

It was a logical place for a wounded brawler to go if he didn't want to get caught. It was also a nightmare for anyone trying to find him. The undercity of any given Station was frequently infested with oversized rats, hybrid molds and slimes, and scalelings and other junkies. Plus, finding one's way around was virtually impossible for someone unfamiliar with the schematics.

Midas heard his thoughts. *"I'll look up a map for this entrance and get the approximate layout. I can help guide you from there."*

"I didn't say we were going in yet." Dante sighed. *"But yes. We are. Thanks."*

He glanced around to ensure no one was watching them. There might be yet another hidden camera nearby, but the feeds were inconsistently watched. Sometimes by AI, which often made mistakes, sometimes by astute professionals, and sometimes by drudge workers who paid as little attention as they could get away with.

Dante opened the hatch with a couple of deft twists of the handle, ignoring the label warning him to stay out, and slipped down into the city's superstructure.

It was dim but not totally dark. Slivers of artificial daylight filtered through cracks or apertures in the street above, and various juncture points in the maze of narrow corridors had built-in service lights which provided steady but dim illumination powered by the "waste energy" of the aboveground. The lights could be brighter when maintenance specialists needed to examine something, but Dante refrained. He didn't want to attract attention.

It was obvious which route Hyde had taken. The upper

reaches of the undercity were laid out semi-logically in a grid, mirroring the city streets above. Cellars sometimes reached the topmost level, sealed off by private doors that their owners locked from the inside. It made for cramped confines. A man significantly larger than Dante but still within the range of normality would find it difficult to navigate. Hyde wasn't normal.

Pipes were dented or slightly bent, wires pulled loose, and pieces of debris kicked aside in ways that a complete neophyte might have missed but were easy for Dante to spot. He was used to examining the landscape around him for hints. He followed the trail to another hatch that opened onto a ramp leading down several more levels.

Past the first two "floors," the undercity ceased to have any rhyme or reason. It became an almost nightmarish jungle of metal, plastic, steam, and static, like trying to navigate the circulatory system of a living thing. And it was darker.

Dante had to admit that he was growing nervous. His nails were digging into the palms of his hands.

Midas reassured him, *"I have been keeping track of your progress so far, although the schematics for these lower levels are, erm, not very helpful."*

"Great," Dante mumbled. He was about to stop and propose a breadcrumbs-type solution when he froze, his eyes fixed on something up ahead, through a half-torn net of hanging wires and shreds of insulation.

A huge indentation, humanoid-shaped, was visible in a broad patch of insulator padding that someone had torn loose from the ceiling. Around it were little irregular mounds of hardened metal, where molten material had re-hardened and was still slick with saline residue.

Dante moved closer, his alertness level rising. "He collapsed here. Passed out. And..." He came to the edge of the makeshift bed and saw streaks and scrape marks on the floor beyond it. "Either he crawled away, or someone dragged him off."

Midas commented, *"That sounds logical. There's, ah, a slight problem, though. I'm afraid we're deep enough into the Station's belly that I'm out of range of any network connection. I still have all my preexisting tools and knowledge, including the downloaded map schematics, but we are bereft of any real-time updates or contact with the outside world. We are on our own."*

Dante said nothing, but Midas felt his grim acknowledgment of the situation.

They followed the scrape marks down a winding makeshift tunnel within the body of Pentapolis, which led to a ragged hole from which a crude staircase, made of random spare parts, led still further down. It was getting colder, Dante noticed, and he reflected on how eerily similar the undercity was, in some ways, to the subterranean layers of Earth.

Slowly and carefully, he climbed down the stairs. Near the base, a human body came into sight, tucked into an alcove and half-covered with a moldy rag. Mold was forming on many surfaces down here, particularly where the vapor was thicker.

The corpse, and it was certainly a dead man, was not Hyde. It was far too small. His chest was caved in, and blood stains trailed from his mouth. Judging by his emaciated, dirty, and sore-covered appearance, he was probably a scaleling. Dante's spirits sank.

Scale was one of the scourges of the modern world, particularly in Pentapolis and other Stations that had once corresponded to North America. A powerfully addictive toxin, the drug spread among the despairing and dragged them further into total degeneration. Scale addicts grew maddened when unable to acquire more of the narcotic and would do anything to fund their habit until eventually, it killed them.

Midas suggested, *"Do you think they might have tried to rob Mr. Hyde? Or perhaps—"*

"Scrap him," Dante deduced, in mental rather than physical

speech. He did not want to make any noise from here on. *"All that crap he's made of has to be worth something."*

Dante drew a long, deep breath. Then he moved faster while keeping quiet. He was back in hunter mode, stalking through the city's bowels as ably as he navigated the wilderness when Dirtside. His knife was out in his hand.

Sounds drifted through the organic-seeming, barely lit, hive-like tunnels and ragged vaporous caves. Human voices muttered and grunted, metal scraped and *clanked,* and the occasional moan of pain, although the last noise had a curious electronic echo effect.

Hyde may have still been alive. He was unlikely to be in good shape.

The mishmash of technological detritus suddenly gave way to a semi-orderly hallway coming from another direction, which ended at a synthetic door. It was ajar. Light and noise wafted from it. According to the faded label, the room beyond was a service hub for construction and maintenance crews. Probably abandoned five or ten years ago.

Dante crept toward the portal, staying low to the ground—which consisted of soft rubber laid atop steel—and moved toward the crack to scout what lay ahead. He peeked around the edge of the door.

Eight or nine scalelings clustered around a low central platform in a loose circle. Half of them worked furiously at something while the other half sat twitching and drooling. Scraps of stolen or discarded food and other refuse littered the floor, but they had at least pushed most of it away from their communal bedding area.

Two other addicts lay in bloody heaps atop masses of cloth and rubber, living but badly wounded. Hyde must have put up a good fight.

A couple of the junkies twisted around in their labors and at last, Dante could see the focus of their activity.

Hyde rested on the platform. At least, what remained of him. He didn't move, his eyes stayed shut, and he didn't speak or groan. The scalelings had largely reduced him to a torso and head. Their disassembly of his entire body was coming along nicely.

They'd cut off both his legs and set them aside for further attention later, as well as his left arm. His right arm must have suffered the worst brunt of the explosion since it was effectively a slag tentacle, the elbow joint stiffened and the once-powerful gauntlet reduced to little more than a narrow, melted stump.

Now, the scalelings were moving in on his face with finer tools—knives, screwdrivers, and a small crowbar.

A tall man with wild eyes and a bushy beard, apparently with a welder's mask strapped to his head, was striding back and forth behind the mutilated cyborg, manic with energy. "We save the eyes," he insisted, in a voice that was like that of a child with severe asthma but louder. "I want his fucking eyes, okay? Everything else is worth something, but we've got to appreciate *beauty*, okay? The eyes. I get the fucking eyes!"

Dante's stomach turned over. Though pitiable, scalelings weren't known as people to easily reason with. The upside was that their mental derangement, physical emaciation, and nervous disposition didn't make them particularly good fighters against someone who knew what he was doing.

One of the other junkies moved toward Hyde's face with a set of pliers. Dante had seen enough.

He sprang up from the floor, flung the door open, and pounced into the room. "*Not* the eyes," he rasped, bellowing as loud as he could, and shouldered aside a scrawny, claw-fingered woman. She crashed into the wall, yelped, and clambered away.

Three of the scalelings nearest him panicked and ran, bolting mindlessly toward the other end of the service depot. Another spun toward the Marauder, wrench in hand, swinging it with surprising speed and force but little coordination.

Dante couldn't risk merely disarming or incapacitating the ones with fight in them. They were too unpredictable. He knocked the wrench wielder's arm aside with his and drove his knife into the chest, twisting it and kicking the addict back in the same motion.

A large woman came at him with two knives, one in each hand, roaring in a ragged guttural way and spitting on the floor. Dante grabbed a metal shelf and dragged it in front of her, blocking her off so her arms got tangled between the shelves. While she tried to extricate herself, he stepped to her flank and stabbed her in the kidney, then dodged her attempted backhand strike and stabbed her again in the back of the neck. She slumped against the shelves, arms now hanging loose.

The others had begun to disperse, making high-pitched mewlings of terror, but the apparent leader held firm. He stared at Dante. "I am in charge here," he insisted. "This is my prize, and you have no claim, okay?" He pulled the mask down over his face and picked up a blowtorch. Not yet lit.

Dante hesitated. The flame from one of those things in an enclosed space like this, with him bereft of eye protection, could blind him even if he avoided getting burned. The scaleling leader tried to ignite the torch but found it stubborn, making only sparks.

Dante moved in for the kill, stepping over one of Hyde's severed legs. Then the blowtorch flared to life.

Dante spun aside, covering his eyes. He'd missed the worst of it but still saw spots and had an abrupt headache.

Then Midas spoke aloud. "How dare you! To steal the eyes of this man! This is my Station. It was built in my honor. You would dare disassemble one of my people here without first seeking my leave?"

He sounded nothing like his usual self. Rather, he sounded like an angry deity, booming and authoritative.

When Dante tried to uncover his eyes, he saw that everything was far dimmer, aside from the white light near the junkies' chieftain. He couldn't look directly at the torch, but he could see well enough to get the job done.

The leader froze in panic. "What? Who are you? We didn't mean it! Why didn't you say so before? We thought this place was *ours!*" He hopped from one foot to the other, looking from side to side, the welder's mask obscuring his obvious fear.

Dante grabbed Hyde's other leg. It was even heavier than it looked, but he could lift it, barely. He heaved it at the scrawny maniac. It fell short of striking him on the chest, as Dante had hoped, but still *clanged* right in front of him and knocked his legs out from under him.

The man's limbs flung out as he toppled, the lit blowtorch falling straight down on top of him. "Oh shit. Oh shit!" His hands fumbled to shut it off as flames engulfed his body.

Dante moved in. He had no desire to watch the wretch burn to death, so he simply kicked him in the back of the neck as hard as he could. Something snapped, putting an end to his thrashing at once. His body continued to burn. Dante kept it away from anything else in the hub that might be ignitable and put a couple of sheets of metal over the top of it to smother the flames. Smoke rose.

The few scalelings who had remained in the chamber were cowering in the far corners, totally incapacitated by unreasoning terror. Dante took note of their positions but otherwise ignored them.

He turned to Hyde. The huge cyborg may have been dead, after all.

The polymer-infused metal that sheathed most of his form was in bad shape, pocked or warped by heat. The little visible human flesh he had on some parts of his face and neck and armpit area had blackened to a crust. His red beard had burned down to charred stubble, and most of his hair was gone. He looked far older when shorn of them, closer to his true, unnatural age. Wires and tubes stuck out of the stumps of his lost limbs.

Dante stared. Then the eye stared back—only one. Dante had forgotten that he'd damaged the other himself back on Earth during their duel, the fight Dante had lost. The lack of natural life in the eyes made it harder to tell unless one looked closely.

The mouth rippled. "Ehh," the reverberant voice buzzed. It seemed weaker than usual, but the corners of the synthetic lips rose in a smile. "It's you, I see. Do me a favor, then. Kill me."

CHAPTER THIRTEEN

Dante stood, doing nothing. His knife was still in his hand. He wasn't sure how he had expected Hyde to react. It wasn't a thing he had considered or prepared himself for.

"You're in pain?" he asked.

A shudder went through the remains of Hyde's body, and a self-echoing cough turned into a low, nasty laugh. He tried to spit, but nothing happened.

"Pain!" he scoffed. "That's fucking stupid. Why would you ask me something like that, Shale?"

Dante grimaced. "It's what I would ask most people in your situation. But you're not most people."

"No shit," Hyde growled. "No, it's not about pain, you dumb bastard. It's about pride. You can understand that, right? Look at me. I can't see myself, but I can guess. I look like shit, don't I?"

Dante spent a half-moment pretending to examine him. "You've looked better. I thought you were dead already."

The cyborg made a vague grunting sound, like an old dog having its ears scratched. "Looked better. Ha, ha. Since when do you try to sugarcoat anything? Is that *chica* rubbing off on you? It's okay. It happens to a lot of men."

Dante did not feel like talking about Nasreen. He wasn't sure what he *did* feel. "Okay, then. You look terrible."

Hyde laughed, and what would have been a shallow wheeze in a normal human became a thin mechanical whine in him. "Yes. I don't want anyone to see me like this. I do not want to be *left* like this, you understand? There's no way to grow back anything I lost.

"It's harder for me to lose shit than it is for most of you people. It's gone for good. Unless I can afford to have it all built again and reattached. Took me a lot of time and money to get where I am now, piece by piece by piece. Not sure it's worth the trouble again. Fuck, I'm old."

Dante had wondered, once or twice, how a creature like Hyde would cope with a truly debilitating injury. The answer wasn't too surprising.

The cyborg went on. "You have plenty of reasons to hate me and want me dead, so do what comes to you naturally. Act on them. I'm okay with it. I'll get to die knowing the only Reaper who's as good as I am—as I was—killed me. Not some low-level *cabrón* looking for cheap street cred."

He stared straight ahead as though he were at peace.

Dante hovered in front of him, the knife held at such an angle that he could plunge it through either of Hyde's eyes or perhaps attempt to cut his throat, though he was not quite sure how well that would work. Decapitation or a brain strike might be the only things that would.

A deep sadness had settled over the old, ravaged face. Dante's skin crawled.

"No," he said. "No offense. You probably deserve it at least as much as Ambrose does. Or more, since he was a decent person before, whereas you've been a piece of shit for a long time. I don't like murdering or executing people in no position to hurt me. It's unprofessional."

Paying no heed to the stunned or panicking scalelings, Dante took a strap out of his jacket and looked around the hovel for some other materials he could use to secure Hyde to his back and carry him to the surface.

The giant's good eye darted around the chamber, and his face fell. "The hell? Fucking bullshit! I gave you *permission*, you stupid fuck. It's not murder! Who cares if it is? I want you to kill me as a *professional* courtesy. Or else I'll tear your goddamn *huevos* off, do you hear?"

He reached out with his crippled, half-melted metal claw, swiping halfheartedly at Dante's groin and midsection, but he couldn't do much since the elbow had fused into relative stiffness. The hand portion was little more than an oversized, blunted, immobile hook.

Dante took two steps back, easily evading the strike. "You said I'm the only Reaper on your level. Well, I'm not a Reaper. I'm a Marauder. I kill things and people when I have to, but it's not the primary purpose. Marauders bring useful stuff back. I'm salvaging you."

Hyde's face, uglier than ever, contorted with helpless rage. "I'm not your fucking salvage, *puto!* Grow some cojones and fucking ghost me, you motherfucker. Dying like that has dignity. You're telling me I'm some trash you're going to pick through? Just kill me."

Dante peered into Hyde's eye. He was using the expression of calm yet intense alertness, the distinctive gaze that had unnerved so many people even when he had not intended to. "If you're not salvage, what are you?"

The eye blinked, and the cyborg's helpless, performative anger began to fade into an unfamiliar emotion—confusion.

"I'm...I'm...I, uh, am..."

Dante suspected they both knew the answer or something close to it. He was the barest remnant of a man, hidden within a machine that no longer worked.

Dante cleared his throat. "If you're a man, you have a chance

—no, that's wrong. You have a *duty* to fight through this, to come back stronger."

Hyde's face inclined forward, and the machine eye drifted down, taking in the sight of his body, or whatever served as his body with its grotesquely twisted metal and dangling bits of wire.

Without looking back up, he queried, "And if I'm not one of those anymore?"

Dante snorted. "Then you *are* fucking salvage, and I can do with you what I want. Either way, stop your bitching, because you're coming with me. I don't want to listen to this crap the whole way back up to the surface. Take some time to make up your mind. Men don't whine and complain constantly, and neither do heaps of metal that are at least worth the cost of scrap. Your pick."

Hyde shut up. He closed his mouth, tightened his jaw, and hooded his eyes. The expression was grim, borderline hostile, but he stopped protesting and sat still while Dante prepared a rig. He wasn't looking forward to what was to come. Shorn of three limbs and some of his exoskeleton, what remained of Eduardo Curtidor still weighed nearly as much as Dante did.

Midas offered his two cents. *"We may find it easier to transport him if we ask one of the local individuals for help."*

Although Dante had kept the dregs of the junkie commune under partial watch the whole time—not consciously but as an automatic, instinctual process—his thinking mind had all but forgotten about them. He examined each of the ones who remained in turn.

"Okay. You." He pointed at a man, the largest and strongest of those who hadn't run off. He was still on the wasted side compared to Dante's relative leanness. "Come here and help me get this fucker strapped to my back. If you follow me and help me with the stairs, I'll give you some money. Then you can come back here and still sell those severed legs and arm for scrap."

The man's eyes rolled around wildly, but he lurched forward.

Hyde made a low growl. "He's the one who cut my arm off."

"Learn forgiveness," Dante said. "Again, if you complain too much, I'm leaving you here. But yeah, we'll rig you up so at least you're facing away from him. Just don't drool on my neck."

Hyde muttered, "Shut up, Shale."

The two days that had passed had given Dante no shortage of time in which to question his judgment. He wasn't usually the type who sat around regretting his decisions. It was better to take responsibility for them and move on to what he needed to do next. Anytime Hyde and Nasreen were together in the same place it became easy to get discouraged.

"You call this shit *soup?*" Hyde roared. "I call it shit. That's what it looks and smells like. What's in it? Rat placenta or something?"

Nasreen's lip curled. "I'm amazed you know a big word like *placenta*, Hyde. Did you pay someone to implant that into your head, or did you accidentally read a book once?"

Dante exhaled, rubbing his eyes and temples with his fingertips. "Be quiet, both of you. Hyde, eat your damn soup and stop complaining. Nasreen, quit taking the bait and entertaining him by arguing. We've got a lot of stuff to do yet and being miserable while we're forced to live together isn't going to help."

Hyde muttered, "Eat your soup. If that's what it is, okay. I will."

Nasreen made a ragged sound of exasperation, threw up her hands, and stormed out of the kitchenette toward the main bedroom. Dante let her go. He'd talk to her about it a bit later. For now, he only wanted to finish his coffee while waiting for Midas to complete an analytical scan of several more news articles and financial reports.

For a moment, it seemed like the truce would last. Then Hyde commented, in a voice many decibels louder than necessary, "No wonder she isn't married. Can't cook worth a fucking Dirtwalker's gangrenous toenail."

Dante pretended to ignore the abrupt sinking sensation in the pit of his stomach. Seconds later, footsteps stomped down the hall.

Her eyes bulging and face muscles drawn with uncharacteristic wrath, Nasreen shouted, "You want the toenail, big man? How about the whole foot!" Then her leg lashed out, striking Hyde in the chest at an angle such that he fell off his chair and crashed to the floor, rattling it loud enough to disturb the downstairs neighbors (if they weren't already pulling their hair out over all the arguments), and rolling over on his face. He lay helpless and sputtering on the tiles, a torso with a head and a single deformed arm, unable to right himself.

Dante rose fast from his chair. "This needs to stop. Both of you." He glared at Nasreen, who stood chewing on her lip and adjusting her hair, then turned his eyes down to Hyde.

The cyborg was grinding his metal teeth and letting out a low, subdued, buzzing growl. His face showed a seething fury, yet it was an oddly cold, controlled anger. Totally unlike the rampaging monster Dante was accustomed to.

The reason for it was obvious. He could barely move. His massive, ungainly torso writhed in place. He reached out with his single remaining limb, the twisted and deformed metal arm, scraping feebly at the floor in a vain effort to pull himself forward. It was the most pathetic he'd looked since Dante had first found him in the undercity.

"Here." He stepped to the giant's side and hauled him up by the shoulders. "You need a minute to sit and maybe watch a stream or something."

Tension ripped in the muscles beneath the damaged metal, and Hyde made a low growling sound in his throat but didn't try to stop him. Dante carried him out of the kitchenette area and into the living room, propping him up on the couch and turning on the viewscreen. He set the controls to voice-activation mode and left. Hyde wasn't the sort to ask him to stick around and talk about his feelings.

When he returned to the kitchen, Nasreen still stood where he'd left her, frowning vaguely into the distance and looking at nothing. In the other room, it sounded like Hyde was watching a news feed.

Dante motioned to the bedroom. "We need to talk."

"Oh, of course," she snapped. "We need to *talk*. Everyone has been talking way too much lately if you ask me."

Ignoring the comment, he put a hand on her shoulder and guided her down the hall. The apartment wasn't large enough for them to have much real privacy, but if they kept their voices low, Hyde would probably have difficulty hearing them over the sound of the viewscreen.

In a harsh whisper, as quiet as she could make it but still sharp and forceful, Nasreen spat, "This is *bullshit!* He doesn't deserve anything, yet here we are taking care of him after saving his miserable, worthless life, and he's treating us like crap. We should dump his ass down an incinerator chute."

Dante sighed. "Maybe. That's not the right option at the current time, okay? We can use him, and we need to be smart, and I need to get through my...whatever it is, my emotional, um, crisis, I guess. The point is, we can't do stupid, impulsive shit until we know what the job has in store for us. Slaine is still out there. He's not going to let up, and neither can we."

Her nostrils expanded as she breathed out, and her eyes seemed to search for a place to focus on, flicking around the room.

"I understand why you're doing this. Maybe that makes you a better person than I am. But *God*. Part of me is still so... I don't know, *hurt*. Part of me wants Hyde to be as afraid as I was. When he almost killed me with his bare hands. Over and over again, I still have nightmares about that. It might be the worst memory out of all the things rattling around in my head."

Dante leveled a cool, critical gaze at her. He'd never seen Nasreen like this. Of course, her loathing and lingering anxiety around Hyde were obvious. He'd seen her get angry at other things and people before. This was different, a helpless hatred linked to something deep within her. It was as though when Hyde had come after her the first time, he'd forced her to confront something about herself that she didn't know and did not *want* to know. She had come back from that encounter in a state of blatant traumatic shock and had taken days to recover fully.

He didn't have the time to help her get the healing she needed. There were still things he could do, related to their present situation.

He rubbed his chin and noticed the stubble. "Letting him live might be closer to revenge in that regard, anyway. Look at him. He's in the worst shape of his life. He can barely function."

Nasreen's lips pressed tightly together. She flipped a lock of honey-colored hair away from her face. "I'm sure he's not happy, but it's not the same. He only has to be more creative about how he inflicts harm on other people for fun."

Dante shook his head. "You don't know the whole story. When I found him down in the Pentapolis undercity, being torn apart by scalelings, he asked me to kill him. Said he'd rather die, killed by a 'worthy opponent,' as he sees it than reduced to what he is now and forced to endure it."

Nasreen must not have expected any such thing. Her mouth hung partway open although she said nothing.

Dante continued. "The only thing Hyde fears is going through life broken and being shown to be vulnerable or weak. He's being an asshole because it's his only avenue of pretending to be strong. If you get mad at him and lash out whenever he does something that bothers you, then on some level that means Hyde still has power over you. See?"

She snapped her mouth shut and looked aside with a sharp motion, narrowing her eyes. She had no comments, but her flaring nostrils told Dante that she didn't like hearing what he'd said. Although she probably would admit later that it was true.

He went on, "By being nice to the bastard and helping him through this, it will demonstrate that he isn't a threat. That will break him to the point that something new and almost decent will start to grow in his twisted old brain, or it will irritate him to no end. So, either way, you win. Think about it."

She did, for nearly a full minute without speaking. Her voice was softer when she replied. "You may be right."

He was about to say something reassuring when Hyde's voice, loud and ragged and surprisingly jovial, called, "Ha, ha! Come here and look at this shit."

He spun on his heel and rushed out with Nasreen tailing him. If Hyde found something amusing, it was probably bad.

Dante usually dampened his reactions to shock. If something flabbergasted him, he didn't react immediately in any way that permitted him to do anything stupid or give anyone else the chance to take advantage of him. He only kept doing whatever he was doing, delegating a small portion of his brain to the task of unraveling the shocking stimulus and reacting accordingly.

Still, there were times that sorely tested him.

Nasreen's eyes went to the viewscreen. "Ahh, here we go. Watch closely, Dante." It was unnecessary to say it. He had already given the monitor his full attention.

Standing there onscreen, brightly lit with his hands folded behind his back and a blank wall behind him, was Ambrose Igento. He stared at a point slightly below the locus of the camera so that his eyes had a distant and dull quality, and his broad, round face was blank of any expression.

He inhaled through his nose, opened his mouth, and began

speaking in a rote monotone. "Hello. My name is Ambrose Igento. I was recently a pilot for a successful Marauder crew, and then, more recently, I was a pilot for Slaine Solar Solutions. I have come before you now to confess to certain crimes I have witnessed or participated in and to 'blow the whistle,' as they used to say, on the illegal and unethical actions SSS has taken."

Dante let out a short, scoffing laugh and shook his head in amazement. "This is going to be big, isn't it? With this going out, everything is going to change."

Nasreen smiled beside him. "Yes, exactly. Now pay attention."

Ambrose had paused for effect, but now he resumed his spiel. "During a joint mission between my Marauder crew and a group of Reapers working directly for Mr. Slaine, we participated in what was nominally supposed to be a raid for lost industrial secrets and minerals, but in truth was an o-harvest of Dirtwalker women."

Dante could imagine the gasps of horror coming from some of the viewers. If anyone was only half-watching the stream while they did something else, most of them were probably now giving it their full and undivided attention.

The pilot went on to explain everything. He avoided mentioning Dante or Hyde by name or anyone else besides Cormac Slaine and himself. He divulged all the details that Dante was aware of. How SSS had paid him and the rest of the crew to betray their captain and keep their mouths shut about the harvest of the ovaries.

Then he related how Slaine had tried to have him, Ambrose, eliminated once he had served his purpose. His efforts to get back in the company's good graces met with nothing but further ruthlessness, including the illegal use of ballistic weapons inside the Stations.

"SSS and those working with them are more exposed by the day," he elaborated. "I and several others have been collecting and distributing data on their many wrongdoings. Now, they are like rabid animals, turning on their allies, including myself. They will do anything to protect their crumbling power. My goal is to bring extra public scrutiny upon them so they will rethink their increasingly violent and erratic actions."

Dante smirked in grim approval. At first, he had been alarmed that Ambrose had tried to bail out and was blowing the lid off things too soon, but no, this was exactly the right action to take. It was putting SSS on the spot, getting them the coverage they *didn't* want at the worst possible time. On Ambrose's part, it was as much a confession as it was a warning. It might help clear his head about all the sleazy actions he'd taken.

Nasreen checked something on her sphere. "Oh, and it looks like this feed is getting a *lot* of attention. Too bad we can't see Slaine's face right now. But, yes. While you were off finding the one-armed wonder, I was busy launching the next attack against SSS." She collapsed her sphere and slid it back into her pocket.

Midas piped up, speaking aloud, which meant it must have been important. Dante had reminded him not to do so otherwise since they still hadn't found a way to avoid the unpleasant skull vibration that always occurred when he used his voice projection module.

"Sir, and Ms. Joelle, and Mr. Curtidor, I suppose. I checked the Industrial Average, and according to it and certain other financial projections, confidence in SSS, and therefore the value of its stock, is dropping by the second. Their partners and competitors must have an instant notification system for any news involving the company, and they are wasting no time in reacting to it."

Hyde glowered at the screen. A nasty expression settled on his brutish face.

Nasreen chuckled. "Our attack is drawing blood. The sharks are starting to circle."

CHAPTER FOURTEEN

Nasreen pulled on her jacket and adjusted her hair. "Okay. I'm heading out. We used secure channels in setting up this meeting, and there are no signs that anyone knows I'm here, so I should be safe. High-end corporate types like them typically use similar security measures. Don't worry. I'm used to this kind of thing."

Dante was aware of that fact. "Be careful. Check in if you need to. I'll be available to reply. In the meantime, I'm going to figure out what to do with the boys. I have an idea or two."

She nodded with a faint smile, then swiveled on her heel and strode out the door. He let out a slow breath as it closed behind her, thankful that thus far, despite all the resources SSS had probably dedicated to finding them, their safehouse in El Dorado had remained secure.

"Now," he groaned and turned back to the rest of the apartment, where his other two companions waited.

Hyde was staring at him, his good eye small and stony under his heavy brow, and his deformed lips curled in a vague snarl. "*The boys*, eh? How creative. I bet you wouldn't have said that when I had a working body."

Dante shot back, "You might be surprised. Besides, it's not an insult."

Ambrose had been even more nervous than usual since returning from the undisclosed location where he'd filmed his whistleblower video. He shifted his weight from one foot to the other in what resembled an awkward dance. "You do not have to do anything with us, Dante. I am going nowhere. That was the last time I do something so stupid. I'm not cut out for it."

He was referring to his recent selling-out to SSS. Again.

"After what I told the world yesterday, there is no going back to Slaine. It puts me on a, um, how do they say it...shoot first, ask questions *never* basis with him and his people. They want me dead as much as you. Maybe more."

Dante stared at the squat man, and the sting of *both* his betrayals came back, sudden and painful. It was all but impossible to trust Ambrose, now or ever again. He knew the pilot well enough to judge when he was too scared to try anything, and now was one of those times. But after all that had happened, they could *never* reform their friendship.

It would be the height of insanity to turn him loose, back into the world. With SSS after his life, he would likely try to flee into the darkest hole he could find. There was a chance he'd join up with someone else at least as bad as Slaine. The mysterious people in the shadows, perhaps. Or if SSS did catch him and try to interrogate him, Dante had little doubt that Ambrose would squeal to them about his and Nasreen's plans if it meant even the slightest hope of mercy.

All Dante said was, "Yeah. Nobody wants you to fall into SSS clutches, aside from Slaine himself."

"Yes!" Ambrose agreed, loosening his collar. "Sticking with you is my best chance to survive this. Oh, I'm sorry. I know you won't accept an apology. But it is obvious at this point that I, ah, made some bad choices."

Dante nodded. "Correct. Right now, I have more important

things to worry about than settling accounts. Don't do anything stupid." He turned to Hyde. "As for you, we're going to find a use for you. We're not leaving you by yourself or turning you over to anyone else, either."

Hyde snorted in derision. "Oh? Why could that be, Shale? I have no idea."

Getting angry would mean that Dante had taken the bait, so in a calm, unruffled tone, he explained, "Because you're in no condition to go anywhere under your power or do much of anything. If we try to ignore you, you become even more loud and obnoxious than usual. So, I think we can kill two rats with one dart, so to speak, by simply having the two of you take care of each other."

He paused and allowed an evil smirk to creep onto his face. "To *depend on* each other."

It was not his proudest moment, but he had to admit he enjoyed the sudden look of dread that appeared on both their expressions. After all the wrong they'd done and all the pain and hassle both had caused him and Nasreen, it was the least of what they rightfully deserved.

In a buzzing growl, Hyde inquired, "What the hell do you mean, depend on? Like putting us to work shoveling sand or something?"

Ambrose swallowed but otherwise said nothing.

"Not quite." Dante motioned them to follow him back into the apartment's living room. While hardly vast, it was the most spacious part of their quarters and therefore best for rigging equipment. He waited while a panting Ambrose dragged Hyde in with him. The giant's leg stumps scraped unpleasantly against the floor.

As soon as the noise ceased, Dante gestured at a large box that had rested in the corner overnight. "Remember that package we put there yesterday and how I'd explain what it was when the time came?"

Ambrose exhaled. "Uh-oh. I knew I wouldn't want to find out."

Dante nodded. "Yeah. It's a magnetic harness. Good one, too. Maybe not the most fashionable looking or the most comfortable, but it has the raw power we need, and that's what's important. It can support a mass of metal weighing up to what you'd find in a typical cab-sized shuttle car. The only problem is having the room to maneuver such a massive object around. With a smaller and slightly lighter load, though, no such problem exists."

Ambrose stared at the box, and his mouth fell open in slow motion, hanging slack as something went dim in his eyes. It was dawning on him. "Ohh, no."

Hyde let out a barking laugh of sorts. "Hah! Are you fucking kidding me?" For once, Dante couldn't tell whether he was angry, sarcastic, or legitimately thought it was funny.

"No," Dante declared. "We are going to set this thing up. We are going to fit it onto Ambrose. Then you, Am, will carry Hyde around on your back until we tell you otherwise. That ought to keep both of you out of trouble, and it will allow Hyde to be a little more useful than he would be otherwise."

Ambrose covered his face with his hands and rubbed his forehead and temples. Dante pulled out his knife, cut open the box, and extracted the main components from the packaging and stuffing. All of it was degradable but still seemed like extra waste relative to the size of the parcel. The actual harness itself was smaller than he had expected.

Midas silently offered a suggestion. *"Sir, it appears to have come with an instruction manual, but I recall how much you despise those things. So, I've downloaded a copy of it myself, and I can simply read the most pertinent parts while you manually assemble the pieces, if you prefer it that way."*

Dante was growing impressed with how well the AI knew him these days. *"Yes, that would be great. It'll save us time. I won't have to switch back and forth between reading and working."* Most devices also came with audio sphere plugins that accomplished much the same task, but half the time you ended up having to download additional drivers or some such nonsense before they worked. Midas' method was more efficient.

At Dante's urging, Ambrose brought Hyde over. The giant used his extremely limited dexterity but still formidable strength to hold the main harness rig in his one deformed hand while Dante and Ambrose did the finer detail work under Midas's guidance.

There was a strong battery. After charging, it would last for about two weeks. Dante activated it first, set it aside, and broke out a set of small tools as he and the pilot set to work screwing, fastening, adjusting, and hooking things up to one another.

Hyde complained the whole while and usually timed his remarks to make them as inconvenient as possible—abruptly saying something in a loud voice while the other two men were trying to concentrate or asking inane questions about simple procedures. By now, Dante was used to the cyborg's immature way of keeping himself entertained. He either didn't respond or gave one- or two-word answers to shut the hulking, deformed man up.

Ambrose sensed that Hyde's current behavior was a preview of things to come. "Do you ever get tired of being an awful person?"

Hyde laughed, the electronic reverb making the sound more loathsome than it would have been otherwise. "No. Besides, you're as awful as I am. At least I never pretended to be anything other than whatever I am."

Dante tightened a screw. "He has a point. Here, Am, hold this and slip your arm through that loop. We're going to need to measure your chest distance. I don't really care what you think about this setup in general, but you'll be able to do things more effectively if the harness is ergonomic."

"I suppose," the pilot moaned. "I do wish the company was better."

A little less than an hour later, it was ready. They had fitted the harness around Ambrose's arms, shoulders, and chest, so it was snug but not overly tight, and the battery was nearly ready. Once the magnets were activated, Hyde's metal-sheathed, half-melted body could be attached to the back panel with relative ease, and Am wouldn't feel most of the weight.

Dante said, "Okay. Once the battery's ready, it makes more sense to leave it on at all times. That will give you two more time to practice working together as a unit on daily tasks and stuff before the fun begins when we move against SSS."

Ambrose's eyes widened behind his glasses. He hunched his shoulders as though his skin was crawling. "Wait. Do you mean that Hyde will be attached to my back when I go to the bathroom? When I'm trying to sleep?"

"Yeah," Dante stated. "Get used to it, old friend."

The pilot looked at the floor in despair as Hyde roared with sadistic laughter.

"Ha, ha, ha! I *will* get some fun out of this. You need to take a piss, *pendejo*, you ask me, and I'll shake it for you. What are friends for, right?"

It took a second for Ambrose to respond. "It will also slow me down. Yes, the magnets will handle most of the weight, but it will still be awkward to move with a giant pile of metal with one arm sticking off my back."

Dante nodded. "All the more reason to practice now, before people shoot at us or we need to get in or out of someplace in a hurry. Right?"

"Right," Hyde agreed. "We should go for a nice morning jog together. You can do the running, and I'll wave at the pretty ladies."

Dante stared at the deformed, lumpy tentacle that had once been

Hyde's remaining hand. "Speaking of which, I've got a power knife I might be able to use to clear some of the slag from that thing and maybe give it enough of a proper shape that you can use it better."

The giant's nasty mirth faded. Focusing on his wretched state tended to shut him up quickly. "Yes. Do that, Shale. Don't fucking worry about the pain. If I can hold things like a human being again, you can cut up whatever you want."

Dante powered up the knife. It vibrated laterally and used low-level, carefully controlled plasma pulses between the serrations in the blade to aid its cutting power and vaporize the debris it created. Rather, it consolidated it into larger chunks via melting since those were easier to clean up than a pile of dust and shavings.

"Ambrose, enjoy your last half-hour of freedom while I give the man a hand."

Ambrose stared at him in shock. "Did you make a *joke*, Dante? Nasreen must have been rubbing off on you."

Hyde chortled. "I'd let her rub me off."

Dante responded by grabbing his arm and shoving the power knife against it. It sheared off some of the half-melted slag, an amalgamation of leftover metal and polymer from the destroyed pool house, metal from elsewhere on Hyde's body, and parts of his arm that had migrated or deformed.

Aesthetics weren't the concern. Functionality was. Dante cleared enough of the garbage material away so the forearm would be more aerodynamic and was at no risk of getting snagged on anything. If Hyde felt any pain, he didn't show it. He only glowered at the floor.

Then Dante moved on to the hand. Hyde didn't offer any suggestions or advice, so Dante simply tried to ascertain approximately where the thumb joint had been and carved out a small hollow next to it, then shaped the rest into a flipper shape.

Now Hyde was gritting his teeth, and shudders went sporadically through his ruined body. At no point did Dante hit anything identifiable as human flesh or bone although some of the debris looked disturbingly organic, and there were a couple of trickles of blood. Still, the brutish man was clearly in well-controlled agony.

When Dante finished, Hyde effectively had two large, flat fingers and a stubby but workable thumb. "There." He shut the knife off. "How does that work?"

His voice sent a subtle electronic echo across the floor as Hyde grumbled, "It feels really fucking strange. Everything is farther down the forearm than it should be since I lost most of the actual hand. But I can move it." He made a couple of pinching and grasping motions to get used to it.

Ambrose came back out of his brief seclusion in the bedroom. "Okay, I guess it's time to put him back on." If nothing else, he'd resigned himself to his fate.

They switched the magnet back on, and Dante lifted Hyde so his midsection rode against the center of Am's back. Since Hyde had originally been much larger than the pilot, he still towered over him from behind.

Dante moved his tongue over his teeth as he inspected their handiwork. "Yeah. This will work. Like the big guy said, Am can do the running, and Hyde can do the waving. Or whatever else we might need him to do."

As Hyde flexed the limb and the makeshift digits, admiring their increased utility and dexterity, something else occurred to Dante. The more power Hyde had to manipulate things—while still being fairly helpless– the easier it would be to keep Ambrose under control. The pilot and the cyborg didn't like one another, and if Ambrose tried to betray them a *third* time, Hyde would be able to stop it.

Hyde leaned forward so his mouth moved closer to Ambrose's ear. Am had the quiver-lipped blank facial expression of an older woman on a shuttle bus who hoped a smelly, noisy vagrant wouldn't notice her if she tried to act invisible.

"Hey, *pendejo*," Hyde gurgled and put his hand on Ambrose's shoulder. "Since we're going to be together all the time, let's set some rules. For starters, I catch you watching any porn that looks sketchy, and I'll rip your *pinga* off and cram it down your throat. You feel me? No cuck flicks for you."

Ambrose cleared his throat. "The thought hadn't crossed my mind, I assure you."

Dante suddenly realized that he was thirsty and could do with some caffeine. "All right, you two keep up the good work and start practicing your maneuverability. I'm going to make some coffee and wait for Nasreen."

He didn't have long to wait. Nasreen came back in through the door as he was finishing his first cup.

"Hi," he greeted her. "There's some junk on the floor in the living room, but I'll clean it up shortly. It was worth it, though. Ambrose! Come out here and show Nasreen what we accomplished."

Both the pilot's and the cyborg's voices tried to respond at once, resulting in an echoing jumble of noises that wafted out of the living room without making any sense.

Nasreen squinted. "I must say, I'm curious. I have some pretty momentous news as well from our corporate allies. Things are coming to a head."

"Good. Tell us all about it. Once all four of us are here to listen."

A moment later, Ambrose trudged in. The harness stayed mostly snug but strained a little as he twisted and turned to keep Hyde's head or shoulders from brushing against the walls, ceiling, or fixtures.

Nasreen blinked. "What the hell? That's interesting. Such a simple idea, but it might work. Ought to keep them out of trouble, I would imagine."

Dante poured himself a second cup of coffee. "My thoughts

exactly. They might even make a great team once they get more practice in."

Hyde patted Am's shoulder. "Hear that? We're a team. Hah!"

"Well," Nasreen added, "as for what I have to say... I'll go over more details later, but here's the essence. SSS is going down. Their value has plummeted into the abyss and the magical spell, so to speak, that protected them from government scrutiny has ceased to function. Officials in multiple Stations, including Londonburg, are discussing opening major investigations into their activities, and their friends are abandoning them."

Hyde had a sly expression, but he kept his mouth shut for once.

Dante suspected the cyborg's thoughts were similar to his. "Does that mean Slaine is going to give up?"

Nasreen folded her arms. "Of course not. He and his most loyal minions intend to go down fighting. They still have enough reserve funds for an impressive war chest. They're lawyering up to stall the investigations and suits, although they probably know they can't win. More importantly, their security forces are making targeted attacks against all their competitors. Of course, they're disguised as mercs or criminals, but everyone knows it's core SSS personnel."

Dante wasn't sure if Slaine would have taken such drastic measures or not. He should have known better than to have doubted the man's vindictive stubbornness.

Nasreen went on. "They're trying to hold the Stations hostage until they get a pardon for SSS and all it's done. It's unlikely to *work*, but it does make everyone's lives far more difficult. It buys them time and increases the chance that some of our allies will get cold feet."

Hyde muttered, "*Papi* was always a sore loser."

Dante asked, "Where is Slaine himself?"

"Not at his office," Nasreen reported. "He fled the tower the instant things went south for them, after the video. This ties into the other interesting rumor, namely that another contingent of SSS' goons might make a final, rushed o-harvest simply to bring in last-minute cash. The proceeds would allow Slaine and the other company higher-ups to purchase comfortable hiding places in some quiet corner of the Atlantica Stations, conveniently safe from retribution."

Dante's hands trembled, and a faint reddish screen fell across his vision. It had nothing to do with Midas. It was all him. He hadn't come this far and carved his way through so many low-level Reapers and the like, only for the individuals responsible for the whole mess to escape justice while everyone else cleaned up their mess.

"*No*," he snarled. "No, they will *not*."

Nasreen raised a finger. "Oh, but there's more. The corporates have something they claim to have received on 'good authority,' whatever that means. Information. They admit they can't reveal where they got it. I suspect it's the so-called big spiders cleaning their webs."

Hyde rumbled, "The big spiders always do, and the web itself remains."

Annoyed by all the evasiveness, Dante snapped, "Yeah, yeah. And?"

"Slaine and his loyalists aren't hiding anywhere in the Atlantica Stations. They're Dirtside, in a compound they built a while back to provide support for and coordinate various efforts of debatable legality. First mining for solar cells, which isn't too shocking, but probably o-harvesting nowadays."

Dante felt his vision clearing. A bright focus replaced the red haze. "Where?"

"I've got the coordinates," she said vaguely. "They expect the location to be heavily guarded and fortified. The corporates aren't looking to engage in a ground war. For all of them to hire mercs to annihilate a competitor's Dirtside operation in a giant firestorm of bloodshed might send the wrong message to the general public."

She sighed. "They said they hoped we would 'figure something out.' You can guess what that means, I'm sure."

Dante responded with a slow nod. "Doing their dirty work for them. They want Slaine taken out, but without having to commit more of their resources to it than necessary, so their hands stay nice and clean."

Nasreen poured herself a glass of water. Noticing how pale Ambrose had grown, she handed it off to him instead, then poured a second.

"Sounds like we'll need an army," she mumbled after her first sip.

While Hyde grumbled in Spanish under his breath, Dante did a quick scan of his memories. "An army. Yeah. I might know where we can get one."

CHAPTER FIFTEEN

"Hey!" bellowed Mr. Hyde, not bothering to keep his voice down. He seemed hungover, although they had not been near alcohol overnight. Dante wondered if someone whose body was mostly mechanical could even get drunk.

Nasreen snapped, "What?" She was busy prepping the shuttle. Due to Ambrose's mobility being limited by having a large cyborg torso attached to his back, she would have to help him with flying.

Hyde responded, "I want to know how much longer I have to wait for my new parts. Yeah, I'm sure it won't fucking be in time to have them for all this shit, but at least it would be something to look forward to."

Dante was looking over their weapons, survival kits, and other relevant gear. He perked up as Midas spoke into his mind.

"Sir, shall I tell him myself, or would you prefer to relay the information?"

He frowned. *"Tell him yourself. It'll save time to inform both of us at once. I'll survive."*

"Very well." The AI switched from neural speech to audible.

His synthesized voice rattled through Dante's skull and sent weird, unpleasant tremors through his whole body.

"Mr. Curtidor, I have checked, and it seems that the first components we ordered are still being assembled or fabricated and will not be delivered for several weeks yet. The craftspeople responsible for them have promised to update us on their status once they are ready to be sent, so we can plan for which ones will arrive first. Is that satisfactory?"

Hyde sputtered, "Several weeks? No, it isn't fucking satisfactory. You think I want to be pressed against this *chingado*'s back and smell his hair for that long?"

Dante called, "Too bad, Hyde. They don't sell cybernetic enhancements of your type at the goddamn supermarket. Especially not in your size. We did the best we could. Now shut up and either make yourself useful or pretend to rest until we're in orbit."

The cyborg replied with a series of animalistic grunting and snorting sounds, made uncanny by his usual electronic reverb, but stopped trying to argue or complain. He knew perfectly well that Dante and Nasreen were doing him a massive favor by investing the time and money it would take to rebuild him, and he would likely not be quite the same creature he'd been before his little accident.

The shuttle came from a small consortium of smugglers. It turned out both Dante and Nasreen knew of them, although they were unaware of the fact until two days ago. Dante's crew had worked with them a few years back, and Nasreen had bought contraband from them through an intermediary not long before her fateful trip Dirtside with Captain Reavo.

The smugglers had lent them a ship without asking too many questions or demanding collateral. It was an "extra" craft anyway, one they planned to sell rather than use themselves. In Dante's opinion, it was subpar at nearly a decade out of date, but it was space-worthy and mechanically sound. It would get the job done.

More importantly, it wasn't registered. They could take off from the Stations without anyone noticing that the shuttle was missing from an inventory or having records of renting it out. When it returned, Nasreen could substitute fake information that wouldn't clash with any dock's preexisting data.

Dante finished doing inventory at the same time that Nasreen came back to help him finish his security check.

"Okay, we're ready to go up front," she reported. "Do you think we have enough gear?"

He shrugged. "I hope so. There's no way to be certain. If there was, I would have made damn certain it was sufficient. But we don't have time to make a scouting trip down there, come back, and gear up at the Stations before we hit Earth for real."

They'd had to estimate how much stuff to bring since they would be supplying not only themselves but also their friends. Getting the shuttle for free, albeit on loan, made it easier to invest in a small army's worth of kit.

Nasreen closed her eyes and nodded. "It's a good amount. It will have to be enough. They have *some* of their own, don't they?"

"Yes," he replied. "They're not exactly unarmed. But we have to assume that this SSS place will be stuffed to the gills with high-end hardware and toys. I don't think we'll get through this one with zero casualties, to be perfectly honest."

He never assumed a job would be easy. It was a major part of why he was still alive after all these years. He had survived so many close calls that would have killed a person who sleep-walked through danger trying to sustain themselves on nothing but the hope that everything would be fine.

Opening her eyes, Nasreen added, "Well, we don't even know if they'll agree to this. Strangely enough, this seems to be the one time when you're better qualified for diplomacy than I am."

He allowed himself a grim smile as he selected a pulsecore carbine for his personal use. "Yeah." There was no need to say anything more on the matter. "Now let's go."

Ten minutes later, the shuttle was powered up. The bay doors opened in front of them, disclosing the orbital band of gravitationally controlled atmosphere surrounding the El Dorado Station. Beyond it lay the strip of space that separated the new home of most of humanity from the mortally wrecked planet known as Earth.

Ambrose grimaced as he sat on his bench—a regular seat couldn't accommodate Hyde, still attached to his back—and took them out of the Station and into the void. Despite the relative age and crudity of the ship, it was holding up well, and neither Ambrose nor Nasreen had much trouble with the controls.

The pair went straight down first as if heading for Central America, which lay below El Dorado. Once they were out of sight from the Stations, they adjusted course, veering north-northeast before entering Earth's atmosphere and braving the usual fiery turbulence.

Ambrose announced, "We're going in. Brace yourselves."

Dante had strapped into one of the rear seats. He inhaled slowly and tightened his jaw. If the shuttle were to develop a sudden "issue," now would be the time.

The whole ship shook as they penetrated the sphere of gas surrounding the planet and flames erupted around them, blotting out most of the windshield. It grew warmer within the cab, suggesting that the shuttle's temperature control system was either weaker than it should be or that something had gone wrong with it. Dante's fingers danced along the chair's armrests.

The heat never became too intense, and the flames cleared as they entered the skies of Earth amid a wispy mass of orange clouds. When some of them parted, they saw a familiar-looking island off the coast of North America, not too far from Nova Scotia and Newfoundland.

Atlantica. The long-hidden and mysterious isle that had given its name to the entirety of the new spaceborne human civilization.

Ambrose gasped. "Yes. Yes. We made it through. Heat shields are thin, are they not? But I don't think we have any problems."

Nasreen added, "Nothing on the readouts as far as leaks, faulty components, or the like, but we'll want to inspect the exterior when we land to be safe."

"Agreed," said Dante. "Am, those coordinates I gave you are an estimate since I didn't have proper ones when I was there. They'll get you within a few miles, at least. I should be able to spot the place once we get close."

Ambrose agreed, although he still seemed nervous. Surprisingly, Hyde had remained silent through the whole descent as though the disabled giant had finally grown bored with complaining and wanted to save his energy for something more fun.

They passed the ruins of what had once been Atlantica Metro. It ringed the vast central crater where the city's bulk had lifted directly out of the earth. Beyond the exurbs was a fairly empty wilderness, shrouded in mists that parted here and there on gusts of dusty wind. Am slowed the shuttle down to make visual confirmation easier.

Dante peered at one of the monitors hooked up to the hull cameras. "That large, square building in the middle of the ring-shaped area. See it? That's our destination. Don't pull up too close. Put us in a holding pattern about a mile away and wait. I'll get on the speaker as soon as the welcoming committee shows up."

Hyde scoffed, "Welcoming committee. You sure they aren't gonna hide like rats running from a car?"

Dante shot back, "They'll hide, but they'll get as close as they can while they're at it. They assume that any ships that come down belong to 'Moonfiends' who want to kill them, harvest their organs, or steal their stuff, so they do recon on anything suspicious in the sky, and they're pretty damn good at it."

Everyone fell silent as they circled a mile away from the

building. It was strange how familiar the place seemed, although it had been months since Dante had been there, and he'd only spent a short time there to begin with. The commune of the Crescent tribe.

Once or twice, he thought he saw flickers of motion along the desolate ground. They were still too high up, and the lighting conditions on Atlantica were still too poor to be certain if it was camouflaged Dirtwalkers or simply the blowing dust and fog. After ten or fifteen minutes, Dante's patience began to wear thin.

"Am, turn on the speaker. Make it nice and loud. I'm addressing them whether they're hiding below us or still in the building."

Mumbling something to himself, Ambrose did as instructed. Once the microphone was on, Dante climbed from his seat and put the attachment close to his lips.

"This is Dante Shale. You know me. You helped me months ago, and we parted in friendship. We come in peace and wish to ask something of you. If you agree to speak to me again, please show yourselves openly."

Nothing happened at once, so they waited a few minutes, then Dante repeated the message. Then a third time, five minutes after that.

Nasreen sighed. "They might think it's a trap. As far as they're concerned, we could easily be o-harvesters trying to draw them out by mentioning the legendary Dante Shale. Unless one of them recognizes your voice."

Dante was about to agree with her. Then he noticed something on the screen. "Wait. Wait. They're coming out. A whole warband, I see."

Two dozen Dirtwalker women emerged, all lean and fierce-looking. The Crescent-Marked sisters. They had emerged from behind a ridge so quickly that they might as well have appeared out of thin air. It looked as though at least half of them carried projectile weapons, either rifles, pulsecores, or crossbows in one or two cases. The rest had spears or swords.

Dante had little doubt that others lay hidden nearby, ready to open fire at the first sign of trouble.

"Okay, good. The fact that they're making a show of force means they're willing to consider meeting us. The extra muscle is in case we turn out to be harvesters. Once we land and they see me, we should be fine."

Ambrose squirmed. "What about me? What about Hyde? Do you think they will recognize us? The last time we were here, we *were* harvesters. Have you thought about that, Dante?"

He had, but he hadn't wanted to mention it earlier lest Am and Hyde get cold feet and pressure him into a different course of action. The Crescent-Marked were their best shot. Maybe their *only* shot at getting help in the battle to come.

He grunted, "Am, you weren't near the action when that all happened. A lot of them probably never saw Hyde, and for those who did, well, he's unrecognizable now anyway."

Shorn of his limbs, with his armor distorted by the explosion and his distinctive red hair and beard burned off, he could easily have passed for a disabled man clinging to life through emergency cybernetics. He was barely the same person as the monstrous entity who had led the SSS Reapers on their brutal o-harvesting expedition half a year ago.

Ambrose said nothing. Hyde quipped, "Ha. Aye, good point. If they do recognize us, this will be a short meeting."

Dante checked his pulsecore. The safety was on, but it was otherwise ready to fire. "Yeah. Ambrose, land."

As the pilot brought the shuttle gently down to the ground, Midas offered to scan subtle reactions, both visual and audible, of the warrior women to help determine if they were about to attack. Dante agreed. It was always helpful to have another pair of eyes and ears or the electronic equivalent in a tense situation.

Dante said through the speaker, "Please stand back about fifty yards." He repeated the phrase in the Dirtwalker Trade tongue, replacing "fifty yards" with "two stones' throw." They had a surprisingly sophisticated system of measurements when it came to certain practices, but in colloquial speech, they tended to stick to rough estimates.

The ship came to a rest about two feet off the ground in a weak hover position, and Ambrose opened the side hatch. He and Hyde would remain at the console, ready to take off if things turned ugly. Dante and Nasreen would do the talking.

Nasreen had a pulsecore carbine as well. They held them at low ready, indicating that they meant no threat but would defend themselves if challenged. Each nodded to one another. Then they stepped out.

The weather was warmer than Dante expected, but the sea breeze still held a cool edge. The island of Atlantica had been known for its strangely mild weather despite being located near a cold part of North America. At present, it was late morning in this part of Earth.

The Crescent-Marked women reacted to them with a faint but perceptible tensing of posture, but they made no move to attack. Out in front and center, holding a spear while those beside her held powerful firearms, was a familiar figure.

She was tall, muscular, and intimidating, with leathery skin and crescent-shaped scars on the sides of her face running from the corners of her eyes down her cheeks. All the warriors had them, but the leader's were somehow the most prominent.

Dante nodded at her. "Urshielle. It's me."

The woman's hard-set face softened and elongated in surprise. "Dante Shale. It is true, then. Welcome back to the world of human beings. You have been long away, on the moon." She frowned. "Things here have grown worse." Like most Dirt-walkers on the isle, she spoke the Trade tongue with an accent that was oddly languid and lilting. They didn't have much contact with the people still on the mainland.

He gave her a sympathetic frown. Some of her companions looked vaguely familiar. Others did not. Quite a few had cheek scars that looked fresh, which meant they had lost their ovaries only recently.

"I am sorry to hear that. We have tried to stop what the worst of the Moonfiends have been doing. We have hurt them badly, but they have responded by committing more evil acts because the harvests allow them to grow wealthy. That is why we are here, now. It's time to stop it, once and for all."

A ripple of excitement went through the crowd, but it was difficult to determine its exact meaning or nature. He suspected and hoped it meant they were happy to hear him joining their fight, but they might have blamed him for driving SSS and their lackeys to step up their o-harvest operation.

Midas remarked, *"Sir, their facial expressions and other body language indicate a mixture of pain and hope, more than anything. I don't think the anger is toward you, at least not most of it."*

Dante replied mentally, *"Good."*

Urshielle leaned against her spear in weariness. "They grow desperate. Desperate and covetous. More of them have come after women of the island's tribes. Each time, they leave us more Crescent-Marked, and in that way, we gain warriors. But the island loses children. Slowly, we are losing. If you, Dante Shale—and you, Nasreen Joelle—have truly come to help, perhaps that may change."

Nasreen didn't yet understand the Trade tongue, but she recognized her name and the tone of half-exhausted determination in the other woman's voice.

"We have killed many of them. A dozen times three, since the last moon," Urshielle went on. "They grow sloppy. In their greed for our eggs, they do not bother to be so stealthy or so well prepared as they once were, simply rampaging around whatever settlement of people they can find. But there are so many of them that we cannot stop them no matter how well we fight."

That was bad news, Dante thought. He'd hoped that Slaine was down to a small cadre of fanatics, or at least the last people he could afford to pay well enough for them to stick around. Still, the Dirtwalkers' depredations might have been at least bringing them closer to that level of desperation.

Urshielle went on. "We fear there will not be enough fertile women left for people to live on this island anymore. Too few children will be born as the rest of us grow older. The land, the Nightmutts, and more of the Moonfiends will finally destroy us altogether, leaving this place barren forever of all we have tried to do."

Silence settled over the group. The only sound was the wind blowing the dust across the bare rock that dominated this part of the island.

Dante bowed his head. "We have come to stop that. The people performing the harvests are the same ones we have a vendetta against, and we intend to destroy them. We have a plan for how to go about it, and we came with as much weaponry and armor as we could get."

Urshielle's eyes grew keener and the depressive haze that had fallen over her thoughts parted and dissipated. "I will see it done. Tell me, and in whatever way we may do so, we will help."

CHAPTER SIXTEEN

Ambrose looked around in wonderment as Urshielle and her two chief bodyguards led them through the halls of the old hospital.

He shook his head, "This is not what I had expected. You people have done quite well for yourselves."

The Crescent settlement had chosen the hospital as its chief headquarters. It served them as a dormitory, academy, meeting place, and fortress in addition to its original main purpose as a place of healing. The surrounding grounds and outbuildings served various other functions, and the place was much like a small but bustling city unto itself.

What surprised the pilot most, as well as the cyborg riding piggyback on the magnetic harness, was how poised the Crescent Dirtwalkers were and how willing to be peaceful and listen to reason. Most people on the Stations grew up knowing exceedingly little about their former, long-lost cousins. The Dirtwalkers were uniformly stereotyped as mouth-foaming savages without any culture, decency, or mercy.

Yet a faint sense of pity and guilt had led to the universal outlawing of o-harvests and t-harvests. A memory, suppressed and forgotten though it usually was, that those who had remained behind on the Earth were still humans.

They came to a foyer within the hospital, where a group of men waited for Urshielle. Dante recognized the one at their head immediately. Raphorien was one of their chief healers, the Crescent-Crowned. Their marks got tattooed around the scalp.

The Crescent-Crowned were men who had been "harvested" in much the same way the women of the community had. This was less common since male fertility on the Atlantica Stations was seldom as badly affected by orbital stress as female fertility was.

"Welcome," the lead healer intoned in his quiet voice. "I am Raphorien. If any of you need care, we can help." Like all of them, he was bald with soft features despite being rather large-framed and gave off an air of gentleness and wisdom.

Dante smiled. "Hi, Raphorien. My leg is better. The rest of us are fine, aside from this gentleman." He pointed at Hyde, who looked more than a little sullen.

Raphorien came forward and placed a hand on Dante's arm in greeting. Then he moved around to Ambrose's side. His eyes widened in alarm as he saw the full nature of the half-man attached to the pilot's back. "Oh. Oh, my. This is beyond my ability to heal, I am afraid."

A series of hushed whispers went through the crowd. Hyde's presence made the Dirtwalkers uncomfortable, and Dante feared it *might* be because they knew who he was. But it was probably the fact of *what* he was.

Hyde muttered, "Yeah, you can't fix me the way you would most people. I need special parts installed. More like fixing a shuttle or something."

Raphorien looked over the rest of them, introducing himself to Ambrose and Nasreen, and concluded that all were healthy.

Urshielle gestured at the pilot and the cyborg. "Good. You two may wait here. I must speak to my warriors, and I wish for Nasreen Joelle and Dante Shale to come with me."

Dante agreed. "Let me talk to them, and I'll be right along. We shouldn't waste time."

The women and the healers all left the foyer, moving into the halls beyond while Ambrose found a bench that would allow him to recline without Hyde's massive, tattered bulk getting in the way.

He sighed. "The magnets support the weight, but it's still heavy. I have to concentrate on where he is all the time. And feel his breath on my neck."

"Hey," Hyde grunted. The reverb in his voice made it louder than he intended, although it was still soft by his standards. "Shale."

Dante moved a couple of steps closer to the broken cyborg, ignoring Ambrose, who faced away from them. "Yeah?"

With his metal flipper hand, Hyde gestured in the direction Urshielle had strolled. "What's that woman's name again? Ursula or something?"

"Urshielle. Why do you ask?"

A crooked smile formed on Hyde's half-melted metal lips. "She's hot as *fuck*," he said. "I mean, yeah, probably not most men's type, but I'm not most men. I'm too big for an average *chica* so I don't mind them being tall. Her being so muscular doesn't scare me. It means she's, you know, sturdy. Solid. Heh, heh.

"She's getting on in years but still in damn good shape, even if she's a little rough around the edges. I like her hair. The braids and all. It suits her, like one of those athletes back in the day. And I love a woman with tattoos. They're the adventurous types, especially if they're tatted somewhere like on their face. Means they aren't going to be afraid of me..."

As he rambled, Dante realized that Hyde was still speaking as though he were his old, intact self. On some level, he hadn't yet fully accepted or internalized what had become of him even though he was attached legless and sans one arm to Ambrose's back.

When he ran out of steam, Dante promised, "I'll talk to her about it. Ask her what she thinks of you or see if I can get some time for you two to talk. If not during all this, at least sometime later, after we rebuild you."

The half-mechanical face fell into a lopsided grimace. "Yeah. I keep forgetting. I'm not in much condition for it right now. But talk to her, sure. Tell her I'm impressed by her."

"I will." He wasn't overly optimistic about Hyde's chances, but Dante had built his reputation as someone who always delivered on his promises. He would try if nothing else.

Ambrose cleared his throat. "That's good of you, Dante. May I have some time to work and relax?"

Dante had to smirk a little. "Of course. Yell, or message Midas if you need anything. The Crescent-Crowned men might be able to help you also. The Dirtwalkers aren't all complete savages. They're peaceful enough if you speak to them right. And they run a tight ship here."

With that, he turned and left.

Walking away from the pair, it occurred to Dante that he had doubted, before now, if Hyde was capable of infatuation or sexual desire. Not that he had devoted much thought to such a horrifying subject, but he'd assumed that Hyde's modifications had left him functionally asexual and that he got his rocks off by killing instead.

Something else far more important popped into his head as well. They had come this far without anyone looking too closely at the pilot or the disabled cyborg and with no ugly incidents resulting from their presence. This meant that no one recognized the two as integral parts of the first major o-harvest that had accompanied Dante's ill-fated trip to the island.

Now it was simply a matter of ensuring that neither of them

fucked things up before the plan against SSS could be set in motion.

Dante glided down the halls, moving at twice the speed of Urshielle's entourage while making no more noise. It wasn't necessary to keep quiet in a place where he was an honored guest, but he wanted to stay in practice.

When he caught up to the group, they had reached the doors to one of the hospital's internal courtyards. They stood before it in a loose throng with Urshielle at the center. The other warriors ringed her with the healers and Nasreen toward the edges.

"...shall never happen again, if this works as the Moonstrider, the Hellcat, says it must. He aided us before, and he shall aid us again, and we him. Let there be no doubt of him unless he gives us cause." The leader of the warriors saw Dante approaching and nodded. "We shall hear out his plan and that of Nasreen Joelle."

Dante returned the gesture, a curt but respectful movement of his head. "I will not waste time. Before I tell you our plans, I have a question. When the Moonfiends come to harvest people, do they come in vehicles? Flying ships, or trucks, or anything like that?"

He kind of doubted they came on foot.

"Yes," Urshielle said. "Usually they are the great metal wheeled carts, the trucks. They are noisy but fast enough to bear down upon a village before everyone can run or hide, even if we hear them coming."

Dante stroked his chin. If Slaine's cronies used mostly land vehicles, it all but confirmed the intel that Nasreen had received from the corporates. SSS's Dirtside HQ was on the island of Atlantica itself. Unless the trucks merely took personnel and booty to ships that went back and forth from the mainland. That would have been needlessly complicated and inefficient. If the compound wasn't on the isle, they would have used shuttles.

He elaborated, according to the rough outline he and Nasreen had come up with earlier.

"Okay, that's good to know. The best way to stop the harvests is a very simple one. We determine where they will strike next, which is something we can do with our tech, plus simple guesswork. Then we ambush the strike team. Or a patrol, if they send one.

"We take over their vehicles, pretend to be their people, and return to their headquarters. Then, with as many warriors as you can spare, we attack the compound and take out Cormac Slaine himself—their chieftain, the one who orders the raids. He has no more friends in the stars. We took those from him, and now he is a hunted man."

He stopped and let his words sink in. He had to admit it wasn't the most brilliantly complex scheme. If they did it right, they would have the element of surprise. The hardware they'd brought would even the odds in their favor. Somewhat.

Nasreen added in English, "I don't know how much technology you people possess. We have things that will allow us to imitate the voices, eyes, and fingerprints of their people and, um, defeat the, uh, automatic security measures they have in place... How do I describe cameras and AI alarm systems? Dante, help me here."

Sighing, he translated to the best of his ability. Some of the warriors looked uncertain, but Urshielle's faith in his trustworthiness and abilities remained firm.

"Yes," the leader announced. "It is true that the moon-people have tools and tricks far beyond anything we can understand. Those of you who came with me to the Gape Mouths, when we took Dante Shale back to the ship that would let him escape into the sky, saw many such things.

"With the weapons they have brought us, we have a chance to win. Some of us may die. That is the fate we expect as warriors. With the enemy defeated, there may come a time when there are no more moon-scrapings, and all our women—and men—can have children as they were born to, at last."

She waited, and it seemed that she looked at each of the assembled women in turn. Only one cringed. Urshielle told her that she could remain behind to guard the headquarters, but she expected her to die in defense of the commune if the time came.

Dante didn't object. They could spare the loss of one fighter if they still had a couple of dozen others, and a person with no stomach for combat might cause more problems than they solved by simply being one more warm body.

Urshielle nodded and looked at her guests. "It is done. All these others shall come, and I will find more if I can."

Motioning to Nasreen, Dante told her, "Show them how some of the tech works. I'm sure there are one or two who understand English so they can translate. I'm going with Urshielle for now."

Nasreen looked dismayed, but pulled out her sphere, drew a deep breath, and began demonstrating to the Dirtwalker women how Stations gadgetry worked.

Urshielle collected Raphorien, and together with Dante, the three strode down the halls toward the far side of the building, presumably where other warriors engaged with some business that kept them from the main meeting.

Dante mentioned, "You know, Urshielle, Hyde—the, um, the guy riding on the back of my pilot—is impressed by you." He felt awkward saying it, but he'd given his word. "He thinks you make an impressive warrior and finds you beautiful."

Urshielle was unfazed. "Some men have said this, yes. He is a broken, metal thing, very strange to me, and I have no time for such concerns. We are going to war."

"True," Dante agreed.

Raphorien sighed. "Oh, and perhaps your friend still has not figured out what it means to be moon-scraped, Dante. The Crescent-Marked women might make wives, but they cannot make mothers."

Dante grimaced. "He knows. We all do."

CHAPTER SEVENTEEN

Up the coast to the north from the desolate coastal region where the Crescent tribe had its base lay the territory of a tribe called the Alstafi, who were sometimes considered kin of the Harij. They were a small tribe that Slaine hadn't targeted for o-harvesting.

Yet.

Dante crouched behind the trunk of an old petrified tree, fingers gently tapping the chassis of his pulsecore. Beside and behind him were five of Urshielle's best warriors, not to mention Ambrose Igento and by extension, Eduardo H. Curtidor.

Hyde kept quiet for the time being, but he seemed tense, as though his immobility drove him mad with the need to act. He would be able to contribute soon enough if their predictions were correct.

Ambrose whispered, "You said these people were related to the, um, Harij? There was no time to ask about that earlier, but it sounded important. Who are they, again?"

Dante frowned. "The tribe you helped destroy." His tone was flat and neutral. The words themselves were harsh enough already. "They lived in that facility where we were supposedly going to pick up that alloy for Slaine."

Am cringed. "Oh. I see. Well, you killed some of their people, too."

"I did," Dante admitted. It was part of penetrating their territory and stealing from them. "They forgave me after things changed. Well, what remained of them. Every one of their women got harvested. Most joined the Crescent-Marked. They ceased to exist as an ethnic group."

He hoped that none of the women nearby were among them, but they didn't quite look like how he'd remembered the Harij.

With Ambrose falling silent, Dante scanned the scene before them. So far, everything was quiet.

The Alstafi lived in a valley in the hills. The location formed the third point of a rough triangle relative to the positions of the Crescent commune and the Harij's former home in the city's ruins. Dante and most of the ambushers waited on ridges above the valley that would be difficult for trucks or even hovercraft to access. The easiest routes into the community had deliberately been left clear.

Down below, some of the villagers were continuing with their normal routines. Especially the fertile women. They had been encouraged to work out in the open, where anyone could see them without difficulty.

Without speaking, Midas provided a small magnification window in the corner of Dante's field of vision that showed what the civilians were doing. Mundane tasks of survival, mostly. These people lived a simple yet precarious existence. He didn't like using them as bait.

It was the best way to ensure that SSS would send its raiders here after Midas had concluded that the Alstafi Valley was the most likely choice for the next harvest.

Many of the women's husbands, brothers, and the like weren't with them in the town. Instead, they waited in the hills along with Urshielle's fighters. Better still, they had picked up another half-dozen volunteers from a recently harvested tribe called the Fengu, men filled with despondent rage.

Dante recognized them as the types who intended to die in the coming fight. Such people could be dangerous. Still, danger was exactly what awaited them and all but guaranteed casualties.

Their force numbered close to fifty altogether. More than Dante had hoped for. The question was whether it would be enough.

The afternoon waned. Midas reported twice on messages from Nasreen, who was on the opposite side of the valley, not far from Urshielle. She informed them that all was quiet on their front too.

It was right around what Dante would have recognized as dinner time—the point at which afternoon gave way to early evening, the traditional time when humans ceased working for the day—that the noise came upon them. It was startling in its volume as well as its suddenness.

Midas advised, *"That is undoubtedly two to three large trucks and at least one hovercraft shuttle. They must have had a silent mode engaged until now and have dropped it for the sake of speed."*

Dante could have guessed all that himself, aside from the number and nature of vehicles. "Showtime," he murmured. "Everyone, get ready."

Below them in the village, the various women, teenagers, and a handful of the more physically fit older folks perked up at the loud rushing and grinding sounds. They made a show of gathering their work and rushing toward the valley's back end, under the cliff where Dante now crouched. The Alstafi and Crescent-Marked had planned it out, then drilled the civilians on how to avoid the coming violence while still putting on a convincing show.

Dante hoped it would work. Most Dirtwalkers were tough and wary to begin with, but even so, he didn't like having noncombatants in a fire zone. At least the young children and very old had been safely lodged at a secret hideaway about a mile off in another valley.

Then the raiders roared into the valley. Out in front was a small, four-person truck. It was light and small, a forward scout more than anything, but closely following it were two other trucks, larger with massive, spiked grinding wheels sheathed in armor. Hovering behind and above them was a land shuttle. It was capable of limited air flight but was primarily for traversing rough terrain without the hassle of physical contact.

Ripples of tension like the subtle charge of electricity preceding a thunderstorm passed between the ambushers. Dante breathed in, exhaled, and left his lungs empty as he aimed through his carbine's sighting system.

The scout truck looped around to the rear of the convoy as the other three vehicles ground to a halt at the village's edge. Women and kids screamed.

Doors *clanked* open on the trucks and shuttle and out streamed men and women in armor, toting various types of guns. The ones in front had riot shields as well. At the rear of the emerging squads were noncombat personnel toting the loathsome devices that would perform the harvest.

Nasreen spoke through the headsets in the helmets that half of the ambushers wore. *"Now."*

Dante squeezed the trigger. So did everyone else.

Pulsecore rounds and bullets streaked down from the ridges. The cacophony of so many weapons firing at once drowned out the noise of the troops below and the purring engines of their vehicles. Dante fired an entire magazine into the cluster of the squad closest to him. He wasn't alone.

Slaine's henchmen barely knew what hit them. The miniaturized plasma explosions and shards of heated lead knocked them around, pierced their extremities, and finally ripped them apart. Their armor might have protected them against a few potshots by a handful of snipers but was rendered useless against the massive rain of death that descended upon them. Entire swathes of the ground turned red and smoking.

Then the scout truck sped away as its driver grasped what had happened too quickly for anyone's liking. Nasreen's unit swiveled to open fire. Dante shouted into his headset, "Wait!" but not in time to stop them.

More bullets ravaged the truck and pulsecore rounds burst its tires, melted parts of its hull, and finally penetrated its fuel system. It burst into flames, sending out a small shockwave and rising cloud of smoke as it exploded. The frame spun end over end while the burning bodies of the four occupants scattered into the pass leading out of the valley.

Dante gritted his teeth. "Goddammit. Now we have wreckage in the path leading out, and we're down one vehicle."

Nasreen responded, "Better than them getting away and warning the base. Let's get down there and check in so Slaine thinks all is well."

As they had the conversation, the half-dozen warriors they'd left in the village proper rushed into the vehicles to finish off the drivers before they could sound the alarm. They were armed with spears and crossbows and had been explicitly instructed not to damage any of the internal equipment.

Dante reloaded his carbine, then he and the others began the laborious climb down into the valley. They had to move fast.

While Ambrose puffed, Hyde cackled. "That was too fucking easy. *Papi* isn't sending his best. They should have scouted these ridges first. And brought more guys."

As Urshielle had said, they were getting sloppy in their desperation to squeeze as much money as possible out of the Dirtwalkers' bodies before SSS finally imploded.

Once everyone was down at the edge of the village and the valley was secure, the local Alstafi men checked on their families and cleared the human and mechanical wreckage aside. Dante took the lead in barging into one of the two big trucks.

The driver doubling as a comms guy slumped over a console, dead with a crossbow bolt protruding from the back of his neck. Dante pulled the corpse aside, let one of Urshielle's women drag it out, and sat before the controls.

"Midas."

The AI didn't waste time with chatter but went immediately to work hacking the network the console connected to. He focused on stored audio files of the crew's voices or other identifying info. Nasreen was doing the same thing in the other vehicles.

Midas spoke within his host's mind. *"I've almost got it, sir."*

Right then, someone on the other end of the vehicle's communications network demanded, "Two-two-seventeen. Report."

To buy them an extra moment, Dante coughed into the microphone as though he were trying to speak but could not for a second. That way, at least it was clear that someone was at the console.

Then Midas spoke up, using his audio module. "Roger, four-thirty, this is two-two-seventeen, we've got an A-F-X. Otherwise all is well. Over."

The voice sounded nothing like the AI's usual. It must have been a perfect imitation since the guy on the other end grunted back with a similarly meaningless string of numbers, letters, and half-assed comments. Then the console fell silent.

Mentally, Dante quipped, *"Nice job. Also, I hope you understood that since I sure as hell didn't. They're using their internal code and lingo. Nothing a Plunderer would be familiar with."*

Midas reassured him, *"Yes, I'm processing it now. I told him that we had a sniper who injured one man but otherwise were able to crush the resistance and that the harvest is taking place successfully."*

"Good." Dante stood and bounded out of the truck to check on everyone else.

His small army was in the process of organizing itself according to the three available vehicles. Nasreen stood near the center and caught Dante's eye.

"Hellcat," she called. "These are quality rides, but there's a slight problem. We can only fit about a dozen in each truck, and maybe a few more than that—sixteen?—in the hovercraft. We'll have to leave at least eight or ten people behind, and that's not counting the locals. We'll have about forty going in."

He frowned. "The Alstafi can stay here and protect their village. Otherwise, we'll go by volunteers."

They decided that the youngest eight of Urshielle's warriors would remain near the valley in case SSS sent more troops and to act as waypoint guides when—if—Dante's forces returned. The half-dozen Fengu men insisted on coming, as Dante had expected.

"All right," he announced. "Everyone pick your ride. We don't know exactly what this place will look like, but it will probably be a hard fight getting through the outer security. Then, whatever we have to do, we get into the inner sanctum. Only one thing matters. Getting Cormac Slaine."

He briefly described the man to the Dirtwalkers, but it was oddly difficult. He'd met Slaine only once, half a year ago. It was hard to remember all the details. He reflected briefly on how such an evil man, who had personally caused Dante so much trouble, could be so thoroughly average and nondescript-looking. Faintly handsome, well-groomed, well-dressed. He could have been any corporate executive, any member of the Stations' de facto aristocracy.

They would know him less by his appearance than by where he was. At the absolute farthest point from wherever the fighting was. Wherever was safest.

"Move out," Dante commanded.

They piled into the vehicles roughly according to the same makeshift units they'd been in while setting the ambush, the exception being that Ambrose took control of the hovering shuttle while Nasreen took the other truck. None of the Dirtwalkers could be relied upon to drive properly.

Once everyone was in place, Dante took a second to familiarize himself with the controls, heeding Midas's advice. Then they set out. Fortunately, the still-burning wreckage of the scout truck proved not to pose much of an obstacle, given how big and well-protected the trucks were. The shuttle simply floated above it.

Then, bumbling and grinding along on the rough terrain, they were out of the valley and into the rugged wilderness of northern central Atlantica. The original Atlantica, the mysterious island never truly tamed even at the height of Earth's civilization.

They followed an approximate course to the coordinates Nasreen had received from their corporate allies. Slaine had built his compound into the side of a mountain in the island's northern part. It would take close to an hour to get there. The Dirtwalkers stood grimly or clung to the sides of the vehicle as the ground bumped them along.

Dante tried to drive gently, but haste was more important. It had been a long time since he'd traveled in this type of old-fashioned vehicle. Most transportation nowadays was hover-based and therefore smoother. It was the one area in which he supposed he was spoiled.

Midas ran the comms system by himself, using apparatuses in the other vehicles to send messages to himself and back in the company's unique lingo. He once reported to base that the harvest was successful, and they were on their way back.

Dante had no idea if the SSS elite guard was buying it. There was only one way to find out. If they *hadn't* fooled their opponent, a military-grade shuttle might intercept them and blast them to plasma residue before they were in sight of the compound.

Nothing of the sort happened. The desolate wilderness fell away. The hills receded to a flatter area while true mountains rose in the distance and Slaine's final hiding place grew closer. Sometimes the cameras showed creatures scuttling through the dying jungles, Nightmutts of various sorts. None of the mutant creatures were brave enough to challenge the three massive vehicles.

Ambrose had the best view, hovering in front of the convoy. He said into the headset network, "We're here."

Ahead of them was a tall fence that blended quite well with the vegetation. Beyond it was a courtyard overlooked by guard towers, then a fortified gate that led into the mountain's bowels. The peaks towered over them, blotting out half the sky. They were deep into the evening now. It was almost twilight.

Dante breathed in and out. They had no real plan to deceive their way in. Assuming they could reach the courtyard, force and speed would be all they had. That and a handful of tech tricks Nasreen and Ambrose had brought, but those alone wouldn't bring victory. Blood was going to flow.

Dante said into his headset, "No one does anything until we're in. Then, as soon as we leave these vehicles, kill everyone, destroy those towers, and blast open those gates. That's all."

A single shuttle circled the compound in the sky, but there were no other vehicles or troops outside the fence. The convoy stopped at the first gate, where Midas took over the comms system.

Dante tried to infer what was going on as the AI conversed in code with the base's defenders. They wanted to know what had happened to the scout truck. Midas concocted a story about how it had taken more damage than expected, and the four men on board had divided between the trucks and the hovercraft. They would go back for it later.

The man on the other end cursed, spat out a few more code terms, and fell silent. The gates slid open.

Ambrose took the hovering shuttle in first, sweeping off to the right, while Nasreen's truck went left, and Dante's truck, the last in, took the center. Behind them, the opening in the fence closed again. The four guard towers watched them. Each was armed with a weapons-grade plasma cutter and manned by two security goons each.

Another dozen troops had emerged from the shadows and crowded around the vehicles in two groups of six each. They could handle that many, Dante knew. There were probably far more out of sight.

His nostrils flared as he breathed in. "Do it."

The trucks and the shuttle opened their doors.

CHAPTER EIGHTEEN

The Fengu warriors, three in each truck, were the first out. In unison, they let out a bloodcurdling war cry and piled directly into the security goons who had appeared to welcome back their comrades. They had only spears. They had insisted that Dante and Nasreen save their substantial but limited stock of rifles and pulsecores for the Crescent-Marked.

"Oh shit!" one of the SSS men exclaimed. "We got a sixty-two plus—" A spear blade took him under the chin, neatly severing most of his neck in one of the few places where his armor was weak.

Cut off though he was, the alarm still sounded mere seconds later. The men in the guard towers must have activated it.

Everyone else tumbled out of the vehicles, guns aimed at the turrets, firing madly, trying to overwhelm the defenders through sheer volume of fire. The SSS shuttle circling overhead descended, trying to get close enough to determine what was going on without putting itself in the immediate line of fire.

By the time Dante's boots struck the ground, all the welcoming committee and half of the Fengu berserkers were dead. Blood soaked into the ground, but the battle had barely begun. Ahead of them, the compound's front doors were opening rather than closing. They must have been sending out reinforcements.

He barked, "Everyone get clear! I'm ramming the doors."

Above and to the sides of them, the guard towers opened up with their plasma cannons. Thick, burning hot beams of green light streaked into the courtyard, incinerating stray Dirtwalkers with horrifying efficiency. Dante tried not to dwell on the sight of the last of the Fengu and two of Urshielle's faithful being swallowed up by the flaming plasma and reduced to smoldering masses of bones in less than a second.

He hurled himself back into the truck and pounced on the controls, shifting into drive and stomping on the gas. The vehicle was already at the courtyard's center, facing the gates that led into the mountain complex.

The entrance stood wide open. A platoon of Slaine's guards were rushing out. Of the three dozen, most toted pulsecores, and at least one carried an old-fashioned anti-armor rocket launcher. None of them had expected Dante to do what he did.

There was visible panic among the mercenaries as the huge vehicle roared straight toward them, closing the distance in the same time it took them to turn around. Green beams from the guard towers fired toward the truck. One from the right missed, kicking up a mass of burning earth to the side. The other, to the left, struck true and cut the wheels loose from the vehicle on that side.

Dante growled as the truck's left side sagged and scraped against the ground, causing the truck to fishtail to the right as its nose cleared the threshold of the gates. The man with the rocket launcher was trapped there and fired but missed in his panic. The projectile sailed over the truck's hood and exploded in an impressive fireball a good half a mile out in the wilderness.

Then the man with the launcher screamed as the truck's front end crushed him and two others against the corridor wall beyond the gate. The others scattered. Half a dozen or so leapt forward into the courtyard, and the rest retreated deeper into the facility.

As the truck smashed against the gates, half-crumpling and sending Dante sprawling to the floor, Nasreen's barely audible voice came through his headset.

"What the hell are you doing, Dante? Oh, fuck fuck fuck. At least they won't be able to close the gates."

He rolled to his knees, overjoyed to discover that his pulsecore sling had remained nicely looped around his body, and he grasped the weapon in both hands as he took in the sights around him.

The truck's interior was badly crunched, but not to the point of crunching *him*, and the door had fallen open again. He dashed toward it as two SSS troopers appeared about six feet in front of him.

Dante blasted them immediately, knowing it was a borderline unsafe range for explosive rounds and not much caring. Both men fell back amid the flashes of green light as the plasma charges burst against their armor, caving in their chest plates and helmets and blowing one's arm off his body. Both fell dead and smoking to the sides as Dante jumped out between them.

The carnage had only grown worse in the minute or so since he'd rammed the gates. The air was full of pulsecore rounds crackling, bullets cutting through the breeze, and the burning beam of the one remaining functional guard tower moving toward a cluster of Dirtwalker women.

Dante was about to empty his magazine at the turret, unsure if small arms fire would be enough to disable it from this distance. An ungainly silhouette lurched out from behind the twisted metal of the truck, which lay like a wadded-up piece of scrap across the main gate's threshold.

Hyde's harsh laughter sounded. "Ha, ha, ha!"

In a brief flash of greenish light, Dante saw Ambrose duck his head and squeeze his eyes shut as Hyde hefted another rocket launcher. Evidently, there had been two men with them among the reinforcing platoon. The single flipper-hand arm squeezed awkwardly at the controls, then the backblast from the weapon whooshed out against the truck's wreckage and the rocket streaked toward the turret.

The tower went up in a shuddering fireball. Chunks of masonry and molten steel flew everywhere. The green plasma beam abruptly died a second or less before it would have incinerated four or five of the Crescent-Marked, who were struggling against a comparable number of Slaine's men.

Dante fired at the SSS guards instead, dropping two of them before ejecting his empty magazine.

Then his head snapped toward Ambrose and Hyde. The pilot struggled to regain his feet after trying to avoid being killed by Hyde's hasty solution to the turret problem.

"Wait a goddamn minute," Dante exclaimed. "If you're down here, who the hell is flying the shuttle?"

Ambrose gestured vaguely to the sky.

Dante looked up and saw the shuttle sailing higher, wobbling a little as it moved closer to the *other* shuttle. The one still controlled by SSS forces had been circling the compound. Midas picked up a garbled message as the pilots of the guard shuttle tried to tell the newcomer to change course. When they realized the craft had no intention of doing so, they accelerated but acted too slowly.

The two shuttles crashed. The nose of Ambrose's shuttle clipped the rear of the other. The thrusters crumpled and spewed flames in different directions. Both spiraled out of control and collided with outcroppings of rock on opposite sides of the mountain, almost in unison. They exploded in impressive curtains of fire.

Ambrose struggled to catch his breath. "Autopilot," he wheezed.

There was no time for Dante to smack his face or congratulate his former partner. Either seemed appropriate. They needed to get into the compound before Slaine could rally whatever defenses he might have left.

He waved his carbine. "Move in! Everyone but Urshielle and a token squad, move in!"

He didn't know how many people they had left, but he guessed with a sinking sensation that they'd already lost half of their force.

Urshielle was bleeding from multiple wounds. She fired a rifle at a couple of straggling mercs as she rallied four of her best surviving warriors to stand guard outside. A few SSS troops remained in the courtyard, pinned down near the wreckage of one of the towers.

The way into the mountain was as clear as it was ever likely to get. The gates kept making high-pitched whining sounds as they tried to close but couldn't, damaged and blocked by the ruined truck.

Nasreen appeared, and so did another eight or nine Dirt-walkers toting spears, rifles, and pulsecores. Dante caught their eye, motioned toward the gates, and plunged forward, trying to let them stay abreast of him so nobody was in anyone else's line of fire.

The tunnel into the mountain was long and deep. It had lights, but they failed to work due to the damage out front. Toward the end of the hall, bright blue-white illumination flooded the space before them. The corridor ended at a broad lobby almost bare of furnishings aside from a security check-point desk and two pillars off to the sides.

Dante roared, "Shoot everything!"

The instant he issued the command, armored figures popped up behind the desk and the pillars, aiming their weapons.

Everyone opened fire at once. Dante and his allies had a slight advantage, but they lacked cover. Bullets and pulsecore rounds cut across every square yard of air, flying haphazardly in any given direction. The lead projectiles ricocheted half the time while the plasma rounds burst against obstacles with concentrated blooms of greenish fire.

Dante fell to his belly as he obliterated the desk with his pulsecore. Something sailed by his face, sizzling a strip of skin off his cheek. In front of him, the desk shattered and men fell dying behind it. To his side, a woman fell screaming with a bloody crater through her chest.

Nasreen threw herself against the wall and riddled one of the guardsmen by the left pillar with plasma rounds, cutting open his shoulder and abdomen from the side and ruining his next shot. He collapsed and fired into the ceiling, dislodging a mixture of earthworks and molten steel droplets that rained down on the steel and polymer floor.

Then it was over. They'd vanquished the five-person ambush force left to deter them, but they'd lost two more Crescent-Marked in the process. There was no time to mourn them.

From the lobby, two halls branched to either side. Nasreen asked, "Do we split up? There aren't enough of us. Wait, I have something that ought to help." She pulled out a small device, a sort of saucer-shaped object with a magnetic attachment.

Dante vaguely recalled that it was some kind of universal door-sealer. "Yeah. Go right and let's see what we see."

They jogged in that direction, coming quickly upon a double door of clear crystal and polymer steel which led into a bunk or dormitory, presumably the garrison's living quarters.

Nasreen smirked. "I bet a bunch of Slaine's guys are waiting there to kill us as we pass. Well, they can wait until after we finish." She activated the device and tossed it against the closest panel of the doors.

The magnets fired and stuck the strange machine in place, where it beeped and glowed blue, then red. The doors slammed shut with a faint sucking sound while the saucer thing hummed.

Nasreen turned. "There we go. Oh, look, some guys are

rushing out. That's all bulletproof and more or less plasma-proof material. They'll have to risk killing themselves with explosives or something if they want out."

"Great." Dante meant it. "Other way. Left hall from the lobby."

The Dirtwalkers looked confused and faintly terrified. They had probably never been inside a human structure as advanced and well-maintained as this one was. Its silvery, antiseptic quality was nearly the antithesis of the decaying ruins and natural landscapes they were accustomed to. They also regarded Nasreen with something like superstitious awe. The sealant device had impressed them.

The left hallway led into a broad area whose overall character became clear at once—research and development, a laboratory complete with reserve stores. Dante's gut bottomed out. He was sure they didn't want to see whatever lay within this place, but it was between them and Slaine. They had little choice.

Past the broad, doorless entranceway and a brief staging area, they came to a wide metallic floor filled with grates to allow liquids to drain. Massive vats rested against each wall, and crystal tubes filled with sparkling fluids ran between them.

Dante raised his carbine as two figures in white lab coats appeared in front of them. The scientists, a man and a woman, approached with their hands raised. Both looked terrified.

"Please," the woman begged. "You can't see them, but they're pointing guns at us. They want you to drop your weapons, or they'll kill us."

The man added, "They forced us to work here. They made us do this, you must understand."

Nasreen squinted. "Do what?" She hopped aside, gun still ready, and peered into one of the vats. Her face fell. "Oh my God."

Two of the Dirtwalker women began yammering in a language unfamiliar to Dante. Perhaps it was their native tongue of whatever tribe they'd belonged to before joining the Crescent.

One of them ran toward another vat while waving her rifle around.

Dante snapped, "Get back here! We can't afford to—"

Someone hidden deeper within the lab opened fire on the impetuous warrior, cracking her head open and sending her spinning through the air. It also shattered the vat behind her. Viscous clear liquid spread over the floor, and floating within it were hundreds of small fleshy objects. Human ovaries.

Nasreen screamed, "Goddammit! You fucking bastards!"

Wishing not for the first time that they'd had time to develop more of a plan, Dante braced himself for the worst as all hell broke loose.

The Dirtwalkers screamed and charged madly into the research area, blasting the gibbering scientists with their guns as the hidden guards opened fire again. This time Dante tried to shoot back. He peppered corners that looked suspicious with pulsecore rounds, hoping the explosions would reach around the edges enough to inflict some damage on their unseen foes. Nasreen did likewise.

The Crescent-Marked warriors fell dead, sacrificing themselves courageously but stupidly in their incoherent rage. Dante couldn't blame them. He would rather have had them around for the rest of the fight.

The other vats shattered, the tubes broke, and various strange and foul-smelling fluids ran across the floor. Where Dante and Nasreen stood, most of it drained into the gratings, but in the other direction, it pooled in place.

Midas abruptly spoke up. *"Sir, I believe that substance is conductive, and there's an exposed bit of wiring overhead. Might I suggest—"*

Dante grabbed Nasreen's arm and dragged her back. "Hey!" she exclaimed.

Ignoring her, he followed Midas's green visual cue toward the wiring and shot it once. Some came loose, descending like a thrashing tentacle and spewing sparks. The voices of two or three men and women cried out in alarm as the wiring struck the floor.

Blue electricity filled the room. Sparks, steam, and gouts of flame rose everywhere as it electrocuted the entire inner lab. Six of SSS' finest fell writhing in agony amid the deadly pool. Their armor was useless against the powerful current. Their bodies continued to spasm after they were dead.

Dante and Nasreen hopped back from the edge of the liquid as it spat out angry sparks. Sickeningly, the electricity had cooked the hundreds of stolen ovaries suspended in the substance.

They waited for the steam and crackling to subside. Then, wary and repulsed, they crept forward into the sizzling morass.

Midas said, *"It should be safe now, but I gather it's unpleasant."*

"Yes, it is." The stuff stuck to Dante's boots, slowing him down, and it smelled awful. The electricity had mostly dispersed, and no other guardsmen were present.

As they penetrated deeper into the labs, things got worse.

Nasreen stared in horror. "My God. Look at this." She pointed at an operating table covered with stains. Beyond it lay jars with strange masses of tissue and a monitor displaying a computer-generated model of a humanoid, but not *human*, figure.

Dante didn't want to examine it in detail. Especially since he wasn't convinced they'd taken out all the guards yet. "What the fuck is it?"

"Human experimentation," his partner proclaimed. "Either they were operating on captured Dirtwalkers, or they were trying to grow their own—I don't know, test subjects? Supersoldiers?—from a lab culture. All horribly illegal. Cloning, maybe. Is this the work of Hyde's 'big spiders,' I wonder? Or is it something Slaine and his cronies were doing to amuse themselves because they're sick bastards?"

Dante grunted. "The two aren't necessarily mutually exclusive."

As they came to the far end of the labs, a short series of steps put an end to the pool of viscous, burned-smelling liquid. They wiped their boots off on the rug beyond. Dante muttered, "Time to cut the head off the snake."

At that moment, a black-armored man leapt out from around the corner of an intersection with a hallway beyond. He had a broad riot shield in front of him and a dart launcher in his other hand.

Dante and Nasreen both fired at him, but the shield had an energy field that reflected the pulsecore rounds at them.

"Oh shit!" Nasreen sputtered, jumping and rolling aside. Her shots streaked past her and burst in the air somewhere in the middle of the laboratory.

Dante narrowly sidestepped his ricochets as the guard aimed the dart launcher at him. He put up his shoulder with the heavy epaulet facing outward as the dart fired, sticking in the pad harmlessly. Then Dante charged the man, sliding under the shield and tackling his legs with his own feet.

The guard toppled onto his ass, gasping and losing the charged riot shield. He fumbled for a knife as Dante plucked the dart from his shoulder pad and stuck its point into the man's semi-exposed ankle.

"No!" the guard cried, frantically grasping at it. Dante rolled away from him as his fingers clutched at the spiked projectile, growing weak as the fast-acting toxin spread through his bloodstream. He pulled it free from his leg in time for the poison to reach his heart and stop it.

Nasreen got to her feet. "Okay. Great. Did that guy seriously *only* have a dart launcher?"

Dante was already past him, peering into the hall beyond, which ended at a strangely ornate yet secure and reinforced door. He glanced down at the dead bodyguard and noticed a cylindrical object attached to his belt.

"No. He also had a grenade."

CHAPTER NINETEEN

Dante hefted the grenade in hand, thankful that his enemies had provided him with something so useful. He walked toward the sealed door.

Nasreen's eyes bulged. "Dante, we're in an enclosed space, you realize. And we're underground. That could collapse the goddamn roof on us."

"Doubtful. These corridors are reinforced all to hell with steel and polymer pylons. It looks like the same shit used on Hyde. The parts of him that didn't melt, I mean. We ought to be fine. Get back, though."

Nasreen turned and dashed back to the intersection, taking cover around the right-hand corner and cursing madly under her breath. "I could hack through, maybe, but no, you have to fucking try this goddamn..."

Ignoring her, Dante activated the grenade. It had a button that could be tapped for a short fuse or held down a second for a longer one. He held it down for a second and placed it at the base of the door before turning and sprinting at top speed.

He got around the corner, going left in plenty of time. A few seconds after he'd taken cover, the grenade detonated.

The blast was predictably deafening although their helmets blocked the worst of the noise. Still, they *felt* it as a vibration. The effect was similar to Hyde's voice but far more intense. Metal screamed, and heat roared down the corridor, scorching the metal while everything around them shook.

Dante stepped back around the corner, aiming his carbine.

A guard in black armor appeared in the opening. His movements were jerky and disoriented, and his face was cock-eyed behind his visor. His pulsecore aimed a little too low. If he'd tried to fire the instant he saw Dante, he would have shot the floor about six feet in front of the Marauder.

Dante shot first. Two pulsecore rounds took the man in the midsection, blasting him back through the shattered and half-molten wreckage of the door where he disappeared into a plume of smoke.

"Come on," he snarled, and Nasreen jumped out behind him. They both plunged through the opening and into Cormac Slaine's sanctum.

Beyond the threshold, they were no longer in a military or scientific base but in a luxury office. Slaine had ensured that he could live in comfort even in a hidey-hole like this.

Before either of them could examine their surroundings in detail, the black-armored man Dante had shot sprang at them through the thinning curtain of smoke. A razorfist blade sprouted from his hand. His chest armor had cracked but wasn't fully compromised. Up close, Dante recognized it as the highest-grade protection available. It would have taken half a magazine of regular pulsecore rounds to destroy it.

He quick-stepped aside as the blade punched through the air where his head had been. Nasreen moved in, deploying her wrist knife and lashing at the man's armpit, but the armor was too thick, and her blade merely scraped it.

The man within the black armor, whoever he was, kept making hysterical howling sounds of rage. He'd lost his gun and knew he was cornered but wasn't about to give up. His razorfist slashed wildly around, but his movements were still quick and precise enough that Dante took a cut along the side that ruined his armor there and opened his skin. It wasn't deep enough for a serious injury, but he had to end the fight *now* before the frenzied bodyguard did further damage.

He tackled the man from the flank, wrapping his arm around the armored neck and using his other hand to seize the razorfist by the wrist. The guard's strength was impressive, but Dante had a better angle and twisted his arm aside.

Nasreen stepped in from the front, nimbly dodging the man's attempt at a front kick. She slammed her wrist knife's blade into one of the cracks in his chest plate. The blade was too short to penetrate much, but it nonetheless punched through his sternum, drawing blood and slowing him.

As the man's snarls became sobs, Dante brought more of his weight down on the blade-wielding arm, so the man shifted posture due to pain compliance. Then Dante threw them both forward, so the man's head connected with a partial wall opposite the melted door that separated the entrance area from the rest of Slaine's suite.

The helmet didn't crack, but the impact was enough to stun the man further. Dante dashed his head into the wall repeatedly while Nasreen ducked in between his legs, unfastened a thigh plate, and cut his femoral artery. Blood flowed in thick waves as the man's life drained out. His hysterical cries of anguish faded, and at last, he slumped to the floor unmoving.

"Fuck," Dante gasped. "Guy must have been hopped up on amphetamines."

Somewhere beyond the partial wall, a voice responded. "Correct. I try not to resort to such crude methods with my personnel, but you left me with little choice. Now it appears that you have won. Let's talk this over, shall we?"

Dante noticed that the suite—in truth, a panic room—was

decorated to resemble Slaine's office back at SSS Tower. The same office where the whole chain of events had begun. A cold hatred suddenly took over. The rush of battle faded and the noises of the rest of the fight elsewhere in the compound seemed distant.

Nasreen exchanged a glance with her partner. Readying their weapons, they both stepped out from opposite sides of the partial wall, covering the whole room beyond simultaneously.

Cormac Slaine sat in a big, comfy chair, and standing beside him were two men who wore suits and headsets but not combat armor. One had a pulsecore pistol. He fired it at the same time Dante fired his weapon. The pistol round exploded two feet over his shoulder, knocking him forward a step, but his shot had already flown true.

The pulsecore round from Dante's gun struck the attendant in the middle of the face. His head vanished, the brief green flash transforming it into a red cloud of mist, and he toppled over sideways.

Cormac Slaine was well-groomed and well-dressed as always. He flinched. Then he resumed his air of genteel unflappability. He swallowed and adjusted his tie.

The other headset-wearing attendant had made no move except to raise his hands slowly. Nasreen covered him with her carbine and motioned for him to step away from Slaine. She guided him into the corner and held him there, keeping one eye on him and the other on their target.

Dante stepped closer. A lovely, plush carpet covered the floor.

"Mr. Slaine," he began. "Our business partnership is over. I never, ever break a deal. You've broken so many that I stopped bothering to count."

Slaine inhaled. He had himself under pretty good control, but his roiling terror was still obvious beneath the veneer. "It would be better if you didn't—"

"Kill you?" Dante cut him off. "Only if you make me. It *would* be better if we hauled you in front of a livestream that everyone in the Stations got to watch as your crimes were listed for everyone to hear about in detail."

The businessman sighed as though exasperated by Dante's stupidity. "No, no. You don't quite understand. All this time, a purveyor of solar power solutions is all I *wanted* to be. The business with the o-harvesting was forced upon me by others.

"I'm sure Hyde blabbed that we have sponsors and backers. People who hold more power than I do. I tried to talk them out of it, but they insisted. The Miracle Makers, they call themselves. *That's* how self-important they are."

Nasreen sarcastically muttered, "Wow, *their* panic rooms must be *better* decorated than yours is."

Slaine kept his eyes on Dante. "Of course. Now listen, Shale. You must be curious about why I had to do what I did, or you would have simply killed me by now. The Miracle Makers were concerned that the population of the Atlantica Stations was collapsing. They might seem crowded, but we faced a demographic time bomb."

Dante listened. He suspected a trick, but the way Slaine spoke suggested that he was trying to quickly confess as much of the truth as he thought he could get away with. He was throwing a bone to his captors to imply that he knew more of value and must therefore be protected.

"Oh," Dante grunted. He tried to sound as though he didn't care—the better to motivate Slaine to say more and be quick about it.

The CEO held up his hands, palms outward. "They demanded that the population situation be corrected at once before it became unsalvageable. I had no choice but to do as they asked. All along, I was a puppet of theirs as you were temporarily a puppet of mine. By eliminating me, you cut the strings that might lead you to the *real* puppet masters."

"I get it," Dante rasped. "You know things. You want protection for as long as it takes to shift the blame up and away from yourself."

Slaine's lips trembled, and his eyes widened with indignation. "Yes, of course, you imbecile! Who wouldn't, in my situation? It's true, though. I *do* know things. The ultimate blame *does* lie with them.

"There are things you don't know. If you turn me over to the authorities, they will bribe or blackmail someone to take me out before *anyone* knows. I must have special, top-grade protection from people you can trust. It's the only way you'll ever know the whole truth."

Footsteps approached, and one of Urshielle's warriors burst in. She carried only a spear, but her face was fierce with battle-lust.

Without looking at her, Dante snapped in the Dirtwalker tongue, "Stop! Stay where you are. Guard the doorway. Watch that man in the corner."

The woman paused, annoyed and disappointed, but did as ordered. Nasreen turned the duty of watching the attendant over to her and moved closer to Slaine.

"Okay," she said to the businessman, "you mention the whole truth. What about *part* of the truth, to prove to us that you know anything? If you can't give us something, Mr. Slaine, you're useless and we might as well turn you over to your puppet masters ourselves."

Slaine looked at her for the first time. His blandly handsome face finally lost its composure as though the emotional under-tows of fear, anger, and relief all crashed, mingled, and left him helpless. His jaw fell open as he tried to find the words he wished to say.

Midas spoke next.

"Sir," the AI piped up, using audio projection. "Something is wrong. There's a signal coming through, and it's trying to, ah, to suppress *me*. It's—oh, dear—it's taking over my communication array."

It took all of Dante's training and experience not to risk losing Slaine by dropping his guard. "What? How? Where is it coming from?"

Midas's voice responded, "I-I-I don't...don't...nnnoooo." His voice changed as the bottom dropped out of it like a drunk man forgetting what he was saying.

"Midas!" Dante yelled. "What the hell is going on?"

When the AI spoke again, he was using three or four voices layered atop one another, as though he couldn't decide which was best. "Everywhere. Inside out. Everywhere! *Slaine!*"

At the final word, the name of the man before them, the voices multiplied again, becoming a chorus of angry growls, terrified shrieks, and the mocking laughs of children all at once. The signal had hijacked every voice module Midas had, imitating demonic possession in projecting them all at once.

Cormac Slaine looked as though he might drop dead of pure fright. The color had drained from his face.

"Slaine," the chorus thundered again. "You faithless coward. Stuffed shirt! Foppish, glorified middle manager. We overestimated you. We will not tolerate treachery."

Slaine fell or slid out of his chair, landed on his knees, and raised his trembling hands, clasping them together as though praying. He sweated so much that someone might as well have been spraying him with a mister.

"Please. Oh, God. Spare me. I'm sorry. I did everything you—"

"Hush!" The chorus, agonizingly coming from within Dante's head, now imitated a chastising parent figure. "You two! Dante and Nasreen. You, on the other hand, have proven your value. We will watch you—eagerly. But your puerile notions could become troublesome if you do not recognize your limitations."

Nasreen stared at Dante in shock, and he wondered how bad he must have looked. The terrible layers of voices bursting from his brain nearly unmanned him. He wanted to do as Slaine was doing. Fall to his knees and beg for it to stop.

The chorus declared, "Miracles can raise the dead, but they can also lay low the mighty. Never forget that."

Then it was over. Dante sensed that the "signal" was gone, as Midas's usual voice, speaking neurally rather than audibly, began to stammer and apologize.

Before Dante could begin to process what in God's name had happened, the other attendant crouching all but unnoticed in the corner of the room, stood, pulled out a tiny pistol, and shot Cormac Slaine in the eye.

"No!" Dante exclaimed.

Slaine remained where he was, his mouth gawking and blood running from it as well as the red hole in his face, and a crimson splatter was on the wall behind him. He slumped, planting face-first on the floor as though collapsing in gratitude that it was over so quickly.

Nasreen spun toward the planted agent, the assassin of the Miracle Makers, but Urshielle's warrior acted too quickly. Roaring in fury, the woman drove her spear through the man's midsection, destroying his heart. He groaned, dropped the pistol, and collapsed against the wall as the warrior pulled the blade free.

Dante let out his breath. It shook.

"Fuck."

CHAPTER TWENTY

Dante found that there wasn't much for him to do besides stand around and occasionally point at things or relay orders between the two groups. He was, after all, an effective translator when it came to going back and forth between English and the Dirt-walker Trade tongue.

Nasreen was the one handling most of the actual oversight job. The volunteers, workers, and managers associated with the Terra Restoration Group were more her sort of people.

She pointed. "Hey, hey! It would make more sense for the breezeway to have its opening *perpendicular* to the wind, don't you think? Usually, the breeze here comes off the sea to the west, right? It'll make it easier for Station volunteers to adjust to the climate. More importantly, that will help keep the dust out."

The five-person crew who'd begun assembling the artificial tunnel stared at her in vague irritation but nodded and adjusted their positions accordingly.

They'd already set up the bulk of the new temporary facility. It had taken the TRG personnel less than a week to get where they were. There were some luxuries, additional amenities, and finishing touches to finalize, but the place was functional.

It was a small complex of collapsible domes, tents, and tube tunnels that collectively served as a medical clinic. The irony of erecting such a place right next to a hospital wasn't lost on anyone, and the crew kept joking about it long after everyone had heard all the jokes they could think of.

The surveyors had determined that a new temporary facility would ultimately be quicker and cheaper than co-opting a century-old building and doing the many repairs it would need to accommodate all the cutting-edge equipment TRG intended to use.

Dante's face softened at the thought of what was to come. He even smiled a little. "Reconstructive implantation" wasn't a very appealing term, but it was more professional-sounding than something like "the gift of life."

Then a couple of TRG accountant types came up to haggle with Nasreen about the cost of power generators and how this affected the resource budget of the Dirtwalkers. They used a very small amount of their self-generated electricity and were willing to share a modicum of it with their guests.

Dante was about to butt in when two approaching figures caught his attention from the corner of his eye. They grew larger amid the blowing wisps of dust and fog. He turned toward them.

"Urshielle. Raphorien. Nice to see you both again." He'd wondered where they'd been lately and what had taken them so long to come out and say hello.

The leader of the Crescent-Marked warriors limped and was still covered in bandages from her various injuries during the battle at Slaine's compound, but she was on her feet and otherwise functional. She seemed tired, but a grim pride carried her through.

Raphorien moved with a lightness of step that Dante had never seen in him before, as though his large, soft, lumbering form was as spry as a kid. He smiled in a way that looked close to painful, and his eyes were a little red, which suggested he'd been crying not long ago.

Dante walked toward them for Urshielle's sake, meeting the pair halfway across the short distance of the rocky plain that separated the hospital from the restorative clinic. Raphorien embraced him immediately, his grip stronger than Dante expected, and the Marauder patted him on the back.

"Thank you," the healer began. "We cannot thank you enough for making this possible. Urshielle and I and the other older people of the Crescent are too far gone, but that is not unexpected. That at least *some* of our brothers and sisters may have hope is something we never dared dream of."

"I know." Dante's voice was soft. "I wasn't sure if it would work. But the TRG doctors are optimistic."

The freshest of the moon-scraped—those who had their ovaries or testicles harvested within the last few months or less—were considered "moderate to good" candidates for re-implantation of their stolen organs. It was impossible to guarantee that all of them would be able to regain their reproductive faculties, but the success rate for such procedures was usually around eighty percent. The bodies of the healthiest ones could likely adapt and renew themselves.

Urshielle drew a long, deep breath. "Yes. If they can restore even one of them, we shall be overjoyed. If more than that, so much the better. Perhaps it is even more important that the harvests have stopped for now. Since these SSS people were overthrown and driven out, there have been no more raids anywhere on this island, and it is our hope that soon there will be none anywhere on Earth."

Releasing Raphorien from his grasp, Dante turned to Urshielle and gripped her arm, putting his other hand on her shoulder. He was careful to avoid her various wounds, although she wasn't the type to cringe away from minor pain.

"That's my hope too," he told her. "Already, it's outlawed

everywhere in the Stations. SSS only started doing it so often because the money they could make was too tempting. They wanted to harvest as many people as possible, then run away with the profits and hope no one noticed what they were doing. It will once again become a rare practice, I think. Everyone in the Stations is learning about Slaine's actions. People will be more vigilant in ensuring it does not happen again."

Nasreen approached, having settled with the number crunchers. Urshielle and Raphorien noticed her and greeted her the same way—the warrior grasping her arm and shoulder, the healer scooping her up in a massive hug.

As Dante watched, Nasreen congratulated them.

"They should be able to start performing the procedures this very evening. After interviewing your people, they have a good roster or whatever you want to call it set up. The moon-scraped who are closest to the, um, the end of their window of opportunity will get the first transplants. TRG will proceed from there to the freshest ones, which will maximize the success rate."

Urshielle and Raphorien understood enough English to get the gist of what she was saying, but Dante still had to translate some of it into the Trade tongue for them to fully grasp what she meant. Both nodded, satisfied.

Nasreen went on. "The Terra Restoration Group is also spearheading the effort to get your story out. To educate the general public about what happened here. It will make it easier to prevent future recurrences."

Urshielle still grasped Nasreen's hand. She looked back and forth between her and Dante. "Both of you are heroes to us, now and forever. Wherever the Crescent-Marked wander, you are welcome. We have some people on the mainland who go among the other tribes. We hope that in time, our order will die off—because we are no longer necessary. Because there is no more moon-scraping."

Raphorien added, "If that comes to pass, all we have done will have been worth it. We would go to our ends knowing that we restored life to others."

Nasreen reacted with a slow nod. "Indeed. Thank you for helping us, as well."

With that, the two Crescent leaders gave their friends a final look before turning back toward the hospital, where they directed their people to cooperate with the Moonfiend workers to the best of their ability.

Dante stood doing nothing and feeling mellow.

Nasreen tugged on his arm. "Hey. Come on. I think we earned a short break. Let's head over toward that cliff. It's been too long since I've been able to watch the sea. I don't believe I've ever done that unless you count a couple of missions where I was looking out for Nightmutts the whole time."

Chuckling drily, Dante joined her in strolling toward the promontory.

Midas asked, *"Shall I go dormant for a while, sir? You seem quite well for the time being."*

"Yes. You've done well, Midas. Take a nice long rest until I wake you up again. Once I check our finances, we'll see about some more upgrades. Deal?"

The AI sounded pleased. *"Absolutely. Good night, or morning, rather. Ping me if you should need me earlier."*

His voice faded and fell silent in time with the rising wind and low sloshing sound of the waves on the rocks below. The clouds and fog were too thick for the ocean to be visible from farther away, but as they drew nearer the cliff, the churning slate-colored waters became visible beyond the edges of Atlantican rock.

Dante turned and looked back again out of habit. He wanted to make sure everything was well before he let himself relax.

A group of men carried supplies into the makeshift TRG facility. Most were employees or volunteers directly affiliated with the group, but also among them were two figures who stood out.

A squat, dark, bespectacled man and another who resembled a bulging armored torso and head mounted upon a stiff, jointed metal skeleton that served as his arms and legs.

"Here." The distinctive electronic growl of Hyde's voice carried it farther than a normal man's. He reached down and took a box from the stack Ambrose was trying to balance.

The pilot said something in return, probably "Thanks." To Dante's mild but pleasant surprise, Am's smile was warm and genuine. Whatever their history, the two seemed to have agreed to make amends in whatever limited way they could.

Dante would never be able to trust Ambrose fully. At least the pilot behaved as though he'd learned his lesson and was smart enough to know that everyone would be keeping an eye on him.

As for Hyde, being taken down to virtually nothing after ruling the proverbial roost for so long had made him less arrogant and belligerent. His current crude mechanical body was nowhere near as impressive as his old one, but it would do until further notice.

"Well." Dante exhaled and turned back toward Nasreen and the ocean. "Maybe this place will end up civilized, after all. Not the whole Earth since it's too big and there aren't enough Dirt-walkers who would want to make an effort. There's no known way to reverse the core damage, but at least it won't be a hellscape for a while yet."

Nasreen tittered. "That's a sardonic way of saying it, but yes. We made a positive difference here, didn't we? Here, and on the Stations as well."

Dante vaguely recalled an old film where a type of white bird, gulls, would typically flap around seashores and fill the air with plaintive cries. There were no such birds here, but it was still a peaceful scene.

"Yeah. For the time being. We had to stop Slaine. I wonder if the 'big spiders' were doing other stuff as bad or worse, and having to cut Slaine loose only spooked them into covering their tracks better. I'm not sure if things *will* get better or if it's the calm before the storm."

The memory of the terrifying chorus of voices, the phantom signal that had hijacked Midas to deliver their cryptic ultimatum, returned unwanted to the front of his consciousness.

Nasreen's sigh held a note of exasperation. "You're not wrong, but you're ruining the moment. Your social skills are somewhat lacking, as always."

"Whatever," Dante grumbled. "Yes, for now things are good, and I'm happy, I guess."

Nasreen put an arm around his waist. "That's probably the best I can expect from you for heartwarming statements, but it will suffice. Thank you for all you've done." She kissed him on the cheek briefly and turned her head back toward the water.

He wasn't sure how to react. It had been a *friendly* kiss or seemed to be, probably. It was the thought that counted.

"I couldn't have done it alone," he admitted. "You've been the best thing to happen to me for a long time, Nasreen. Thanks." His gaze drifted up to the new civilization that humanity had built amid the stars. "Whatever comes next, we'll face it together."

Thank you for not only reading this book but these author notes as well!

I'm presently leaving Holland (Rotterdam) on the train heading to Paris. This train is very full, and we aren't the first stop. What this means (I am now very aware) is that luggage storage for big bags is at a premium.

I had to take my luggage (two large bags) and race down to the next coach to see if there was any space. In short, NO space where you should be able to store your bags, and I had to use the location in front of the other door to exit. I sure hope that we don't stop at a location where they need to get off that way.

If they do, it's not only our bags but those bags others stacked on top of ours.

Holland has some of the best foreign food.

I have visited Spain, Italy, England, Scotland, Switzerland, Germany, France, and now Holland. If you had asked me which country was best for foreigners (who like to eat food they are accustomed to in the United States I would have suggested Spain.

Which I still like.

But I have to say, after staying in Rotterdam for a few days, my stomach now prefers Holland for eating other choices (than the local food). Italy is now my third choice since I have figured out I need to ask for Pizza Diavola when ordering a pepperoni pizza.

We had some amazing Chinese food and Argentinian steak while staying in Holland. Plus, there were plenty of US fast food (Burger King, McDonald's, Subway, Taco Bell) and other restaurants catering to those who wanted foreign cuisine. I feel like I could easily have stayed another two weeks if food selection was my main criterion.

And let's face it. If you have read enough of my author notes, you probably know food *is* a major consideration for me when I travel.

I shall see if my top three countries (Holland, Spain, and Italy) change next year.

Enjoy your day, and talk to you in the next book!

Ad Aeternitatem,

Michael Anderle

MORE STORIES with Michael newsletter HERE:
https://michael.beehiiv.com/

OTHER ATLANTICA BOOKS

John Chambers Books

Her Mother's Pendant (Book 1)

The Mystery Deepens (Book 2)

One Last Choice (Book 3)

Valentina Winters

The Red Countess (Book 1)

One Night to Kill (Book 2)

One Death Too Few (Book 3)

Terra Kris

She is the Law (Book 1)

Law or Justice (Book 2)

Justice Served (Book 3)

Santana Sokolov

Law of the Jungle (Book 1)

Inner City Jungle (coming soon)

Rumble in the Jungle (coming soon)

Justice Begins

The First Executioner

Aiming Blind

High Lead and Low Deeds

No Backing Down

Justice is Not Blind

Scorched Earth

BOOKS BY MICHAEL ANDERLE

Sign up for the LMBPN email list to be notified of new releases and special deals!

https://lmbpn.com/email/

For a complete list of books by Michael Anderle, please visit:

www.lmbpn.com/ma-books/

CONNECT WITH THE AUTHOR

Website: http://lmbpn.com

Email List: https://michael.beehiiv.com/

https://www.facebook.com/LMBPNPublishing

https://twitter.com/MichaelAnderle

https://www.instagram.com/lmbpn_publishing/

https://www.bookbub.com/authors/michael-anderle

* 9 7 9 8 8 8 5 4 1 6 7 7 1 *